How I Pawned My Opals and Other Lost Stories

By Catherine Martin

Edited and introduced by Katherine Bode

Obiter Publishing

Published by Obiter Publishing
PO Box 5133
Braddon ACT 2612
info@obiterpublishing.com.au
www.obiterpublishing.com.au

Copyright © Introduction Katherine Bode 2017

The introduction to this book is copyright. Apart from any fair dealing for the purpose of private study, research, criticism or review, as permitted under the Copyright Act, no part may be reproduced by any process without written permission. Enquiries should be made to the publisher. The moral right of the author has been asserted.

A catalogue record for this book is available from the National Library of Australia

ISBN 978-0-6481742-0-2

Cover design by Giraffe
Design by Karen Downing
Printed by Ingram Spark

Series introduction: 'To Be Continued . . .'

The 'To Be Continued . . .' series publishes fiction discovered by literary scholar Katherine Bode and bibliographer Carol Hetherington. They used new digital methods to search the National Library of Australia's *Trove* database to uncover over 21,000 stories published in Australian newspapers between 1828 and 1914. Although fiction is a rarity in newspapers today, prior to World War One Australian newspapers routinely published fictional works, and in the nineteenth century, were the main source of fiction for colonial readers. Some of the stories discovered in this project are short, amounting to only one or two columns on a newspaper page; some are lengthy novels, published over multiple newspaper editions.

Fiction in Australian newspapers came from around the world: from Australia, Britain and America as well as France, Germany, New Zealand, Russia, and beyond. All of the titles discovered – with an interface for readers to interact with *Trove* to discover new stories and correct the newspaper text – is available at http://cdhrdatasys.anu.edu.au/tobecontinued.

The 'To Be Continued . . .' series focuses on Australian fiction not previously known about, or published, beyond the original newspaper pages. It thus uncovers lost pieces of the nation's literary heritage enabling new understandings of the way Australian literature developed and how early Australians understood themselves and their world.

Contents

Publisher's note

'How I Pawned My Opals' appeared in the Adelaide's *Evening Journal* in 1881; 'A Stray Kitten' appeared in the *Adelaide Observer* in 1883; 'Mrs Archibald Thorndale's Dog' appeared in the Melbourne's *Leader* in 1890; 'Hänslein's Disappearance: A Story of Saxon Switzerland' appeared in the Adelaide's *Chronicle* in 1897; and, 'Teresa's Betrothal: A Tale of the Coral Fishery' appeared in that same newspaper in 1898. No changes have been made to the original formatting apart from obvious typographical errors.

From Adelaide to Genoa:
Locating Catherine Martin's Lost Fiction

Katherine Bode

This book collects for the first time and restores to readers five previously lost stories by Catherine Martin: South Australian feminist, socialist, world traveller and one of Australia's most significant nineteenth-century authors. In literary criticism of the 1890s, Martin features alongside writers such as Rolf Boldrewood, Ada Cambridge, Henry Kingsley and Catherine Helen Spence as a key figure of the emerging Australian literary tradition. Indeed, Spence singled Martin out from all of their contemporaries as the only 'Australian novelist of genius'.[1] Like all of these nineteenth-century authors, Martin's fiction was published in newspapers, with Adelaide publications especially important for showcasing her writing and supplementing her income as a journalist. But Martin's habit of publishing anonymously or under pseudonyms means that these stories have until now been unknown to contemporary readers, even as her major works – *An Australian Girl*, *The Silent Sea* and *The Incredible Journey* – have continued to be reissued, read and discussed. In collecting these stories this book enables a fuller sense of Martin's literary career, including the important connections between her major works, life and newspaper fiction. It also presents for the first time a selection of nineteenth-century Australian stories that are intrinsically interesting, often humorous and always thought provoking.

Martin's journey from childhood poverty to international renown as an author itself suggests the narrative arc of fiction. Martin was born

---

[1] All citations from Spence's letters are taken from Margaret Allen's 'Biographical Background' in the Academy Editions of Australian Literature volume of Catherine Martin's *An Australian Girl*, edited by Rosemary Campbell, and published in 2002 by the University of Queensland Press.

Catherine Edith Mackay in 1847 on the Isle of Skye and moved, aged eight, with her family to Australia. In Scotland the Mackays were poor crofters: tenant farmers working a small landholding. They made the journey to Australia with assistance from the Highland Emigration Society, a philanthropic organisation that promoted and assisted emigration as a solution to economic destitution. Just months after the family arrived in South Australia and settled in Naracoorte in the colony's southeast, the father, Samuel, died of dysentery.

What would seem a very poor and unlucky start in Australia was transformed by the family's hard work and perspicacity. The Mackays began as farm labourers. However, by the time Catherine Mackay moved to Adelaide in 1876, aged 29, one brother was a respected teacher and at least two others were leading pastoralists. Martin, herself, was well educated, fluent in a number of modern languages, particularly German, and widely read in literature, theology and philosophy; she had helped to establish and had taught in a school with her mother and sister; and she had published her first book, a poetry collection entitled *The Explorers and Other Poems*. Such was Martin's education and bearing that, upon encountering her for the first time at the University of Adelaide's inauguration in 1876, Spence thought her 'the daughter of a wealthy squatter of the south-east', only later discovering that she was, like Spence, 'a litterateur trying to make her living by the pen'. Spence – a respected journalist, Unitarian preacher, social advocate, philanthropist and suffragist, as well as an esteemed author – became an important mentor, close friend and intellectual influence for Martin.

It was probably Spence who introduced Catherine Martin, then Mackay, to her future husband Frederick, an accountant, social reformer, writer and member of the Unitarian congregation where Spence attended and preached. Catherine and Frederick were married in 1882, when she was 34. The marriage seems to have been a happy and equal one. They were 'comrades', Martin was later to write to Spence, sharing a belief in social justice, a desire to write and, as their life together showed, to travel and to see the world.

In 1888 Martin travelled alone to Europe to study and write, and it was in this period, and prior to her return to Australia in 1890, that her most celebrated work, *An Australian Girl*, was written and published. Though this novel is a romance, it is far from formulaic, and features a compromised marriage as well as extended reflections on philosophical and theological themes. In 1891, the Martins together departed for Europe, where they remained until 1894; it was during this period that Martin's second major work, *The Silent Sea*, was completed and published. Part thriller part romance, *The Silent Sea* drew on Martin's experience living at the Alma gold mine near Waukaringa, where Frederick was the purser or accountant. The Martins made other extended trips to Europe, to study and to write, until Frederick's poor health led them to return to Australia where he died, in 1909, of tuberculosis. After Frederick's death Martin continued to travel. Her final novel, *The Incredible Journey*, recognised as the first Australian work to centrally feature an Aboriginal character, was finally published (after rejections and revisions) in 1923. In 1932 Martin returned to South Australia for the final time, dying in Adelaide in 1937.

The stories collected here were originally published in three distinct periods of Martin's writing career. The earliest two, and the first two in order of their appearance in this collection, appeared in the early 1880s, immediately before and after Martin's marriage to Frederick and at a time when she was publishing other short fiction for the Adelaide press. 'How I Pawned My Opals' was published in the 1881 Christmas Eve issues of the weekly *Adelaide Observer* and its companion daily paper, the *Evening*

Journal, under the pseudonym 'H. Derwent'; 'A Stray Kitten' appeared in the Christmas supplement to the *Adelaide Observer* in 1883, without attribution but with a note describing it as by the author of the earlier story. The middle, and longest, story collected here, 'Mrs. Archibald Thorndale's Dog', was published almost a decade after these two short stories, as the Christmas Story in the *Leader*, Melbourne's major weekly newspaper, in 1890. It thus appeared just after *An Australian Girl* had been published, and as that book was garnering critical acclaim in the British and Australian press. The story was published anonymously but described as by the author of that major work, as were the final two stories collected here. 'Hänslein's Disappearance: A Story of Saxon Switzerland', and 'Teresa's Betrothal: A Tale of the Coral Fishery', were published almost another decade later, in Adelaide's *Chronicle* in 1897 and 1898, respectively, during an extended period the Martins spent in Australia prior to their final trip together to Europe.

Although separated in time, these stories share a number of themes that characterise Martin's other, known works. As is often noted in discussion of *An Australian Girl*, all of these stories have an independent and strongly delineated female character at their core. These characters are different in many ways. The protagonists of 'How I Pawned My Opals' and 'A Stray Kitten' are both Australian; but Nell is middle class, the daughter of a rural doctor, while Helen is a rich Adelaide heiress. The other protagonists are not Australian: Lily, in 'Mrs. Archibald Thorndale's Dog', is a wealthy American living in Paris who travels to Adelaide with her new husband; Marie, in 'Hänslein's Disappearance', is an Englishwoman, daughter of a classics scholar, living in Germany; and Teresa, of 'Teresa's Betrothal', is an Italian peasant girl. Despite these differences, all of these central female characters are decisive and determined, and resist or actively go against the mores of their respective societies.

With the exception of the Italian Teresa, who has little formal education, all of these female characters are also highly opinionated, outspoken, intelligent and well read. Nell quotes German poetry to her sister's fiancé, Dick, translating it for him when he admits, 'I understand "das" and "Sie", the rest of the meaning is a little vague'; Helen mocks the pessimism of modern writers, while Lily is conversant with the habits of Bedouin Arabs and argues vigorously with her husband-to-be about the depiction of feminine virtue in French playwright Molière's *L'Ecole des Femmes*. Marie translates and supports her father's work on contemporary German politics. For her depiction of Stella Courtland in *An Australian Girl*, Martin has long been seen as responsible for creating a uniquely Australian form of the New Woman. These stories show that she conceived of this figure as a global phenomenon, an emerging sisterhood of women independent in thought and action.

Two other, common threads often remarked on in Martin's known works and present in these newly discovered titles are explicit references to European intellectual traditions and debates, and a concern with poverty, social justice and equality. Literary allusions suffuse these stories, with references to Ancient Greek plays, Norse legends and German poetry alongside allusions to numerous British playwrights, poets and novelists. Martin's knowledge of German, French and Italian is on display, as is her familiarity with key theological, philosophical and political debates of the time. The depth of learning in Martin's writing is often presented through the thoughts and actions of the female protagonists – they are the ones who quote Shakespeare or reference German philosophy – and the same is true of the commitment to social justice.

In all of these stories the female protagonists have, or come to have, an appreciation of the difficulties of poverty, whether because they are poor and must work hard to earn a living (as is the case in 'Teresa's

Betrothal'), because they encounter people in desperate need (in 'A Stray Kitten' and 'Mrs. Archibald Thorndale's Dog') or because an event occurs that means they run out of money and have to budget and plan for how to acquire some more (in 'How I Pawned My Opals' and 'Hänslein's Disappearance'). Although Martin escaped the extreme poverty of her childhood she had to work to support herself for much of her life and this understanding of financial necessity and insecurity clearly informs these stories.

More broadly, they demonstrate Martin's sharp eye for social pretension and injustice. Much of the considerable humour in the earlier stories is directed toward deflating social pretensions, whether of the self-importance of the citizens of Hamlington in 'How I Pawned My Opals' or of the faux modesty of the 'respectable matrons' of Adelaide in 'A Stray Kitten'. Particular satiric bite is reserved for those who profess religious belief without humility or compassion for others. Thus, in 'Mrs. Archibald Thorndale's Dog' we are introduced to an Archdeaconness who alludes to 'the Almighty as the Great Disposer of Events with a certain air of patronage, as if she had promoted Him to the Directorship of a Joint-Stock Company', and to Lady Keightley, 'a stanch churchwoman, and, as we all know, the first instinct of most orthodox Christians when aggrieved by any one is to visit the offender with pain in mind, body or estate'.

Such deflations of titled characters signal Martin's rejection of colonial social hierarchies based upon old-world models, a characteristic of her writing also widely noted in her novels. At the same time, and as funny as many of these asides are, their focus on female characters introduces something of a discord into the feminism of Martin's fiction. The status quo in all of these stories is represented and rejected in terms of the narrow-minded censoriousness of older women, not the social power and freedoms accorded to men. Accordingly in breaking free of social mores, the young heroines inevitably clash with older female characters, and Martin presents these clashes with a derision of – even a certain ire for – older women that never extends to the male characters. One might say that Martin largely reserves her anger for the assistants rather than the chief beneficiaries of women's social and political inequality in the nineteenth century.

Where the earlier stories use humour, the final two explore social justice and inequality with a more serious tone. As well as foregrounding the economies and sacrifices arising from Teresa's family's lack of money, 'Teresa's Betrothal' describes the hard labour and poor conditions of men on ships sent to harvest coral for the jewellery market. In 'Hänslein's Disappearance' the concern with social inequality is particularly earnest, and expressed in terms that allude to Martin's husband, Frederick's, political activities and writing. While Martin spent their European trips writing fiction and meditations on daily life, Frederick learned and wrote about industry and labour in the countries they visited, publishing at least sixty-three articles in Melbourne's *Age* newspaper under the heading of 'Labor in Other Lands'. In 'Hänslein's Disappearance', Marie's father loses his job and is imprisoned for writing about the 'military burdens of Germany' and how these fall 'heaviest … upon the poorest'. The eventual title of this treatise – 'The Conditions of Labor in Germany' – echoes the title of Frederick's work and suggests the importance Martin attached to socialist politics.

A commitment to social justice perhaps underpins an unusual theme common to three of these stories: the central female character's devotion to an animal or animals. In 'A Stray Kitten', Helen rescues a cat from being strangled by street urchins and becomes deeply attached to it; the title of 'Mrs. Archibald Thorndale's Dog' expresses some of the centrality

of that animal to the story, as well as the complex threesome presented by Lily, her enormous St Bernard Gustave and her husband, Archie.
For much of the story Lily's devotion to the dog is contrasted with her
aloofness to her new husband. The title of 'Hänslein's Disappearance'
likewise references an animal: Hänslein is one of Marie's two much-loved
kookaburras, given to her by a Brisbane cousin. Characters' integrity,
and particularly their relationship to superficial social opinion, is largely
indexed in these stories by their tolerance or lack of tolerance for these
animals. The animals' freedom to express loyalty, love, joy or disdain also
signifies and celebrates a space beyond social strictures. We are told this
directly, though jokingly, in 'Mrs. Archibald Thorndale's Dog', when Lily
excuses the St Bernard's tendency to knock over ornaments with his tail
by reflecting that, 'Gustave has too strong a sense of virtue. He would
like to destroy all that is vicious in art and life. Of course, the thing is
impracticable, for what would be left?'

Contemporary literary critics often frame Martin's commitment to
social justice in terms of her sympathetic portrayals of Aboriginal people.
There are no parallels in these stories to characters' ethnographic interest in Aboriginal culture in *An Australian Girl* and *The Silent Sea*, or to
the depiction of Aboriginal motherhood in *The Incredible Journey*. And
the only reference to Australia's Indigenous people, in 'Mrs. Archibald
Thorndale's Dog', is somewhat ambiguous. As the ship bringing Lily,
Archie and Gustave to Australia comes close to the shore another passenger asks: '"Are there no natives – no little villages anywhere?" … with
that sinking of the heart which a wide expanse of desert country awakens
in those who see it for the first time'. No commentary is made on this
question beyond Archie's blunt reply that: 'We have killed all the natives
… and the villages have not yet begun'.

While this reference to Aboriginal genocide is almost certainly intended as a critique of colonisation, in contrast to Martin's reputation for progressive depictions of different races and cultures, these stories contain a number of racist character portraits. The xenophobic descriptions of Chinese and Arab characters occur in passing and represent common nineteenth-century prejudice about people of non-European descent. The anti-Semitism on display in two of these stories, and particularly in Martin's portrait of the avaricious Jewish pawnbroker in 'How I Pawned My Opals', is more marked and extended. This element signals the dark side to Martin's interest in socialism and German and French culture, reproducing widespread negative associations of Jewish people with capitalism and/or greed.

Although sharing major themes, these stories also demonstrate distinctive features, with particular shifts in the centrality of Australia to these narratives, and in the meaning and importance of romance to female characters' lives. 'How I Pawned My Opals' and 'A Stray Kitten' have a humour and lightness of touch that resembles some of Martin's other early newspaper fiction, including two stories previously published in 1878: 'A Bohemian Born' and 'After Many Years'. But unlike these fictions, and the later ones collected here, 'How I Pawned My Opals' and 'A Stray Kitten' are set entirely in Australia and offer vivid portraits of colonial life. The former moves from the peace and beauty of a rural garden crowned by Nell's favourite Moreton Bay fig tree to the 'spectacle' of Melbourne's Elizabeth Street the day after Melbourne Cup. Adelaide is the setting for 'A Stray Kitten', which gently satirises a society that imitates 'the modes in which the aristocracies of old countries kill the time' at night – with balls and cards – while having, unlike those aristocrats, to work for a living during the day.

As with their depiction of Australian settings and society, these early stories resemble *An Australian Girl* in the centrality of the romance plot. However, where the marriage in that major work was unfortunate and unsettled, the romantic relationships in these stories are much more orthodox. The romantic narrative in 'How I Pawned My Opals' is characteristic of nineteenth-century women's writing (and indeed, of contemporary romance fiction). After misunderstandings arising from the heroine's stubbornness and the hero's jealousy, love is declared and the story ends with engagement and a ball.

In contrast, and despite its somewhat saccharine title, 'A Stray Kitten' offers a thoughtful critique of relationships between men and women. Its first part establishes the paucity of typical relationships of this type, where social mores and the separation of the sexes prevent meaningful connections. The story's second part uses conversations between the independent and intelligent Helen Seymour and the somewhat curmudgeonly but accomplished journalist Gabriel Thornton to show the potential of relationships between men and women to be the most enriching of social interactions. This prospect is inflected by a fair degree of intellectual superiority: it is 'men of limited intelligence, who have associated only with women of inferior intellect and narrow minds', who have unfavourable views of women and vice versa. But the meeting of minds and hearts that is portrayed – Gabriel's dream for their future together features Helen 'glancing over his proofs, and making the most astounding suggestions' – offers a remarkably modern notion of marriage between intellectual equals, based on shared interests and mutual admiration and encouragement.

A marriage is also central to 'Mrs. Archibald Thorndale's Dog'. But this story bears little resemblance to a conventional romance plot. While nineteenth-century romance fiction typically ends with a marriage, the formal union of Lily and Archie occurs very early in the story – preceded by arguments rather than declarations of love – and once conducted does not appear to bring Lily much happiness. Rather, the relationship is rendered with deliberate distance from romance conventions, and with an ambivalence about marriage reminiscent of *An Australian Girl*, published only months prior to this story. In that novel, Stella Courtland has to decide between two suitors: Anselm Langdale, an intellectual English doctor, and Ted Ritchie, a poorly educated but rich Australian pastoralist. Her choice of Ted is shown to be a mistake when he is revealed as an alcoholic as well as her intellectual inferior. The marriage in 'Mrs. Archibald Thorndale's Dog' is a similarly complicated three-way affair: not only does Lily show more affection for her dog than her husband, as noted already, but the St Bernard is a gift from a previous suitor, a 'young attaché, at the British Embassy, who lost his life in the Bernese Alps'.

It is not at all clear that Lily felt any affection for this earlier suitor, and Archie has no similar affliction as alcoholism. Although Archie is something of an intellectual follower in contrast to Lily's radical independence of thought, his honourable character and devotion to Lily and her dog make her coldness to him all the more apparent due to the lack of a clear cause for it. And where Stella Courtland is noted for her nationalism, in 'Mrs. Archibald Thorndale's Dog' Lily appears to strain against the limitations of Australian society as much as those of marriage. Lily is a citizen of the world. An American who has spent most of her life in Paris, she has also lived in London, Vienna, Rome, Dresden, Florence, Japan, Norway and 'the East'. While she is distanced from Archie from the first moments of their marriage, that disconnection seems to grow with her vehement dislike for her husband's Adelaide friends and family: their pseudo intellectualism and snobbishness as well as the demands they place upon her.

In a thoughtful reading of *An Australian Girl*, Amanda Nettelbeck describes that novel's ambiguous and unsettled marriage as a conflicted response to the limited opportunities available to female protagonists in nineteenth-century fiction. Stella Courtland's situation at the end of the novel – of marriage to the wrong man, coupled with a newfound devotion to social justice and religion – both frees her 'from the narrow limits of the romance plot' while tying her to other ideals of Victorian womanhood.[2] 'Mrs. Archibald Thorndale's Dog' concludes with a similar sense that Lily's potential can be realised elsewhere than in romantic love: with the possibility of helping the poor. But in contrast to *An Australian Girl*, there is also a sense of love blossoming between Lily and Archie (although the reason for this situation is open to interpretation). Despite such differences, both works' treatment of women's complex relationship to love and marriage suggest the value of reading *An Australian Girl* alongside this previously unpublished story in understanding Martin's distinctive contribution to both Australian literature and nineteenth-century women's writing.

If the romance plot in 'Mrs. Archibald Thorndale's Dog' is a compromise between the expectation that women marry and the limitations of this state, the final two stories collected here imagine fulfilment for female protagonists in ways that decentre romantic love and marriage. The end of 'Hänslein's Disappearance' suggests the potential for future romance. But this vague possibility is entirely subordinate to the fierce satisfaction that Helen gains from supporting her father's work, through intellectual contributions and by her companionship. Although this female character finds self-worth in supporting a man, the story privileges an ideal intellectual partnership rather than a romantic one. In 'Teresa's Betrothal' the love between Teresa and her *fidanzato* Carlo is, in one sense, the impetus for all events. But the story unfolds almost entirely in Carlo's absence, and focuses on the religious sustenance that Teresa gains from her faith in God and devotion to the Virgin Mary. In these

---

[2] See Amanda Nettelbeck's 'Introduction' to *An Australian Girl*, edited by Graham Tulloch and published in 1999 by Oxford University Press.

stories the intellectual and spiritual life, respectively, is upheld as the basis for women's fulfilment rather than the more traditional routes of love, marriage and motherhood.

These final two stories also differ in being set outside of Australia. 'Hänslein's Disappearance' alludes to that country in the presence of the two kookaburras, whose fits of 'prolonged hooting and jeering' ring out across the Saxony landscape, and in the late arrival of the Brisbane cousin and his mother to the narrative. But Australia is a spectral presence in comparison to detailed descriptions of Dresden and the cultural riches it offers, as well as of the natural beauty of the landscape surrounding the country retreat of Wehlen. Australia is completely absent from 'Teresa's Betrothal', which immerses the reader in a richly depicted Italian landscape and way of life, especially through the prominence of Italian language and cultural practices in the story.

These detailed accounts of other places can be tied to Martin's travels in Europe, where she was known to spend time writing observations from life. Two years prior to the publication of 'Hänslein's Disappearance' and three years before 'Teresa's Betrothal' Martin published a 'Vignettes of Travel' series in Melbourne's *Age* newspaper. These brief, evocative accounts of scenes and events from Martin's time in Europe resemble the detailed descriptions of Germany and Italy in these stories, with both indicating the importance of European travel to her writing. While these vignettes rarely mention Australia, one of them mocks the fatuousness of Australian travellers, 'ignorant of any language save the Australian variety of the English tongue, and … chiefly anxious that they should get a due return for the money they are spending. As they spend so much', Martin writes, 'and are so impervious to most of what they see this is rather an unequal contest'.[3]

---

[3] This description comes from Martin's entry on Freiburg and can be read in full in *Trove* at: http://trove.nla.gov.au/newspaper/article/193980701.

In light of these disparaging comments on Australians in Europe, the move away from Australia in these stories perhaps suggests an ambivalence in Martin's relationship to her adopted country. Spence once remarked of Martin that, 'Europe and especially Italy seems to call to her – and she does not love Australia as you and I do'. The nationalist proclamations of Stella Courtland in *An Australian Girl* mean that Martin is often viewed as a distinctively – even a polemically – Australian author. In contrast, the stories collected here progress from the quintessential Australian girl who is the central character of 'How I Pawned My Opals' to the protagonist of 'Teresa's Betrothal', who knows nothing of Australia and is quintessential Italian. This is not an absolute trajectory; Martin returned to Australian scenes and characters in her final, major work, *An Incredible Journey*. But it is a different version of nineteenth-century Australian fiction to the one we often hear: wherein writers are either assertively Australian or timidly follow the models of other places. Martin's work suggests, rather, a thoroughly cosmopolitan author and world view, bound to but not bound by the emerging Australian nation.

How I Pawned My Opals

Chapter I
In Hamlington

A few years ago there was not a railway station within a hundred miles of Hamlington. But we had a daily mail from Melbourne, which was delivered at 7 p.m., when the coach arrived at the fixed time. In winter, however, this was very seldom, and the safety-valve which was thus afforded for the ill-temper and uncharitableness of the township was invaluable. "What I want to know is, how much longer are we to put up with this sort of infamy?" Captain Goring would say, with an incipient tinge of purple on the tip of his nose. It was rather a prominent organ, and was always the first to show any emotion in the old Captain's face. That he rarely got letters from any one beyond the confines of Hamlington, and that his correspondence was chiefly confined to missives which had a neat slit at each end, and "Invoice only," printed on them, did not in the least allay the old gentleman's wrath.

The "shameful irregularity" of the mail was a kind of red rag, which he kept by him for chronic use, and waved vigorously when the monotony of life at Hamlington threatened to derange his liver. For no doubt Hamlington was monotonous, though those of us who were bred in its atmosphere of quiet and leisure were not much affected by the want of excitement. We had croquet and evening parties in abundance, and twice a year we launched into the extravagance of subscription balls, after which two certain events happened. The Rev. Nicodemus Pash delivered what his admirers called an "earnest and stirring discourse" on the evils of dissipation, in which "ashes and cinders," and "apples of Sodom," and many other striking metaphors figured largely if not very coherently, for the Rev. Nicodemus was a man with a large gift of fluency which was repressed by no consciousness of limited knowledge or necessity of logical sequence. He prided himself upon being low church, and particularly insisted on the certainty of damnation for the large majority of his fellow-beings. But on the other hand he was much given to dwelling on the joys of Paradise, and used to draw most florid pictures of the felicity of eternal reunion with our "beloved ones." As the Rev. Nicodemus was married to his *third* wife, it was a moot question with Bess and myself how *he* would manage about reunion. We had a very vivid mental vision of Nicodemus with the three Mesdames Pash in a circle round him. The other event was that Mrs. Squareup emphatically declared to each of her friends in confidence, that she really did not think she could allow Emmeline and Jane to go to the subscription balls any more. Too much champagne was drunk, and the young men—"now, didn't you notice yourself, my dear, some excitement in their manner before the ball broke up?" Mrs. Squareup would say in a tone of the deepest concern, as if fearful that Emmeline at thirty-six and Jane at thirty-eight might discover how black was the world from which she protected their dewy innocence.

And then amateur concerts were by no means rare, at which our music-master Herr Bohn used to play severely classical music for an unbelieving and unregenerate audience seeking novelty and fireworks, and where Mrs. Warbler, after pressing solicitation, sang "Why do summer roses fade?" in a pale-blue silk dress, with what is technically termed a V, and a surprising train, "So unbecoming to her, you know, a woman of her age," Mrs. Ashgrove would invariably remark. But this was such a constant phrase with the latter that no one attached much meaning to it on her lips, except, perhaps, her husband, who understood it to mean a young and rather pretty woman. Mrs. Warbler really dressed well, while Mrs. Ashgrove, with three sandy-haired, freckled daughters, was always making frantic efforts at once to lead the fashions and make their dresses at home. "Ah, yes, my dears, they are pretty dresses in a way; but to my mind the Melbourne dressmakers always give a frivolous effect to the skirts," she would say, when Bess and myself returned from a visit to the metropolis. But next time we saw Mrs. Ashgrove and her daughters ten to one if she had not clothed them in disguised copies of our Melbourne dresses, "with all the frivolity in the skirts and the good taste left out," Bess declared. Mrs. Ashgrove was not the most favourable specimen of Hamlington society; but as her husband, Dr. Ashgrove, was in partnership with our father, we were in a manner obliged to see more of her than we wished. This partnership had been entered into three years previously on account of our father's delicate health. It was this delicacy of constitution—weak lungs—which had in the spring of 187- decided father to take a trip to England "and the Continent," as we have learned to say, with a kind of vague grandeur. We were all to go, that is all of us who were at home, besides our parents, to wit, Bess and myself. The eldest of us, Mabel, was married to a doctor, settled in Queensland, and James, an only brother, was making his way as a squatter on a small scale in the same colony.

We were within a week of leaving Hamlington, when father lost a large sum of money he had invested in Ballarat mining shares. The day after this news reached us something occurred that put an end to all prospect of travel and sight-seeing as far as I was concerned. I left my mother in the dining-room with her accounts, and went out to Bess in the garden, where I had left her half an hour previously. In that interval she had been joined by Dick Fitzgibbon. Parentheses are hateful, but I must explain that Dick had come to the National Bank in Hamlington five months previously, that he was the son of an old College friend of father's, and had been in consequence a constant visitor at our house since his arrival in the place. He was a merry good-looking young man of twenty-two, Bess was a girl of twenty-one with a ready wit and lovely brown eyes. Dick had nothing but a miserable salary of £90 year; of course they fell in love, and of course the approaching departure brought matters to a crisis. Dick had "spoken" to Bess five days ago, and Bess though she was reckless enough to admit that she returned the young Irishman's passion, was not quite hardened enough to add to her father's troubles by allowing Dick to speak to her parents. They were standing beneath the Moreton Bay fig-tree—the pride of our garden—when I came out, with a look of ineffable "spooniness" on both their faces. Needless to say that they tried to look as grave and abstracted as if they had been discussing conic sections. As Bessie was my senior by a year it was only fitting she should set me an example of unimpeachable decorousness.

"Well, Nell," she said, with a surprising assumption of not being caught, "have you been reading Murray and making the sign of the cross over ancient cathedrals."

"Nothing of the sort, I am not going at all."

"Not going at all!" echoed Bess and Dick simultaneously.

"Oh, but what a shame, Nell," continued my sister.

"No, it's my own fault," I replied drearily. "Oh dear, what a dreadful thing it is to be such an idiot as I am. Five minutes ago I suddenly volunteered to stay, and now I'm in such a state of despair I can't even cry."

"But how came you to make such a melancholy offer, Nell?" asked Dick.

"Well, mother sat there adding up columns of figures, and looking so worried and horribly meek and long-suffering, as if she felt acutely how criminal it is to have two expensive girls to take abroad, but could not really help it. I thought of offering to go as a stowaway, but the thought of the aldermanic rats with a paunch, 'wie Dr. Luther,' that infest the holds of ships damped my spirits; then I felt sorry she had not sent us to a baby-farm in our infancy. I could not get a gleam of satisfaction out of our existence from any point of view."

"Oh, you raging heathen," said Dick folding Bessie's hand in his long brown fingers.

"Now don't you interrupt, Dick," returned Bess gravely. "Well, Nell—I understand—you were rather low-spirited all day, and I notice it is always when one is most depressed that one is apt to rush unthinkingly into the vortex of virtue. But go on."

"At last mother laid down her pencil, and gave a great sigh that turned the scales. 'Mother,' I said, 'will it make much difference if I stay.' 'Oh, my dear, you would not like to do that!' said the mother with a sudden light in her face. 'Yes,' I said quite brazenly. 'I can pay my long promised visit to the Harrowbys, and then go to see Mabel. I shall be quite happy.'"

Here Dick threw up his hands with an expression of tragic horror at my mendacity.

"And what did mother say then?" asked Bess.

"She thanked me in a broken voice and folded me in her arms, and then the last lingering hope died out of my heart. You know when one contemplates a stupendous piece of self-sacrifice a mean expectation remains that at the very last something will interpose to save one—like the clod that hid Sphigenia from the sacrificing priests."

"I didn't think the loss of a thousand pounds would have reduced us to such abject poverty," said Bess reflectively. "Perhaps I ought to offer to stay as well?"

"Oh, no, that little cough you luckily get occasionally will save you," I returned, half indignant at the robustness of my own constitution which obstinately refused to betray the slightest symptom of delicacy in any direction.

"Well, now, Nell, it's really frightfully good of you to give up your trip like this," said Dick in a tone of mournful sympathy. "And will you really like staying with the Harrowbys?"

"Oh yes; the only drawbacks are that Hester and Louise are ferociously learned, that John Harrowby and Nell hardly notice each other of late, while the Professor is simply oblivious of the existence of anything more youthful than a Sanskrit verb. He is a Professor of the Dead Languages, and has an abstracted dried-up look as if he lived on Greek and Latin roots; and Mrs. Harrowby (she is mother's first cousin, you know) considers that the whole of us are brought up on wrong principles," said Bess, answering for me.

"Faith, you wouldn't be so plump, my pigeon, if you weren't brought up on something more nourishing than principles," returned Dick laughing.

"Well, Bess, it's hardly fair of you to sum up the family like that," I put in. "Certainly, John and I are not such fast friends as we used to be; he has had too much to take up his attention, what between his work as a rising lawyer and his engagement, and breaking it off."

"That is such an odd affair you must know," said Bess, addressing Dick. "John Harrowby two years ago got engaged to a Miss Vandome— an heiress with thirty or forty thousand pounds of her very own. She is rather good-looking, but with such a very strong dash of vulgarity. John is extremely fastidious, and you couldn't see them together without being conscious that she was constantly irritating him in one direction or another. They had been engaged for six months when quite suddenly it was broken off, and no one ever knew who took the initiative. Miss Vandome went with an aunt for a trip to the old world. She returned six months ago, and now she and John are quite good friends again, and what will be the end of it no one knows, except perhaps Mrs. Harrowby, in whose eyes thirty or forty thousand pounds is an ample atonement for all kinds of deficiencies."

"Louise—that's the one I saw here when I came first to Hamlington, I think—is a very nice girl, only you always felt that you stood upon a vast abyss of ignorance into which you might at any moment plunge headlong when you were talking to her."

"Oh, but you know, Dick, it's the proper thing for girls now to be up in the sciences and the old religions and the modern languages and mathematics. I feel quite ashamed when I think how Nell and myself idled away our time over the old poets and writers, and a little French and German. Sometimes we made up our minds to attack Euclid, and so we used to begin a preparatory course of arithmetic, but oh dear, we *are* so shamefully backward in sums. There is one about so much money to be divided among men, women, and children."

"Bedad, I wish there was a little more of it floating about. But, my angel, what would become of a poor ignorant spalpeen like me if you were perched up on the topmost bough of the tree of knowledge? I'll never forget the shame and confusion that fell on me once talking to a sweet girl graduate a few weeks before I left home. She was my brother's sister-in-law more by token, and I felt no diffidence in trotting off on the broken-kneed old conversational hacks—the weather and the shooting. In fact, I had just launched out in the history of one of my father's old parishioners, when she brought me up short with some quest about the Archaeological Society. A party of them had been prowling about our district looking after some 'remains' or another. Did you ever hear of such a term? I get a kind of clammy feeling at the very mention of it. Well, in a few minutes Miss Gray was soaring miles above me. Yes girls, dear, it was exactly as if she was at an immense altitude overhead; now and then some such term as 'cosmic emity' and 'protoplasm' came booming down on me, and I just sat there with my mouth agape, vowing cartloads of the largest tapers to all the saints in the calendar if only they would deliver me. You know how in what the novelists call a supreme crisis one involuntarily goes back to the old faith. Well, there I sat, and never a saint took pity on me, and at last I became dimly conscious that Miss Gray asked me a direct question, ending in microcosm. Microcosm? I grew hot and I grew cold, while a wild whirl of thoughts passed through my brain. Was it a new tribe of savages discovered by Herbert Spencer? a modern sort of wall-paper? or stay, was it not a kind of biscuit? Ah, thank goodness, I had it at last. Miss Gray had taken pity on my darkness and at last broached a subject on which I could make a rational remark. 'Yes they are very nice,' I responded cheerfully. 'What is very nice?' retorted Miss Gray with a look of profound amazement. 'Microcosms' I faltered out, and then a horrible suspicion flitted through my brain that there *might* be no real connection between maccaroons and *microcosm.* Ah, but that was a *mal quart d'heure.*"

There was an irresistible drollery about Dick's method of telling a story, a raciness in his brogue that always provoked laughter of itself.

"Well, it seems to me we shall all be very dull after the jolly times and the fun we have had; the father and mother are always so wrapped up in each other, I shall feel little like a third party in a honeymoon trip," said Bess, rather drearily.

"Faith, we'll have no third party when our honeymoon comes," said Dick, looking unutterable things.

"Dick, don't you think you had better speak to father before he leaves," I said, prosaically breaking in on this rapturous prospect.

"Ah, my dear girl, that's what I want to do badly, but Bess shrinks from the thought of it, while your father has so much on his mind; if I could only get that rise of £15 or £20 a year I should pluck up courage at once."

"Well, how an additional £15 a year could appease the anger of an indignant parent, I am at a loss to understand," I answered, a little crossly.

"Ah, but it does Nell," answered Dick, earnestly. "I have written heaps of letters, and it's always when I come to that part I get stuck. And how often have I, in thought, and with Bess, rehearsed the scene till both our hearts beat. I would come outwardly resolved to speak to the Doctor, but inwardly hoping he was away. Just as I came in at the gate here, however, there would be a light in the surgery. As soon as I asked for your father, and find myself shown in, there every scrap of my native eloquence would desert me. Nothing of the English language would remain in my memory, save the most brutal idioms and proverbs which attest to the grasping Saxon's adoration of wealth. It would be with difficulty that I should say 'how do you do?' instead of 'when want comes in at the door, love flies out at the window.' Then your father would notice an unusual pallor on my manly countenance, give me one of his rapid professional glances, and say:–

"'Well, Fitz, has the muscular Christianity of the period been too much for you, knocked yourself out of gear with cricket, eh?'

"'Well, no Sir, but the fact of the matter is—I—my heart.'

"'Pooh, your heart—what about it?' your father would say, taking up his stethoscope.

"'What can minister to a mind diseased?' I would gasp.

"'Tush, boy, it's nothing more than a slight derangement of the digestive organs, a couple of liver pills.'

"'Oh! not liver pills, Sir, but Miss Bessie,' I would at last stammer out, and then the Doctor would plunge his hands deep into his trousers pockets and smile that half ironical little smile that fathers keep in stock for such occasions. 'So that's the way the land lies, is it? And what do you think Miss Bess herself will say?'

"'Oh, Sir, we adore each other—we have loved from the first moment we met.'

"'Indeed! Well, Fitzgibbon, you're the son of my oldest and dearest friend; personally I have no objection to you as a prospective son-in-law—but what is your income? how do you purpose to support a family? what prospects have you?'

"'My great aunt has a tidy little property worth five hundred a year; she has quarrelled with all her relatives except myself. Never having seen each other we are the best of friends.'

"'Yes, yes, but in the meantime—now?'

"'Now, Sir, I have a sage-green tea-cosy, with a sunflower on it—bought at a Church bazaar, and £90 a year;' and then, girls, would come that awful glance of your father's, under which I would feel myself slowly dwindling into nothingness—my last recollections of this sinful world being that strange enlargement cut off some unfortunate man's tibia, that your father keeps in spirits on one of his shelves. Now, girls, I put it to you—what man could stand such an ordeal as that? But, Bess, if you'll allow me, I'll speak to your father this very evening."

Everyone knows how obstinate a girl can be. Bess had taken it into her head that Dick's proposal on his very slender income would be the last straw in the culmination of troubles that now worried our father.

"Nothing of the kind, Dick," she said, promptly getting up from the rustic spindle-legged bench, on which we had been sitting under our favourite fig-tree. "Some day when we are on the voyage," she said, picking a leaf to bits with her pretty filbert-nailed fingers, "when the sun is shining, and the waves are dancing, and father has recovered some of his old spirits, and is rejoicing at the prospect of soon seeing grandma once more—then I'll tell him all about it, and I'll forthwith write a letter to you both, that will make you weep for joy—at least Dick will—as for Nell, she's an awfully hard thing at times—no sentiment can melt her."

Chapter II
An Unexpected Meeting

I had been just four weeks in town, when to my amazement one afternoon I suddenly met Dick Fitzgibbon in Elizabeth-street. I had been writing letters all the forenoon to my parents and Bessie, and as the mail was to close at 5 I went out at 4 to post them. Hester and Louise were constantly at some class or attending one of a course of University lectures, so that I had frequently to go out alone. Not that I minded—what girl bred in the bush does? But Mrs. Harrowby had at first made a point of my not going through the streets unaccompanied. So on a few occasions Blanche Maud, the under housemaid, decked in as much finery as she could possibly smuggle on her person, had gone out with me, and bestowed most affable bows on divers postmen, bakers, and policemen, who had returned the salutation with benign grins, and in some instances come to a dead pause—no doubt with the object of giving "Blanche Maud" an opportunity of introducing them to her *friend*. It was too absurd—and of course in a short time I dispensed with such a grotesque imitation of protection. It was the day after Cup day—that great Youmanhoo festival at which Dean Swift's satire is literally realized in Melbourne—when the horse is the proud master of the situation, when he receives the homage of feverish thousands, and is paramount in so many hearts, loud on so many lips. The streets of course were much more crowded than ordinarily, and the contrast between them and the leisurely semi-deserted thoroughfares of Hamlington gave me a keen enjoyment of the spectacle. At the Post-Office there was a perfect cram, so that it was a matter of time to get my letters posted. After accomplishing this feat I turned homeward, amusing myself with speculating about the divers types of faces I met. There was a hawk-eyed Jew whose Semitic nose would of itself have traced his lineage straight back to Abraham; his quick dark eyes seemed to search in the multitude round him for the Gentiles who were so ready to become the debtors of his race; jostling on his heels came the well-dressed, somewhat reckless looking young squatter, who habitually haunts town when races are on, and who as habitually comes down a "cropper" before he returns to his pastoral possessions in the heart of the placid solemn woods; beside him goes hurrying on a thick-lipped, heavy-jawed man with a flushed face and an evil look in his eyes—a man who has long fed on the husks that the swine did eat; on the opposite side is a wan-looking girl in a shabby dress, carrying a portfolio of music. I recognise in her one of the voluntary martyrs who advertise to give music lessons for one guinea a quarter; she is hurrying on to the dwelling of some small shopkeeper or artisan, whose daughters are taught to draw villainous trees and impossible bridges, to play inferior music on a bad piano, and to consider themselves entitled to be styled "ladies" in consequence of these superlative accomplishments; and here is a happy family from the country of three sons and four daughters, youthful copies of their treble-chinned parents, who have that look of dull content which is characteristic of people whose mental out-look is immovably stationary —blocked up for all their lives by an all-sufficing answer to the question—What shall we eat, and what shall we drink, and wherewithal shall we be clothed? And in contrast to this numerous family comes a solitary looking young man with a painfully depressed aspect. He is distinctly gentlemanlike, and there is something in his gait and the cut of his garments, and the freshness of his complexion, which marks him as a new arrival. Has he spent all his money on the passage out, and already found that for a penniless man who cannot dig and is ashamed to beg the *struggle for existence* in this large over-populated city of the 'under world' is as dire as in the old country? And who is this with the white face and the downcast look? Another young man with a most unhappy countenance. It will serve to show the absolute change in Dick's face when I say that for one brief instant I did not know him. As for him, he did not notice me; I doubt if he really saw anything that was round him. A sickening feeling of apprehension—a dread of some evil rushed through my mind. He would have passed me in the crowd but I hurried up to him and touched his arm. He turned round with a quick start.

"Oh, Nellie," he said, and his voice was as much changed as the expression of his face. It was hard and metallic, with all the jovial careless music of youth and high spirits gone out of it.

"Dick, you are surely ill," I said, looking into his face anxiously.

"No, that is I am not very well," he answered slowly. He turned and walked up Collins-street with me, and I waited for him to speak, to tell me what ailed him. But he volunteered no explanation; he absolutely began to say something about the weather.

"Oh, Dick what do I care for the weather? Tell me about yourself. When did you come to town? Why didn't you find me out?"

"I only came the day before yesterday," he answered, "and—the fact is, Nell, I've got into a horrible scrape, and there's no use in telling you about it, poor dear; it will only make you fret."

"But, Dick, I'll fret all the more if you don't tell me. The look of your face is as bad as anything you can tell me. Have you—resigned your place in the Bank?"

"No; I've received my promotion at last, and have been sent into town. Yes, just fancy how jolly we would have been only for this. Well, of course, I must tell you now, Nell. I arrived in town, as I told you, on the 3rd, the very evening before Cup day. On Queen's Wharf, just as I landed, who should I meet but Harry Quin. He was a shipmate of mine, and we were both very glad to meet again. He came out to a bachelor uncle, a rich old squatter in the Riverina District. He had come into town to dispose of a mob of cattle, and see to some other station business. I went with him that night to the hotel at which he stayed, and next day we went to the races together. He introduced me to some of his friends, and all went right enough. I betted a little, as every one else did, but nothing to speak of. Harry had to leave that evening, and half an hour before he went he asked me if I would oblige him by taking charge of £200 and depositing it for him next morning in the Bank—the National— you know, my own Bank, as he did not want to travel with so much money on him, though, probably, he would draw it in a few days, as he was going to buy some stud rams on his way back for his uncle. I ought to have placed it in the Bank yesterday, but I was not in town in time," he said. "Of course, I took charge of the money, and"—

"Dick, you have lost it," I said quickly as Dick paused.

"Well, Nell, it would be easy for me to say I lost it," returned Dick in a profoundly dejected tone, "but, then, I know that I am miserably to blame."

"But surely, Dick—oh, no?" I was not so ignorant of masculine human nature as to be unaware that men—and young men especially— will sometimes overstep the bounds of moderation, but I could approach the subject only in gasps.

"Well, not quite," answered Dick, to whom the pauses were eloquent, "but just that stage when one feels as mirthful as a harp in the hands of an angel in Paradise without the least logical reason in the world. Oh, Nell, I'm afraid you'll think me a worthless beast: but it was an exciting kind of a day, and a fellow takes a sip of this and of that, and then I was with a lot more young fellows in a billiard-room, till some one proposed we should go to the theatre. I went and put on another coat, and left my pocketbook in the one I put off. This morning I woke up at 9 o'clock, dreaming I had lost Harry Quin's money. I got up at once, and went to search my pockets, and found the pocketbook was really gone!"

"Oh Dick, how dreadful, what will you do?"

"The first thing I did was to tell the landlord, but the only result was a surprising amount of profanity, but he finally put the matter into the hands of the detectives. However, I don't expect ever to see the money again. When a man makes such a glorious fool of himself, he has no right to expect the interposition of Providence in his favour. In the meantime a cheque may come in from Harry Quin at any moment. Of course, if I knew whereabouts he were I would not have the slightest hesitation in writing and telling him. He would give me time to refund the money."

"But, Dick, why don't you tell the Manager all about it?"

"Because, my dear girl, so much embezzlement and money sharping of all sorts goes on at race time among young men in town, that confessing to any money trouble is like taking out a patent for a bad character. And I'm quite a stranger here, with my way to make. As ill-luck would have it, Frank Hamilton, who could at once help me through this scrape, is ill of a fever. All the money I have in the world is £60."

We had almost reached the gate opposite to the Harrowbys' big handsome house in Fitzroy-terrace. Some dim purpose was forming in the back of my head to help Dick, what I could hardly say, as I knew that my pocket-money in all could not be more than £35.

"Nell, I'm almost sorry I met you, you look so troubled and miserable," said Dick, as we stood by the gate.

"No, don't say that, Dick. I can, I must do something. Will you meet me near here tomorrow about 3 o'clock?"

"Yes; but, Nell, don't ask your friends for money for me," said Dick, flushing up painfully; "don't tell them anything about this."

"On, no, Dick, I don't mean to," I answered, with an inward shudder at the bare thought of telling Mrs. Harrowby of my perplexity and Dick's trouble. I could feel the calm, astonished gaze of her pale, prominent eyes riveted on my face as she asked me:—"And pray who is this young man whom you call Dick?" And if then and there I told her that he was to be engaged to Bess when their parents gave their consent she would have regarded me in the light of one of the evils that threaten the stability of society.

As soon as I got to my own room I turned out my purse, and found it contained five pounds in notes, two half sovereigns, and some silver; I then took my pocket-book out of the recesses of my trunk and subjected it to a rigid scrutiny. When going away my father had given me my half-yearly allowance on a much more liberal scale than ordinarily, and I am sorry to say that I had in consequence bought more pretty things to wear of late than there was any absolute necessity for. I thought of this with remorse, as I counted all my money like the king in the nursery tale. My pocket-book contained a roll of twenty one-pound notes, one 10-pound note, and some change. So at that moment I had exactly £30 15s. 6d. Then if I lent Dick £25, along with his £60, there would still be £115 needed to make up the £200 he had lost. There was a tap at my door.

"I have brought you a cup of tea, Nell; the tray had just gone out of the drawing-room when you came in. We were wondering where you were."

Louise sat on the side of my bed as I sipped the tea.

"By-the-way, Nell," she said as she was going out, "what are you going to wear this evening? You know there are some people coming to dinner."

"Oh, anything," I answered wearily. If one is planning to save a fellow-creature's life it is hard to have one's thoughts distracted by such irrelevant questions. No wonder some women who are anxious about their souls retire into secluded convents.

"But that's just what you musn't do. Jack was wondering the other day what you had done with your opals. Wear them to-night with that pale-blue silk of yours. Ah, why do you blush so furiously. Is there any history connected with your jewels that you are keeping a secret?"

"Only the old history, that they were left to me by the most benevolent of godmothers," I answered, laughing joyously, for the word "opals" had touched the secret thought that had been slowly developing in one side of my brain. I suppose the want of scientific precision in this is something terrible. But how else shall I describe that troubled vague groping after a fugitive thought, which some choice allusion all at once makes distinctly luminous?

In a trice I had taken out the quaint old oaken casket that contained the opal necklace, bequeathed to me by my godmother. They were of the kind called noble opals; in their youth they had reposed in the recesses of Simonka, in Hungary. How long they had been journeying among the children of men it was impossible to say; probably more than a century, to judge by their old-fashioned *pavè* setting of plain gold, of that deep yellow which the old ballad writers call "the red, red gold." My father had often laughingly said:—"Well, Nell, you have always a few hundred pounds between you and want in that necklace"—a sentiment which had seemed to me little short of sacrilege, so fondly did I love those gleaming gems, which seemed to hold in ambush all the tints of sky and flower and rainbow, flashing and blushing out suddenly as one looked at them, like meteors playing at hide-and-seek. It was anguish to think of parting with my necklace—but I need not sell them, I thought; I can pawn them. All the confused memories I had of pawnshops pointed to the fact that they were kept by harpies who thirsted for profit and were ready to cry "naught, naught" to the most precious heirlooms. But surely the most godless pawnbroker alive would advance at least £130 on my opals?

I had loved them for their beauty, because they had in them the bright fiery flame of the carbuncle, the fine refulgent purple of an amethyst, and a whole sea of the emerald's green glory, while behind all this fitful brilliancy spread a soft delicious milky-way of bashful serenity. Now I could have gone on my knees with thankfulness that they were so costly. The temptation rose strong before me to steal out there and then and hie to one of the numerous pawnshops which I had noticed in going about Melbourne. On several occasions I had scandalized Mrs. Harrowby when out with her by standing before the pawnshop windows and regarding their contents with undisguised interest. They seemed so full of pathetic stories—those pledges from the homes and lives of human beings. Unhappily it was frequently my fate to shock Mrs. Harrowby. But the habit was hereditary; indeed, nothing in our intercourse with each other annoyed me more than a habit she had of saying, "Your poor father," when talking to me of him. I suppose the chief cause for this element of chronic compassion was his steady avoidance of church-going. During one of his visits to Melbourne, at Christmas time, Mrs. Harrowby had pointedly asked him if he would not go to Church—*at least on* Christmas Day. To which my father had replied, "My dear Jane, though I am naturally of an economic turn of mind, I prefer not to mix up my swearing and praying in a sporting lot, so to speak." This allusion to the Athanasian Creed, filled the measure of my father's iniquity in Mrs. Harrowby's mind. Thus it will be seen that she was the last one to whom I could confide any perplexity, and I felt it would not be fair to tell Louise and Hester anything that must be kept a secret from their mother.

It was not a large dinner-party—ten in all. The principal guests were Archdeacon Tumsim and his wife. The Archdeacon was a smiling cherubic-looking little man, in whose mouth such themes as sin and sorrow and death seemed like pale traditions of things that could have no existence.

His wife was large and serene and masterful, always carrying a complex kind of handbasket containing generally a yard or two of coarse flannel to be manufactured into petticoats for destitute babies. Of course this was very good of the Archdeaconess, but one could have wished that the flannel was not of quite such a penitential kind. Indeed, some of the worthy woman's most impressive stories were of the ingratitude often displayed by the recipients of her bounty. "I am very poor, certainly, but I am not going to tear my baby's skin off with that." "Yes, my dear, these were the woman's very words," speaking of some delinquent with a solemn shake of her head, and then she would say something abstrusely pious about people not taking trouble, as it was meant for their good. The Archdeaconess had a way of alluding to the Almighty as the Great Disposer of Events with a certain air of patronage, as if she had promoted Him to the Directorship of a Joint-Stock Company. I did not have an opportunity of profiting by her discourse, as John Harrowby had taken me in to dinner and monopolized most of my attention.

"What a howling swell you are, Nellie; those opals of yours are real beauties."

This was the very opening I wished. I tried to speak carelessly as I looked down and answered, "Yes, they are great pets of mine. I have often wondered in a vague way what kind of emergency would make me sell them, and if the necessity arose how much I could get for them."

"Have you now? Pray what leads your thoughts to be sicklied o'er with such a pale hue of avarice?"

"Avarice do you call it? If you were such an ignoramus as I am you would often find yourself conjecturing what you could do if you hadn't a crust to eat and your last penny was spent."

"By Jove, what a touching picture of misery," returned John, smiling and pulling at his long tawny moustache. "I should think that to wear opals so gracefully is one of the best sources of income a young lady could desire."

"But, joking aside, what do you think a pawnbroker, for instance, would lend me on my necklace?"

"Upon my word you shock me with the mercenary spirit you display. Well, I suppose a man like Zaki Judah—you know the large Mont de Piété at the corner of—street—who does a respectable business in his way, would lend £140 or £150 on it—that is about a fourth of its value."

I could not very well under pretence of making conversation ask for farther particular regarding the practices of pawnbrokers, but as Zaki Judah was supposed to have a respectable business of "its kind," and as I knew where his establishment was situated, I resolved to take my necklace to him as early as possible on the morrow.

Chapter III

Judah of the House of Israel

The children of men are an ungrateful and stiff-necked race. If forty-five days are calm and prosperous, and the forty-sixth day rough and disastrous, they straightway write melancholy histories of that last day, and say, "Life is a cheat and a burden." We remember but too well the hours in which "Time was a maniac scattering dust, and life a fury slinging flame;" but we do not always remember with equal distinctness the halcyon periods in which no fateful messengers came to tell us that the Sabeans, the fire of God, the Chaldeans, and a great wind from the wilderness have utterly destroyed our dearest hopes, all our chances of earthly happiness. I always notice that when essay writers and moralists in general decry the human race and hold its weaknesses up to profound scorn, it is invariably on the consoling assumption that they (the writers) are exempt from such lamentable shortcomings. I avail myself of such illustrious examples, and openly protest that, however ingrate my fellow-creatures may be, I at least shall always recollect with thankfulness how Hester and Louise were occupied with the higher mathematics, and how providentially Mrs. Harrowby went away with the Archdeaconess to look after a woman whose husband had sold the blankets, and beaten the children, and torn up the tracts that had been bestowed on him for his conversion, leaving me absolutely to my own devices on that special morning when I wanted to pawn my opals. I gave them a long fond look when I took them out of their casket, wondering a little sadly when and how I should recover them again. But I drove this melancholy foreboding away, wrapped them in tissue paper, and put them in my sealskin portemonnai along with the £25 I would lend Dick in case the pawnbroker declined to advance £150 on my necklace.

Judah's Mont de Piété was at the end of a long careworn-looking terrace in one of the principal business streets of Melbourne. The main entrance was from this street, but there was a small dingy door at the side, opening on a rather squalid little off-street, and over this small and dingy door was inscribed the legend "Private." This was no doubt a thoughtful stroke of diplomacy for the encouragement of those faltering souls who, like myself, went shamefacedly to the place. My first impulse was to avail myself of the concession thus so kindly provided. But a nearer view of this door made me change my mind. It was a door with an incredible amount of freemasonry about it. It had originally been drab, but much use and little cleaning had told severely on its complexion. It had a large square pane of glass let in at the top and hung with a little faded green blind, which was pinned up at one corner. The aspect of sly craftiness which this imparted to the door is indescribable. It seemed not to wink, but to leer with a knowing mockery that was appalling. And withal there was an air of patronising fellowship about this door as though it would say, "Come on, you young spendthrifts, with your dis-honoured cheques and your interminable drafts on the future. I know ye of old coming with a watch given you by a fond mother, and your dead father's rings, and the sapphire-cross returned by the broken-hearted girl who was compelled to take back her troth. Bring them in, bring them in, gather them into the bosom of Abraham; you will come back again many a time and oft; but your jewels, when will you redeem them?" An uncanny kind of a door decidedly, and not to be entered lightly. I glanced furtively up and down the street, fearing the approach of some one I knew. Then I abused myself for an abject slave of Mrs. Grundy, and finally I marched in by the front entrance, trying to look as if trans actions with a pawnbroker gave the finishing grace to a young lady's education. The place was rather dim; it had wide counters running up two sides. Behind one of them stood a short stout youth with oily ringlets and a guileless smile, whose attention was engrossed by a thin woman in a draggled dress and a tartan shawl talking most volubly. There were two or three others standing round, evidently waiting their turn. "I'll take my davey on it that yer best give me back that ring," said the woman shrilly. "Mind, we ain't under 'Ebrew lawses in this colony. It's agin the British Constitution to take wooman's weddin'-ring 'less she gives 'erself—and that you'll find. Why, you might as well take my married lines—not as I would care if they was burnt, tho' I keep's 'em in the lining o' my best gown. Spike, he's a heavy-fisted loafer if ever there was one, but I never could ha' believed he would sneak away with the ring, and me to think I'd lost it when I was out washin', my finger being nothing to speak of but skin and bone, though it were that podgy the day I married 'im I scarce could get it over the knuckle. And then to come along and see it as bold as brass shinin' in your winder. Oh yes, I knows it right well. I'd know it anywheres, not bein' a weddin' ring at all, but the only one to be got, as we was up the Wimmera a hundred mile from any township, and Jeremiah he begged it from Dandy Bill, who ran through a fortin' with blackleggin', but 'ad 'ands like a femyale through it all."

At this point of Mrs. Jeremiah's eloquence, a door at the back of the shop was opened, and a second youth, if possible more guileless in his appearance than the first, entered. He gave me a quick scrutinizing look, and then came up enquiring whether I wished to see Mr Judah. I answered promptly that I did, and he then asked me to step this way, and preceded me down a long ill-lit passage past the "private" entrance to a dismal little room at the end, into which he ushered me.

"Sit down, Miss, my father will come to you in a few minutes," he said, and then closed the door. How my heart thumped when I found my-self alone in that room. It was dimly lit by a window which seemed to be let on lifelong lease to some enterprising spiders that were evidently making a good thing out of it. The only prospect it afforded was of a high blank wall and a few hundred chimneys. The light came timidly in like a banned creature on whose lips a price has been set. There was a large elaborate clock with figures in relief in silver, on a background of ebony, quite new and shining, standing on a mantelshelf. No doubt a pledge from some impecunious householder. And high above the mantelshelf hung a wonderfully ornate little French cage, glistening in blue and gold, containing a canary on a hoop that ceaselessly swung backwards and for-wards. What made it swing so frantically without uttering a single note? And why did those little eyes glitter so unnaturally? It was a painted bird in a painted cage. What an appalling fancy to make a sham bird—a ghastly image of the very incarnation of life and motion—and set it rotating dismally in a forlorn room! The sight repelled yet fascinated me, and I was still staring at the small noiseless phantom when the door was opened abruptly, and a short thick-set man with a beaked nose, enormous cheeks, and small piercing black eyes, overhung with long bushy eyebrows, came in. He bowed and smiled at me encouragingly, but my heart seemed to sink down to my boots.

"Vot gan I do for ze young lety?" he said, displaying a row of large irregular carnivorous-looking teeth.

"Can you—I—you lend money on jewellery, don't you?" I gasped, turning hot and cold by turns.

"Zhes, zhes on any dings," he returned, rubbing his hands in a gleeful kind of way. I tremblingly opened my portemonnai, unwrapped my necklace and handed it to him. He held it in his fat grimy hands and looked at the glowing iridescent stones with a ravenous kind of look.

"Zhu vant how mooch?" he asked, scanning my face with his suspicious little eyes.

It sounded so horribly like selling them!

"I require £150, and offer you the opals as security," I answered with as much determination as I could convey.

He gave a low long whistle and promptly handed me the necklace.

"Imbossible zat I coot gif so moooh," he replied. "Vat do you dinks I coot get for den ven you don't reteem?"

"I know they are worth £400, and of course I shall redeem them in a short time," I answered with indignant emphasis.

"Ov gorz, ov gorz, my young lety, eferybody reteems eferydings, zat is drue, and so comes it zat my whole house is vool ov dings zat a git money for zat I gannot get again; no nefer."

"Oh, if you cannot advance what I want I need not trespass further on your time," I said, rising and holding out my hand for my opals. There was such a horror in the prospect of leaving my beautiful necklace in the hands of this rapacious old man that for the moment I felt almost glad at the thought of taking it.

"I gan advance you £113 at dirty shillings a week interest till you reteem the necklace," he said quickly, holding the opals up in the light again. "No vone gan do fairer vor you; and I gan assure you I do it because you are von young lety in tisdress. You nefer have bawned nodings before, no?"

"Thirty shillings a week interest." I tried to reckon what rate of percentage this was but my arithmetic was too vague and my agitation too great to make any very precise calculations. I could only be sure that it was most sinful usury.

"Is that the proper charge?" I asked in as severe a tone as I could assume.

"Any dings lower would simbly ruin me," replied Judah with such solemn pathos that for a moment staggered me, and made me wonder whether I was not robbing this charitable son of Israel of his daily bread. But a glance at the vulture-like way in which he looked from me to my opals was enough to dispel this childish delusion. But I reflected that John Harrowby had spoken of this man as a "respectable pawnbroker." Of what use would it be to go wandering about from one plunderer to another only to sound the depths of pawnbroking greed? And how could I bear a succession of such interviews with the possibility that I might after all fare worse?

"Zhu will take dat amound, zhes?" he said in an insinuating tone.

I faintly murmured "yes," and he went at once to a chiffonier that was in the room, unlocked it, and took out a massive-looking money-box, which he pressed at the side on a particular spot, and the lid flew open. He took out little bundles of Bank notes, which he smoothed and counted out with a tremulous kind of tenderness. What a sinful world-weary existence many of them must have led! They were so soiled, so battered, so altogether disreputable, and departed from the purity of their youth.

It was easy to see that they had seldom been within sound of a Church-going bell; that they were privy to felony, and had been seasoned by topers in grimy public-houses.

"Vor how long do you bledge the obals?"

I had not the remotest guess how long it might be before my necklace would be restored to me. But I could not bear the thought of consigning them to Judah for an indefinite period, so I said "for a month," and then he took a square reddish ticket, inscribed a number on it, and handed it to me, and I counted over the notes of value, ranging from one to twenty pounds.

"A huntret and dirteen bounds; and now will you blease bay the inderest for four weeks. Zat will be sixch bounds."

I returned him six of the most hardened-looking sinners, and placed the rest in my portemonnai. I feel ashamed to confess it, but as I gave a last lingering look at my opals the tears came into my eyes. There they lay in all their sparkling yet soft elusive brilliancy, seeming to remonstrate with me for leaving them in such an uncongenial atmosphere.

I was glad to be out once more in the bright warm sunshine, and the fresh invigorating air away from the misty atmosphere of that close dim back room, with its glass-eyed little sham canary. I reached the rendez-vous in the Gardens a little before the appointed time, but Dick was there before me, looking more miserable, if possible, than he had done on the previous day. It somehow seemed as unnatural to see Dick unhappy and haggard as it would be for a joyous child. I could not bear to keep him in suspense one moment longer.

"Dick, I have got the money for you," I said, and then and there I pulled out the bundle of notes Judah had advanced, and with it the £25 of my own money. Dick stood quite still, his face flushing a deep red all over it.

"Nellie, darlint, where did you get this?" he said, in a slow pained voice which sent a pang through my heart.

"Oh, I robbed a Bank—you would be surprised to see how civilly they allowed me to present a pistol and take my pick of their notes. Quite an opening for young women in want of employment." Dick smiled, and when I saw him look a little like his old self I rewarded him by telling the truth—the whole truth, and nothing but the truth.

"But why did you go, Nell, it is bad enough to take your beautiful opals to a pawnbroker, but that you should go to such a place by yourself—and for me."

"Oh, Dick," I said, "it was such fun. Do you know I think it is very stupid only seeing people who read the same books, and wear the same kind of dresses, and speak the same kind of grammar as oneself;" and then I went on to tell Dick of the slatternly woman whose husband had pawned her ring. I could see the comical element in it now far more than I did at the time. I fear I imposed upon Dick, and that he really believed I enjoyed going to the pawnbroker's.

"But Dick, there are only £132 here, can you"—

"Yes, Nell, of course I can make up the rest—but to think that you should have done this for me. Oh, Nell, I can't bear to say just 'thank you,' as I would if you passed me the salt."

Dick clasped my hand in his, with a perceptible moisture in his eyes. We had wandered down by the little creek that babbles through the garden, and stood now beneath a large magnolia-tree, and while Dick held my hand in speechless gratitude, who should pass within a few yards of us but John Harrowby! He looked from me to Dick, and from Dick back to me again with an expression of cold and haughty amazement that made my cheeks tingle. I gave him a frigid little bow, to which he responded with a stern punctiliousness, and went on his way, towards home evidently.

"Nell, has that masterful-looking young man any right to look at you with such an air of outraged ownership?" asked Dick.

"Oh, that's John Harrowby," I answered with studied indifference, and then a comical look came into Dick's face which I did not quite understand.

"Then I suppose you're fast friends again—you and he?"

"Yes, moderately—but Dick, I'm afraid I must make haste home."

"But, Nell, you'll be sure to tell John that I'm your sister's sweetheart—and whatever else you may think fit. I won't mind his knowing about my scrape, for though he looked very black at me I like his face."

"Dick, if you mean that I'm to cry 'peccavi' to John Harrowby and tell him about your affairs because he saw me talking to you, why you're making a mighty error," I said warmly. I don't know which vexed me most, John's impertinence or Dick's quizzical smiles. There is no doubt that if the Lord had not made men the chief source of discipline in a woman's life all would be lost.

"Come, come now, my own good little sister, don't be cross with me whatever happens. It's no use my trying to say how I feel what you have done for me, Nell. I'm just in old Pash's plight. Ye remember how after he told us about the harps and the palms, and had pumped himself dry, he gave a little cough as though a crumb stuck in his throat, and said, 'But my brethren, we won't enlarge upon that.'"

I would certainly have been much happier going home if that *rencontre* with John Harrowby had not taken place. Should I not after all tell him the proposed relationship in which Dick stood to me? He came home that afternoon rather earlier than usual, and I was annoyed to find that I awaited his entrance into the drawing-room with a fast beating heart. "Just as if I were afraid of him," I said to myself scornfully. There were only Louise and myself in the room. Hetty had gone with her mother to a Dorcas meeting.

"Well, Jack, you are really getting into civilized habits again—coming home at half past 5," said Louise, looking up from her book.

I was sitting on a low chair in the bay window, partially hidden by the ample tapestry curtains.

"Is Nellie at home?" asked John abruptly.

"I'll go and see," answered Louise gravely, although she knew perfectly well where I was. "If she's not we had better invent a town crier. 'Lost or strayed—oh yes, oh yes—Helen Maxwell Derwent, when last seen, arrayed in brown eyes and a peacock-blue cashmere,'" and with that she left the room. Louise, despite her mathematics and ancient languages, had a spice of wickedness that was always more pronounced in her sister's absence.

By this time John had seen me, and sitting on an armchair within a few feet from where I sat, he favoured me with a long, searching gaze, under which I grew hot and uncomfortable, and doggedly obstinate in my inner heart. Outwardly I was calm, engaged in crewel-work, finishing the heart of one of a series of golden sun-flowers on pale-blue Roman satin couch-back.

"Let him think what he likes, I shall volunteer no explanation," I say to myself, threading my needle.

"So you really tore yourself away—got home after all," he says, bending slightly towards me.

"Why, did you expect that I would be swallowed by a cassowary, like the missionary of Timbuctoo?" I ask, just raising my eyes to his face.

He tugged at his moustache, got up and talked across the room; came back and stood near me with folded arms.

"Do your parents know of this affair?" he asked in a less saturnine tone.

"What affair, pray?" I asked with an accent of extreme astonishment.

"Oh, of course, you do not know what I refer to," he answered quietly.

"Why, do you mean my having worked the frog's leg out of drawing on my last piece of crewel?"

"Good heavens! how exasperating a girl can be," he said vehemently. Then he placed his hand over my work, forcing me to look up.

"Nell, who was that you were talking to in Fitzroy Garden?"

"A friend from Hamlington—Dick Fitzgibbon."

"Ah! and does my mother know? Have you told her?"

"No: she has not been in since I returned and if she were I don't think it is necessary to mention every one I may happen to meet."

"*Happen to meet!* Do you mean to say that you did not meet that fellow—the Fitzgibbon—by appointment?"

I was thoroughly angered by the tone of this question.

"I decline to answer you," I answered, and swept out of the room with imperial dignity. As I am not very tall, I was very glad I had a trained dress on, which I notice always lends a certain distinction when one leaves a room in wrath. But this air of dignity did not prevent me from being thoroughly vexed with myself for not being more amiable. And then I discovered that I had half expected John to ask me in the old cordial manner, which had lately been revived, 'Who was the friend you met this morning, Nell?' and that I was to have told him in confidence that it was Dick, Bessie's future fiancé, when father was robust enough to bear the shock of finding that his daughter wished to be engaged to a man whose wealth was comprised in a £100 a year, and an aesthetic tea-cosy. I found that we would be much tickled by this; that John would then ask for Dick's address, call on him, and bring him to the house as an old Hamlington friend. Of course, I would not dare to refer to the future connection till we heard from Bess that Dick's suit was favoured by her parents. "It might all have been so different," I said to myself pathetically, as if the history of endless processions of ancient and modern nations were not written to show that men invariably fail to take the course they should pursue.

Nor were my troubles over for that day. As we were at dinner Mrs. Harrowby, who always heard dreadful tales of human depravity when she went out on missions of benevolence with the Archdeaconess, recounted a thrilling story of a burglary in a friend's house, which was supposed to have been effected with the connivance of one of the housemaids.

"It made me feel that we are not half-careful enough in locking up, my dear," she said to the Professor, who looked up with a slightly scared expression, as if he feared that the wife of his bosom proposed to count him and wrap him up in chamois with the silver spoons. As he was prosecuting an exhaustive pursuit of a root that had viciously broken out in Sanskrit and the Chaldean tongue in totally different meanings, such a proceeding would have been disastrous. Of course, a moment's reflection showed him that there was no accommodation for him in the pantry; so he smiled vaguely, and said—

"Well, my love, shall we get more locks?"

"I decline to give up my latchkey, mother," said John, who held by that hard-won insignia of his liberty as tenaciously as the Barons clung to Magna Carta. Mrs. Harrowby had learned that though a husband may be trained to play the part of a Greek chorus in the domestic economy, it does not always follow a son will inherit the gift of submission. So she deigned no reply to this demonstration of chronic insubordination, but fixing her gaze on me said—

"Helen, you had better give me your opals to lock up in my jewel case; you have a careless habit of leaving your things about. The other day I went into your room, and saw a quantity of silver lying loose on your toilet table."

If Mrs. Harrowby had not been a woman of the most implacable resolution, I would have assured her that I kept my opals locked in their casket in the innermost recesses of a trunk hermetically sealed, or murmur some indefinite excuse. But I knew too well that whatever it was possible for me to say would straightway strengthen her in the conviction that it was a sacred duty to take charge of my jewels at once, and that as soon as dinner was over she would straightway march me into my room to give them to her. Strong as the temptation might be to a different course, honesty was now the only possible policy. So with something of the calmness of despair I replied—

"Thank you very much, Mrs. Harrowby; but I have not got my opals in the house just now." I felt myself turning into stone under the glance with which Mrs. Harrowby regarded me.

"You have not got them in the house," she answered slowly, with a little gasp. "Then, pray, where are they?"

A terrible silence fell on the room. I looked up helplessly to meet John's keen enquiring eyes full on my face. It is said that fashionable doctors have the medical accomplishment of looking grave whatever nonsense is talked to them. I fancy lawyers have a faculty for suspecting villainy when any little mystery crops up. I felt my face reddening horribly as I replied—

"They are quite safe, but if you will excuse me, Mrs. Harrowby, I would rather not explain why I haven't got my opals just now."

Chapter IV
John

Two days afterwards I got a letter from Dick that somewhat consoled me for the disgrace which hung over me for my missing opals.

"My dear Nell.—No pen has yet been invented that could express the feelings of gratitude which fill my heart for the deliverance you wrought for me. Never shall I forget last Wednesday morning. I met you with a miserable conviction that the Day of Judgment had come, and that I was the first criminal to be judged . . . To-day a cheque of Harry Quin's came in for £85. You can imagine how thankful I am that all has been arranged. Indeed, it seems as if my gratitude is too great—as if I could not recover from it. But then, I think of your destitute condition, and that helps me to touch the ground again. I know that as soon as ever Hamilton recovers he will advance the money to me on reasonable terms, and then I can get your lovely opals back from that old rascal—not that I should abuse him. But what I want you to tell me, Nell, is, have you enough money to go on with? I know the miraculous way in which a woman can go through a week with dignity, and spend perhaps only threepence. But have you the threepence? You would confer a great favour on me by stating the real state of your finances. You can have no conception of the manner in which I am saving money. The way I manage it is this:—I take every morning one shilling and sixpence for my lunch—not another sous. Billiards are cinders and ashes to me; as for beer, I never tasted it for a week till yesterday, and then it was cider—the day being so hot. The only redeeming little vice I cling to is a smoke now and then. And there is nothing like a pipe to console a man in affliction. Faith—not that I'm afflicted though—I can hardly explain it to you, Nell, but there is a certain desolation in saving money so ferociously. However, I mean to persevere, and so you see, my dear girl, I am quite in a position to be your banker."

But I decided that I could manage without trenching on Dick's hardly saved store. I could not help being sorry that he had to be so painfully economical. It might be pleasant to be stingy if one could live long enough. But there is a certain wastefulness about hoarding-up money when you may never have the pleasure of spending it. I used to think Bess and my-self managed with a very moderate allowance. But on reflection I found that mother must have paid for nearly all our dresses, and any girl knows that this is a considerable item in her expenditure. It was when I found all my remaining money melt away on trifles light as air that this fact was forced on my recollection. In three weeks I found that thirty-seven shillings had been frittered away with very little to show for the money. I took a pocket-book and pencil and began to make a solemn entry of all I could remember. A feeling of intense virtue suffused my frame, but nevertheless I could not get on with the list. Collection three Sundays, three shillings; Marabout feathers for white toque, sixteen shillings; a beggar with one leg, two shillings. There was a slight tinge of regret in my mind about this entry. John had asserted that all beggars in Melbourne were imposters. "But the man with the one leg who plays a barrel-organ, he is not an imposter," I had said. "Oh, yes he is, the other leg is doubled up in his pocket." I did not believe this at the time, but now when I regretted to find my money fading away like last year's roses, it occurred to me that John might be right. Where was the rest of the thirty-seven shillings? I raked my memory in vain to answer this question. The upshot was that I had to be extremely saving, not only had I to think twice before spending a shilling, but I had to think twice, and then not spend it. As I had not from the first allowed Mrs. Harrowby to bear the cost of my amusements I had now to make excuses, and steadily decline going to the theatre, opera, or even concerts.

"Is it that you are turning serious?" said Louise in an awestruck tone, one night when they were going to the opera, and I, as was becoming my wont, stayed at home.

"Who knows?" I answered laughingly. And, indeed, I began to enjoy having so much time to myself for reading. There are so many delightful old and new books that one should read and meditate over—not once, but a great many times. As Madame de Sévigné said—"It is to the interest of those I talk to that I should read beautiful books." So I read "Seven Lamps of Architecture" for an hour and more, and then I bethought me of a piece of work I had to do—the trimming of a hat. So I took it into the drawing-room and set to work. I had a yard and a half of white silk gauze, some pale blue sarcenet silk to line the wide brim, a few ears of corn and a scarlet poppy with which to drape the unadorned nakedness of the straw. Who, without trying it, could believe that to loosely twist a length of gauze round the crown, and catch the silk up at the side with a flower in a graceful manner, was almost beyond one's highest skill? I found it hard to believe I had been brought up a Christian, as time after time I pricked my fingers, and puckered the gauze. In the midst of this who should come in but John. Sometimes when he was more than ordinarily busy he did not come home to dinner, and would perhaps be not seen by the family till breakfast time next morning. On this evening he had not been home to dinner, and it was nearly 10 when he came in. Ever since the passage at arms I have recorded we had been coldly civil to each other, and that was all.

"I suppose the rest are at the opera," he said, after a formal salutation had been exchanged.

"Yes," I answered, fixing my slight, foolish flower on the side of the hat.

"Why didn't you go with them?"

"I'm not sure that I am very fond of operas, especially 'The Grand Duchess.'"

"So you stay at home *à la* Cinderella and trim a hat for a few orphans—of course that thing must be meant for more than one."

I think a man reaches the maximum of his odiousness when he stands in the Briton's typical attitude with his back to the fireplace, smiling at one's hat, and calling it "that thing."

"You are mistaken," I answered gravely. "It is not for an orphan asylum, but for a family. The father wears it and goes first, all the rest follow in his wake and are completely protected."

"In that case I must see whether it is adapted for a masculine head." He took my hat, and with the deftness peculiar to his sex he put it on back to front. It was too ludicrous. The sight of his big moustache and brown face under the flowing gauze and delicate blue silk completely upset my gravity. I burst into a peal of laughter, in which he joined, then returning my hat, he said:—

"Are you sure it is because you are getting indifferent to the pomps and vanities of this life that you stayed at home to-night?"

It is easy to make a lofty and dignified excuse when you are very indignant; but if an ancient feeling of kindness stirs the heart it is more difficult.

"Well perhaps not altogether," I replied, holding "that thing" at arm's length to decide whether the poppy was not too far to the back.

"You are very mysterious of late, Nellie," said John, sitting on an ottoman at my side, and speaking more in his old tone than he had done for a long time

"We used to be very good friends at one time. Do you remember when I went down to Hamlington three years ago, just before I went to England?" he went on, lowering his voice as if he were going to tell a secret.

"Yes, of course, when you were so proud because the tips of your moustache when pulled very hard reached your ears."

"Ah, little slanderer. Is that all you remember about my visit?"

"Oh, no. I recollect very well how you took me out on rides on Jill and taught me to jump brush fences to the utter ruin of my riding skirt. And one Sunday you gave me snuff in church, and when I took a tiny pinch I had to keep my face buried in my handkerchief for fear of sneezing. The Rev. Nicodemus was preaching one of his periodical sermons on the bottomless pit, and the next time I met him he said, 'My dear Helen, it gave me a thrill of pleasure to see how deeply affected you were last Sunday; such tears are a sign of grace!'"

"Yes," rejoined John, laughing, "and do you remember the day I went with you to Sunday School, and Mrs. Ashgrove insisted on my taking a class? There I found myself with eight little beggars punching each other on the sly, and then staring blankly in my face. I knew I ought to tell them about Adam or Jonah, or some old patriarch; but I felt awfully mixed up. I could not be sure what were the proper anecdotes to tack to the names. At last I said, 'Who was it that went into the lions' den?' There was a perfect uproar. 'Abel, Sir.' 'No; please Sir it were Joshua and the ten spies.' 'It warn't, it were the ten tribes of Judah.' 'It was Noah and his seven wives.' And then they began to quarrel over it, and give each other furtive kicks just like grown-up Christians:—

"Fighting each other for conciliation

And hating each other for the love of God."

And there I sat confused and helpless. There were so many persons who might have been the victim that I could not be sure who it really was. And the little imps were making such a noise every one in the school was looking at us. At last, in despair, I told them about the 'House that Jack Built.' Next week an irate mother complained to the Superintendent. She said she sent her children to Sunday School to learn hymns and Pharisees (she meant paraphrases), and not worldly rhymes."

We both laughed heartily, and then John said rather abruptly, "Do you remember the morning I left?" My heart gave a sudden leap. I did remember it—perhaps too well—but all things considered I did not see that John should bring it up.

"Yes; you left early in the morning, didn't you?" I said carelessly, bending over my hat, and stitching in the last ear of wheat.

"A little after six; but early as it was a certain young lady was up to give me some breakfast. What delicious coffee it was to be sure. I drank three cups of it; before I finished the third the young lady looked at the clock with a little cry.

"'Oh Jack!' (she called me Jack in those days) 'you must leave in four minutes. The coach passes Aaron's corner at ten minutes past six.' With that she handed me my gloves and"—

My face was getting intolerably hot.

"How absurd to recall such trifles," I said, making a desperate attempt to cut short these reminiscences.

"Trifles! ah, but wait till I tell you all. This charming young lady gave me my gloves, and bade me put on my greatcoat (it was a cold winter's morning), and then I was quite ready to go—but oh how loath. You must picture to yourself that the breakfast-room was warm and cosy, with a great fire of split fragrant blackwood crackling in the wide chimney, and that the young lady—she was just seventeen if I remember rightly—had the brightest eyes, the sauciest smile, and such roses in her cheeks. I believe I can even describe her dress. It was a lovely soft blue—a morning gown, you know, with a delicious little white fur collar and cuffs. Her fair hair had been hurriedly wound up, and as she flitted about a benevolently-disposed old hairpin slipped out of its place in that unobtrusive way in which true charity is always performed, and there the thick soft fair hair fell over her shoulders in beautiful rippling waves. 'Oh, Nell, why didn't you wear your hair like this before?' (her name *was* Nellie, by-the-way—curious coincidence, isn't it?) You must picture to yourself that the cares of this world and the deceitfulness of the law had not then taken hold of me, and that I was the fellow who in all the world least liked going away from this young lady. 'Never mind my hair, you really must go.' 'It's all very well for you who see your hair like this every day to say "never mind it." Did you keep it as a surprise to the last moment?' 'Oh you goose; must I drive you out of the house? Really, Jack, good-by,' she said, giving me her two soft little warm hands. 'I suppose I'll not see you for a woeful long while,' I said, unable to take my eyes off her hair. She came a little nearer, with a beautiful moisture in her bright eyes, and then I drew her still a little closer, stooped down, and"—

"You tell the story nicely; no doubt you have had practice in relating it," I said, half choked with contending emotions.

"Nellie, you should not say that," returned John in a subdued kind of tone. "If I have vexed you I am sorry, but that parting has come up in my mind so often of late, and—Well, at least after being such good friends at one time, and cousins always, I think you might be a little more open with me. I don't want to force your confidence. Of course I saw at a glance the relations between you and the gentleman you were talking to in Fitzroy Gardens"—here John paused, and though in my heart I would have been glad to disabuse him of his mistake, two or three contending emotions sealed my lips. Perhaps the most potent of these influences was the half bitter thought that as John himself had been engaged without even writing any of us a friendly note on the matter, he would more readily believe that I could adopt the same course, and of course eventually he must know the truth.

"What I want to say," he went on, "is that if I can do anything for you I shall be very glad. It strikes me that you have not been in smooth water of late."

"Thank you very much," I replied, hesitating whether I should say any more.

"Oh, confound it," broke in John impatiently. "I beg your pardon, Nellie, but if you don't give me any bread, don't offer me a stone. That conventional 'thank you very much,' is too absurd. It would be far less aggravating to hear you say, 'Please, mind your own business.'"

There was a ring at the gate, and the entrance of the family saved any further altercation.

"The mail is in, Nell," said Hester. "I suppose you'll get your letters to-morrow."

Mrs. Harrowby looked at me and then at John in an enquiring sort of way.

"I suppose you were too busy to come to the opera, John," she said, slowly drawing off her gloves.

"Yes, and that woman howls at you so when she is dying. I can't stand her."

"What woman? No woman dies in 'The Grand Duchess.'"

"No? I never go to the opera without seeing some woman in lace and jewels dying gracefully in time to the music, or a fool of a tenor in black velvet assassinated under cover of the ophicleide and big drum—only unfortunately he never *is* really stabbed."

"Miss Vandome was there to-night with her mother. That girl really seems to grow handsomer every day," said Mrs. Harrowby, calmly ignoring her son's bad temper.

I gave an involuntary glance at John, he was looking straight at me. It may seem curious, but the mention of his *ci-devant fiancée* made me feel pleased that I had not taken him into my confidence, as I had felt tempted to do.

Chapter V

What Came of It

I got my letters next morning at breakfast—a delightful batch. I forgot all my troubles, my pawned opals, Dick's increased poverty, and my own destitute condition, while reading them. Most of Bessie's letter was devoted to Dick; how she loved him, if possible, more than ever, how dear the old times in Hamlington seemed to look back upon, how she was writing a journal, and meant to persevere to the end, though jokes and sights always seemed a little stupider after writing about them; and most important of all, how mother and father knew of the attachment between Dick and herself, and were not—oh, not half so cross as we feared. 'I am afraid you'll have to wait a long time, Bess, before Dick's ship comes in,' the pater said to me quite kindly. But I know Dick will be very economical now, and we'll be able to manage quite well on £200 a year to begin with, &c. I feel thankful that I had been able to serve Dick so effectually. What a blow it would be for Bessie if he had lost his position in the Bank! But the afternoon post brought an invitation to me in common with the rest of the family, which changed the complexion of my thoughts from gratitude to regret. An invitation to a great ball, given by the Grantleys prior to leaving for a trip to Europe. Now a ball at Grantley's was quite an event in Melbourne society. From the moment you drove in at the gate and up the immense blue-gum avenue, lit with glorious lights, that looked like globed pieces of vivid starlight; and heard the soft musical rippling of innumerable fountains, it was like a brief sojourn in an enchanted land. Instead of the heavy splendour of costliness that one so often finds oppressive in the surroundings of the *nouveaux riches,* one found an etherealized kind of beauty, which seemed in no way associated with material wealth. Naturally all Melbourne was eager for invitations. Those who were disappointed at once remembered that Mrs.

Grantley was the daughter of an Irish labourer, "a man who broke stones, my dear, for seven or eight shillings. The mother took in washing, and Mrs. Grantley and her sister no doubt helped." "And where is the sister now?" "Oh, she married one of those millionaire Americans—they live in Paris in the utmost magnificence—not that I suppose for a moment they are received by the very best society there." This supposition was mere malice. The American millionaire's unlimited means, coupled with his wife's beauty, her supreme tact and unerring taste, had opened to them the most exclusive representatives of the ancient Fabourg St. Germain. It was there, no doubt, Mrs. Grantley had learned the rare secret of giving a ball that was like a page out of the "Arabian Nights." But quite apart from this divine gift, I liked Mrs. Grantley immensely. She was so witty and vivacious, and yet withal there was a grave depth in her beautiful Irish eyes that made one feel she was never ashamed to remember the old homely days when her father delved and her mother span—or washed, which, after all, is much the same.

"Of course you will go, Nell," said Louise, and without waiting for an answer she hurried away with a portfolio under her arm to take drawings of the ancient gods.

"Of course I can do nothing of the kind," I thought bitterly. For a moment a vision rose up before me of myself in shining raiment, with my opals gleaming in their marvellous way round my throat, and John coming up to claim the first waltz, and then I returned to prosaic reality and reminded myself that my opals were pawned, my purse all but empty, and that my last evening dress was shabby beyond redemption. Though outwardly I shed no tears, I felt that kind of inward chill which has all the melancholy of weeping without its pathos. Then I grew ashamed of myself; I remembered how many things there were that should weigh on my mind more than the fact of being unable to go to a ball. I reflected how high the percentage of paupers, lunatics, and criminals is all over the civilized world—how short and fleeting life is, how one should strive after goodness, and try to improve the time.

The result of all this moralizing was to leave a general flatness, which induced the feeling that after all nothing mattered so very much. Under these circumstances one may imagine my joy at getting a note from Dick by the afternoon post saying:—"My dear Nell—By this morning's mail I received a letter from my great aunt enclosing a draft for £300. At last a merciful Providence has put it into her heart that a fellow cannot go on existing indefinitely on nothing, that it is possible he may not be vowed to celibacy and that tailors have a superstitious habit of looking for payment. I never thought I should be so glad to get money. Dear girl, let me go with you to-morrow to redeem your opals. I shall be at the corner of —street at half-past 3 precisely."

I was only too happy to obey. Poor old Dick looked quite himself again.

"Do you know, my dear girl, I was beginning to be quite sceptical as to the very existence of happiness," he said, as we walked onto Judah's. "'Fairies, witchcraft, happiness,' I used to say to myself, repeating a melancholy little litany of the belief of early days; but now begad I feel that misery is nothing but a disease; the worst form of any, because, you see, having it once or twice is no manner of protection against the old baggage again."

"Do you remember what Heine says about the matter, Dick?"

"Das Glück ist line leichte Dirne,

Und bleibt nicht lang am selber art,

Sie streicht das haar Dir von die Stirne.

Und kusst Dick rash und flaltert fort

"Frau Unglück hat im Gegentheile,

Dick liebefast ans Herz gedrückt—

Sie sagt sie habe keine Kile,

Sitzt sich zu Dir ans Bett und strickt."

"Come, now, Nell; don't be after giving yourself a sore throat, but put it into decent Christian words. Although I understand 'das' and 'Sie,' the rest of the meaning is a little vague."

"But it is so hard to translate, Dick; the nearest I can get to the first verse is:—

"Joy is a maiden free as air,

Who does not long in one place stay.

She from thy forehead smoothes the hair—

Gives thee a kiss and flits away."

"The other verse defies me; the meaning of it is:—'Mistress, unhappiness on the other hand clasps thee lovingly to her heart. She says she is in no hurry, sits down by thy bed and knits.'"

"Faith, the old harridan turned the heel of her stocking well before she left me this time," said Dick.

Thus laughing and talking we reached the Mont de Piété. We both thought Judah looked a little dejected when Dick produced the ticket and explained that he had come to redeem my opals.

How delighted I was to see them once again. They blushed and smiled, and grew red and white, and took sudden subtle changes of yellow and green and fleeting scarlet on themselves as of old. It was delightful to fold them up tenderly and put them into my portemonnai once more. But a terrible thing happened as we were going out. Just as Judah was opening the side door for us, one of the assistants came up the gloomy passage—into which the side door opened—ushering two ladies and a gentleman into the sitting-room we had left. It was John followed by his mother and the Archdeaconess. The two ladies were talking, and a few paces behind. John with a glance took it all in, he looked from Dick to me without a sign of recognition, then stepped back and stood facing the ladies, asking some questions, and barring the way till we went out.

It was all over, and arranged in the most satisfactory fashion, and yet all through I had not been so exquisitely uncomfortable as I felt when John came into dinner that evening. He was behind time, and as he sat down he made some brief apology for being late. He sat just opposite to me, but he never once allowed his eye to wander in my direction. Absurd as it may seem, an overwhelming sense of confusion fell on me, when, as I sat there, I fully realized the equivocal light in which he must regard my conduct. A girl who, in the absence of her parents, made assignations with a man unknown to her relations, made assignations, and went with him to a pawnbroker. What did he think? Not the least chance of finding out. He hastily ate his soup, listened with half his mind to his mother's reiterated expressions of horror as to the wickedness of a man named Jorling, who had deserted his wife for six months, then returned and lived upon her earnings, spent all the money she had, and finally stole all her jewellery—a gold watch and chain and some rings, which had been traced to a pawn-broker's. This was the reason of the visit which had been paid by herself and the Archdeaconess under the shadow of John's legal pinions.

"And you actually went into a pawnbroker's, mother," said Louise, "what fun! I wish I had been with you."

"Indeed, my dear, I am at a loss to know what fun there could be in visiting such a place—the resort of criminals and vagabonds of every description," returned Mrs. Harrowby severely.

"Surely, my love, yourself and the Archdeacon's wife cannot be placed in either category," said the Professor with mild deprecation. Louise and Hester tittered, but John looked as impassive as if he were a Sphinx in the Libyan Desert. Did my abnormal iniquity so prey upon his mind that like the King of old he would never be seen to smile again? I am afraid I half enjoyed the thought of the way in which I would scatter those gloomy visions of his by the simple statement—"That was Dick Fitzgibbon—my future brother-in-law. He was in temporary embarrassment for money so I pawned my opals, and to-day he went with me to redeem them." For I really felt that I must offer John an explanation this time. The opportunity offered itself in the course of the evening. I had been playing and singing to "an audience composed of the performer," as Dick used to express it, when, as I sang that old pathetic Scotch ballad,

> "Sweet the lavrock's note and lang
>
> Lilting wildly up the glen,
>
> But ay to me he sings ae sang,
>
> Will ye no come back again?
>
>> Will ye no come back again?
>>
>> Will ye no come back again?
>>
>> Better lo'ed ye canna be,
>>
>> Will ye no come back again?"

I felt rather than saw that John had come in and stood a few paces behind me. As soon as I finished the song I turned round and said—

"You saw me to-day at Judah's?"

"I did."

"I was grateful that you sheltered me from your mother's observation. She would have been astonished if she had seen me."

"I should say she would rather."

"I daresay you guessed what took me there."

"I never guess."

Now I put it to any one whether with the best intentions in the world, such curt rejoinders, coupled with a demeanour closely resembling that of

an iceberg in the Arctic Ocean, are not enough to repress the most determined friendliness. It is all very well to plan a reconciliation and repeat a
confession beforehand, but after all anticipating a conversation is something like trying to answer a letter before it is received. I sat quite still, hon-
estly wishing to explain but quite unable to call up the necessary amount of
humility—to eat dust like the serpent as it were. And then John spoke:—

"I said before that I have no wish to force your confidence, but there
is one thing I *must* say."

He paused, and the beating of my own heart was the only sound I heard.
Then John went on, every word dropping from his lips like a separate icicle.

"While your parents are absent you are supposed to be under my
mother's protection, are you not?"

"Yes, I suppose so."

"Then I ask you in all fairness is it consistent with your ideas of propriety
to make assignations with a young man who is a complete stranger to her."

"That depends on"—

"It depends upon nothing," interrupted John vehemently. "There is
nothing to excuse a girl for doing such a thing. And to go with him to
a pawnbroker's of all places in the world. You credited me with guessing
the purport of your visit. What was it?"

"To redeem my opals."

"I thought as much. Yet during the last three or four weeks you have
had so little money that you have been obliged to deny yourself all cus-
tomary amusements."

I made no rejoinder.

"What conclusions am I to draw?" looking at me with a world of
wroth blazing in his eyes.

"Knowing nothing you will of course think the worst," I answered,
looking at him with the fearlessness of injured innocence.

"Shall I tell you what I am forced to think?" said John, with a sudden calmness of manner which I knew was forced.

"Yes; if it gives you any satisfaction."

"Then I think you are a misguided, over-credulous girl, who allows herself to be blinded and duped by a foolish attachment."

I maintained an obstinate silence.

"Answer me one more question, Nellie. Do your parents know of your engagement?"

"My engagement? well, it would be an extraordinary thing if they did, seeing I don't know of it myself," and with that I made a clean breast of it. John's face was a perfect study; amusement, indignation, and some other curious expression strove for mastery. When I finished he stood looking at me for a minute or two without saying a word.

"Well, you are a most determined wicked little minx," he cried at last, but there was a smile lurking round his mouth. "What pleasure could you find in torturing me like that?"

"Torturing you?"

"Yes, come, Nellie, I'll stand no more nonsense. Oh, hang your letter-writing. You don't go out of this room till you give me an answer."

"Good heavens, how many more questions have you to ask. You're like a catechism and a Royal Commission rolled into one."

"Well, I'll ask only one. Do you know what made me so mad about the pawning business? Now no evasions, Nell—look at me straight in the face."

John was standing beside me now, looking at me in a way that made my heart beat and my cheeks flame.

"Shall I tell you. Nell"—he said almost in a whisper, "because, my darling, I love you."

"Oh, Jack!"

I went to Mrs. Grantley's ball after all, and danced with Jack so often that I am afraid every one must have guessed we were engaged.

A Stray Kitten

"Going anywhere this evening, old man?"

"Yes, confound it, I have to go to the Cornflowers' dance."

"Merciful heavens. This is Friday. On Monday you went to a ball, Tuesday ditto, Wednesday a carpet dance, Thursday an at-home, and this evening again! No wonder that the little intellect you have is rapidly vanishing. When I come to look at you narrowly there is an expression of rooted imbecility on your face. Beware, young man, of the baleful results of constant dancing, simpering, and tea drinking."

"It's all very well for you, Thornton, to indulge in such everlasting chaff, but I would like to know what would become of society if every one were as selfish as you are."

"Oh, come, this is too rich. Are you really going to pose as one of the modern martyrs of altruism? Ha, ha, ha! Fancy all these delicious little bouquets, white gloves, faultless ties, and late hours being for the good of society. Do you know I was so coarse minded as to fancy that they were for your own personal amusement. But now, when I come to think of it, of course it's all self-sacrifice! But seriously, Browne, how can you stand it night after night? The mad galop, the seductive waltz, the unwholesome supper, the cloying inanities of bread-and-butter misses, the bitter gossips of the old campaigners, whose sole claim to originality is their belief that they are youthful."

"Well, Thornton, of all the bitter old cusses I ever knew, you're sometimes the worst. Is there a gully breeze to-night, or has your liver gone back on you, or what? There may be nothing very grand or elevating in the commonplace amusements of commonplace young men like myself, but how does the general current of my life compare with yours?"

"General current of my life is a good phrase," murmured Thornton.

"Come, now, as you have been so unsparing with me, let's see what kind of picture may be made out of your own pet amusements. None of your friends can depend on you for a social gathering of any kind. Why? Because an evening coat and the amenities of civilized life are despicable in comparison with lager beer, cards, tobacco, and the savage freedom of the clubs. You wonder I don't get tired of dancing with girls. By Jove, I do wonder how it is you don't get sick of old Harley and Yap and Mac. I heard Yap tell a story about a piebald horse the other evening for the twenty-fifth time. Does he always tell it, and do you listen and laugh over and over again just as politely as if you submitted to the indignity of changing your coat before dinner?"

"Well done, young one—go it—I admire your pluck," laughed Thornton.

"And as for that Girder who is eternally with you," said Browne, speaking with all the warmth of long-restrained dislike, "why, the very turn of his nose makes my gorge rise. He is for ever sneering and carping at something. Whether a woman, a horse, a game at billiards, a book, a picture, or an investment. Girder treats all with ineffable condescension. If an angel appeared to him (not that I can in the wildest flight of fancy imagine one of the heavenly host with such frightful want of taste) the only thing Girder would be capable of saying would be—'Ah, a secondhand pair of wings; bought them up cheap!'"

There was no withstanding the tone in which Charlie Browne mimicked Girder, and Thornton laughed with real enjoyment, and then said rather gravely—

"Well, well, my boy, we neither of us make a very shining tale out of the life that now is; but you see Girder and Yap and the rest of us at least interchange good literature and such ideas as our brains are capable of conceiving. The work of the world and the problems of life may not be greatly advanced by our discussions of them, but they at least in some measure help us to keep some hold on the vast interests of the world at large, instead of sinking submerged in a flood of frivolous trifling, in one stifling narrow groove; and, joking apart, it seems to me one of the most appalling modes of killing what little intellect a young man may have, this apeing of the modes in which the aristocracies of old countries kill the time. Now, if you were a member of an old European aristocracy, you might go to balls and routs, and shoot, and run after opera singers, and still have heaps of time left to save your soul and improve your mind. But here, where we have no leisured classes as such—where every man, unless he is a born loafer, has some kind of work to do—to devote so large a portion of the margin you have in life to the most frivolous and objectless pursuits, is simply destruction to any mental development.

"But, seriously speaking, now," said Charlie, with a very impudent imitation of his friend's graver tone, "don't you think that your own partial seclusion from the society of ladies is rather a hindrance to that all-round development you speak of?"

"Yes; yes, it may be, nay it *is*, but it has been my unfortunate experience that most of the women I know have 'no character at all.' What I mean is that our well-to-do British matrons have an unhappy knack of becoming submerged in household details or in endless gossip of their neighbours' concerns in a way which to most rational out-siders is simply the acme of boredom. To give up a favourite author or the prospect of an evening's good whist-playing in order to hear for the five hundred and twentieth time of Johnny's measles or the extraordinary recklessness of Mrs. Robinson's party giving is a little too thin. Between that and being stuffed into a room where a num-ber of young men and women are hopping about with more or less celerity is certainly to most men who have outlived their salad days a choice of mislikings."

"You speak as though you were an Eastern potentate with rows upon rows of nautch girls around you at whom to throw your pocket handkerchief. Pray publish a recipe for training women in the art of conversing with all the piquancy of a grisette in a French vaudeville, and after that you will perhaps find society a little more tolerable."

"Let me explain"—

"Well, you must explain yourself on some future occasion. I have not a moment more to lose. You are aware that there are seven Miss Cornflowers, and that the number of men who are basely wanting in a proper sense of their social duties is largely on the increase." With this Browne left the room, and Thornton, who still had an hour on his hands before he met his friends at the "Barbarians' Retreat," poked the fire and fell into a reverie.

Rendered into words, it was something after this fashion:– "Partial isolation—yes, say what we will, the lack of any close friendship with women who are pure and noble makes a fellow's life very sterile. Has not some one said that between man and man there is an insuperable gulf? They can never quite grasp each other's hands, and therefore man never derives any intimate help, any heart-sustenance, from his brother man, but from women—his mother, his sister, or his wife. Wife! well, sometimes there is a sort of magic in the word, a thrill; and again when one looks round among his married acquaintances what a miserable procession of failures, looked at from any ideal stand-point, wives are. One is deplorably ugly; another hopelessly commonplace; a third has a shrill voice and talks nothing but measles, or whatever infantile disease happens to be going; a fourth is pretty but vain to the verge of imbecility. Bah! the man who sold all that he had to risk his wealth in a grand lottery ticket, and drew two red herrings and a crooked sixpence, was lucky compared to the man who makes a mistake in the choice of a wife . . . And most men make a mistake. What a frightful sell life is on the whole . . . When one thinks of the hordes of human beings who live in mud hovels, or the damp cellars and bleak archways of overcrowded cities—of the children born only to shame and pollution, with no hand stretched out to save them—yes, and the still greater number who are doomed because some near or remote ancestor had a passion for champagne and truffles, or some more disastrous vice. Truly our pet sins are chickens that infallibly come home to roost. Who says that most men and women are only just one couple more? It's true, and all this shine we kick up about our progress and—Bah! I'm actually moralizing."

Chapter II

Charlie Browne did not indulge in any reveries after he left his friend. He dressed with the rapidity which is insured by constant practice and the absence of any distinct amount of vanity, and hastened to the hospitable mansion of the Cornflowers. He was not conscious that Thornton's words made any lasting impression on him. Yet somehow he took up an attitude of criticism which was certainly the result of repeated conversations much in the same vein as the one that has been recorded. "*Do* these girls really talk such pitiful nonsense as Gabriel Thornton thinks?" he said to himself; and the next girl he danced with was subjected to very unfair analysis. She was rather short and thickset, with small eyes and a not lovely complexion—facts which no doubt enabled Charlie to be more impartial in his observations than he otherwise might be. There were live couples on the floor in excess of what the room would comfortably hold, so the pauses in which conversation is possible in the course of a polka-mazurka were not infrequent.

"Have you heard that Willie Merton is engaged, Mr. Browne?"

"Oh! yes; he told me of it himself. Very nice girl Miss Harker is, too. Don't you think so?"

"Yes, no doubt; but you see she is not in our set. I don't know her very well. But fancy Willie, you know; he is asked everywhere, and to marry on £300 a year! How do people live who marry on that? Do they take a cottage in the hills, and grow cabbages and a pig and some chickens?"

This no doubt was meant to be very amusing, but instead of laughing Charlie recollected that this young woman's father had been a grocer's assistant; had married his employer's daughter, and lived for the first decade of his married life on a weekly wage of fifty shillings. Then the champagne was inferior, so that next morning Charlie woke with a bad headache, and was inclined to moralize. In fact, the habit stuck to him all that week; so that towards the end of it he said to one of his boon companions who was in the same Bank with himself—"I say, Anthony, don't you think a fellow might do better than all this dancing and liquoring up, and all the rest of it?"

Anthony did not take readily to new ideas, so he gave his friend a blank look, and then said, "What the deuce do you mean?"

"Oh; do you never get a little sick of things in general, and long to do something else?"

"Yes; I get pretty sick of being in the beastly Bank at £150 a year. I'd like to make a travelling menagerie of the Manager and the Directors, and charge the public a shilling a head to look at the vermin, who expect a fellow to pay his tailor out of three notes a week. If the Governor didn't shell out now and then where would I be?"

"Well, you see, perhaps if you gave up a few expenses and took more to reading, and that sort of thing"—

"Oh, what put such a frightful thought in your head?" groaned

Anthony. "Perhaps you mean to go on the same tack as Barringer, who began to learn French without a master. You know we lodged together for a time, and he used to wake me up in the morning, making the most unearthly sounds. I used to offer to run for the doctor, or get him a mustard-plaster, or anything in life to stop that ghastly howling. Oh, no; he wasn't ill; it was the letter *u*. And then he used to explain that this vowel in French should be uttered with a greater effort from the pit of the stomach, and conveyed through the nose, taking care to keep the tongue down. 'There is no similar sound in English,' he would say, proudly. Oh, but I know what's spoiling you—you live too much with that newspaper fellow Thornton. He shuts himself up for a week at a time, writing tales, doesn't he?"

"Not quite so bad as that; but he does write a good deal between one thing or the other. By-the-way, there he goes to Munch's—we may as well go and lunch with him."

When they got in, however, they looked in vain for Thornton. Charlie looked from one table to the other, but though he saw a great many of the men he knew, he saw no trace of his friend.

"I say Dick, have you seen anything of Thornton here just now?" Dick was a young man with a florid complexion and a long drooping nose, who was what the reporters call 'doing justice' to his viands.

"Oh, Thornton doesn't condescend to grub with a lot of unselected mortals like us. He has had the audacity these last few days to go straight up to the ladies' room. I believe he spoons on that pretty little rich widow. She is a stranger here—you know who I mean—the little party with the eloquent brown eyes."

"What, a Madame Pousard? Why her husband has been dead only four or five months!" ejaculated Charlie, and then a sudden conviction seized him that there was something in this insinuation.

"All the more reason why she should want the consolation of a refined and cultured Job like Thornton," said an elderly man, who was the beau ideal of a sucking Mayor—sleek, obese, and smiling.

"And he never breathed a syllable when I chaffed him the other day after seeing him with a charming young widow," said Charlie, with a sense of grievance strong upon him.

"I say, though, wouldn't it be rather a jolly lark to spring a mine on him," said Anthony, who had ordered a plate of the veal and ham pie for which Munch is renowned.

"What do you mean?" asked Charlie.

"Well, you know what an embodiment of all the cardinal virtues old Munch is. Has to obtain a certificate of character from a fellow's godmother if he speaks to one of the waitresses, and all that sort of thing. If some one goes up to him and says 'Look here old fellow, my wife used to come to your room upstairs regularly when she went shopping with my three eldest daughters. Of late, I am sorry to say, she has been forced to cease patronising the room.' Old Munch would get as red as a turkey-cock, and gasp 'What's wrong—the soup?' 'No, the soup is beyond criticism; so is the cold lamb; so is the salad; so is the pepper; and, likewise the waitress; but'—an awful pause there, and then as old Munch is on the point of choking, in a low sepulchral voice—'so is not the gay Lothario who, without wife or child, goes up there day after day and scandalizes all the respectable matrons who are the guardians of our hearths and homes.'" Young Browne, the sucking Mayor, and Dick, all laughed, and voted this a good idea.

"Gad, you better go and make that little speech at once," said the elderly man.

"Me!" echoed Anthony. "Why, you darned old innocent, there's a bit of my skin nailed up on every domestic door in the place. I'm an example to every harassed father who has a son going to the bow-wows. Look at

Anthony Talbot—that's what you'll come to if you don't look out. Thus I'm made to point a moral and adorn a tale. Now you could without the slightest trouble take upon yourself to speak 'seriously'—isn't that the phrase?—to old Munch."

"I don't quite see it," answered the elderly man, rather stiffly. He had reason to believe that Anthony was trying to get up a kind of private pantomime, and resented being selected as the hero.

"Look here," broke in Charlie with eager face and voice, "I've thought of a plan much better than any personal steps in the matter. Let's draw up a letter for the *Guardian*; it can appear in tomorrow's issue." He took out his pocket-book and pencil, scribbled on a leaf for a few minutes, and then read aloud—"Sir—As a member of the Social Purity Society, I beg to address a few lines to you on a matter which is not without some importance to the general public. There is a certain restaurant in this town that has long been regarded with favour and confidence by respectable people. And deservedly so; for in this restaurant the unholy sound of bacchanalian laughter is never heard, no billiard room is attached, and the menials are without exception, like Caesar's wife, above suspicion. Of late, however, a change is noticeable in the room devoted to the use of ladies. In this room wives, mothers, and daughters have hitherto assembled when the necessity arose, without fear and without reproach. For they were well aware that no clandestine male dared to enter the room unless his morals were satisfactorily vouched for by the presence of a wife, a sister, or a daughter. Of late, however, this sacred confidence has been rudely disturbed, and if a change does not speedily take place, the irreproachable British matrons, who have hitherto been secure in the well-known respectability of the restaurant in question, will have to seek some retreat secure from the insidious presence of unwedded flirtations.

I am, Sir, &c.,

MATERFAMILIAS."

"Bravo! that's the very ticket," cried Dick,

"It will do admirably—admirably," said the elderly man.

"Yes," chimed in Anthony, "with one or two corrections. 'Clandestine male?' Is there any reasonable being who could attach a meaning to such a phrase as this?"

"Certainly," said the elderly man. "A 'clandestine male;' well, I can't quite explain it, but the phrase will go down with every respectable person."

"Well, every respectable person must be a precious fool, that's all," said Anthony, moodily. "And 'unwedded flirtations;' surely that will cover the letter with ridicule. Who ever heard of people flirting after marriage? You might as well expect people to be in love with each other after the honeymoon."

"Now, Anthony, have you ever been married?" said Charlie solemnly.

"No, thank heaven; various as my mishaps have been, I have not come to that yet," replied Anthony.

"Very well, then, my boy, you shut up. It may be epigrammatic and *French* to assume that there is no love nor flirtation after marriage, but I assure you that coquetry over a butcher's bill is by no means unknown in British married life."

"Hear, hear," said the elderly man with enthusiasm.

"Then this letter is to be sent to the *Guardian* intact?" said Charlie, addressing himself to his audience of three with a most business-like air.

The table at which the four sat was near the door leading into the shop, where buns, custard rolls, meat-pies, ice creams, and various other delicacies too numerous to be mentioned were retailed to the public. Now, between them and this door was the staircase that ascended into the ladies' room, and at that moment who should come down but the pretty widow with eloquent brown eyes, followed by Gabriel Thornton. She was clad in black, with the conventional heavy veil. But the latter was thrown back, and revealed an extremely pretty and almost youthful face, lit up with brown eyes that were indeed eloquent, not to say enchanting. The two passed out through the shop, attracting the attention of many besides that of the four men, who looked after them with so much interest.

"Now, Marion, I must go back and get some lunch," said Gabriel, taking out his watch as they reached the street.

"Very well," returned the young widow with a decided pout. "Then am I to understand that I can get no money beyond the paltry £500 a year mentioned in the will?"

"Certainly not so far as I and your other trustee are concerned. Five hundred pounds a year for your personal use, £100 for each of the children. It is impossible for us to make any advance on that. And I must again say that I think Pousard was more liberal than most men would have been under the circumstances."

"Oh yes, Gabriel, I understand the insinuation. 'The circumstances' —that means you think I am altogether to blame because Pierre and I could not quite hit it, and had to live apart for the last year before his death."

Madame Pousard drew out a delicate looking heavily laced handkerchief, and held it elaborately to her eyes, under the crape fall which she had now drawn over her face.

"For God's sake, Marion, don't make a scene in the public street," said Thornton, hurriedly.

"Oh, I have no intention of making you ridiculous," said Madame Pousard, withdrawing the handkerchief. "I thought that you, as my second cousin, and nearest living relation, would stand up for my rights, and make the other trustee see how really unjust poor Pierre's will is; but it seems I am mistaken. When can I see you again?"

"Any time you wish—but, wait, to-morrow and to-morrow night I have special engagements, and the day after is Sunday."

"On the 13th, then—that will be Monday—meet me at Munch's. I will be there at half-past 12. I'll bring the accounts I told you of, and show you how desperate my case will be if I can get no more ready money."

The two parted with a silent handshake at the corner of Königin and Wendel streets, and Thornton returned to Munch's *café* with a clouded brow. He made straight for the table at which he saw Charlie Browne sitting.

"Well, young 'un, how goes it with you," he said, with a somewhat unsuccessful attempt at hilarity.

"Ah, tolerably," said Charlie, a trifle stiffly.

Thornton, however, was too preoccupied to notice this. He glanced over the bill-of fare and ordered a roast teal.

"We did not look for the pleasure of *your* company down here, Mr. Thornton," said Anthony demurely.

"Why not?" asked Gabriel absently, and then, without waiting for a reply, he took out his pocket-book and totted down some figures.

Anthony elevated his eyebrows. "Adding up her income," he whispered to Charlie. And this was really nearer the truth than the young man imagined.

"The woman is absolutely rapacious for money," was Thornton's mental comment as he reviewed his cousin's financial position. She had returned from England only a few weeks ago, where she had been for nearly a year; incompatibility of temper had led to her separation from her husband, who, during her absence, had sold a valuable property in an adjacent colony, and bought a station in South Australia. She now visited Adelaide for the first time, and was staying with some friends seven miles out of town. Thornton had seen very little of her, but after Pierre

Pousard came to South Australia the two men formed a close friendship, and hence the trusteeship which was likely not to be a sinecure. Thornton was a reticent man, and hence very few of his friends knew as yet that the pretty young widow who was credited with so much money was a connection of his, and that he was one of her two trustees, the other being a squatter whose property adjoined the late M. Pousard's station.

Chapter III

Mrs. Seymour was a widow past fifty, with ample means and an only daughter. It would be hard to say which caused her the greatest anxiety. Yet an independent fortune is not an unmixed affliction, and Helen Seymour was a truly charming girl. What then marred the serenity of Mrs. Seymour's enjoyment of such important blessings? To begin with Helen. She had from her earliest youth an amazing fund of high spirits, and as she grew into womanhood she developed a sense of humour which was so foreign to her mother's nature, that the worthy lady had a perplexed feeling of insecurity as to the light in which anything in life might strike her daughter. Most things struck Mrs. Seymour as being very serious. After being left in the possession of a liberal income, unhampered by restrictions of any kind, she took most seriously and laboriously to philanthropy. She embraced it as a profession, and the more she became entangled in a network of Societies and organizations for the relief of the poor and the reformation of the vicious the less there seemed to be in the world to treat as a joke. It was certainly trying to a woman of her temperament to have a daughter who constantly saw a comic side to most of the daily routine of life. "Helen, I have often told you what very bad form it is to show any signs of levity in Church," she would say, severely. "What induced you to smile so broadly to-day in the very middle of the sermon?"

"Did I, mother? Oh, I am so sorry. I remember now; it was when Mr. Proser was speculating as to whether the stars were inhabited, and if so, what the inhabitants were like. I thought how very awkward it would be to have disused fireirons and empty kerosene cases come floating down on us from Jupiter and Mars. But of course, being so many millions of miles away, there's not much danger," she added, sobered by the unrelaxing gravity of her mother's face. Or again: "Helen, I think it is hardly becoming in you to laugh so boisterously talking to the new gardener. If it were old Miles it would not matter."

"But, mother, dear, old Miles is about as amusing as the gate-post, and this new man, Schulze, is just delightful. Now, let me tell you. He has been in the country only a year, and he told me how when he first came out he went up on a station in the bush. 'I knew but vere shmall English, and one of the men when first I did see him I wondered that when he choined me the vere first tings he said was did my mother know about me—did she know that I was out. I egsplained to him that my mother was not in this gountry, but in Chermany. I haf often vundered that he was so kindt, for he was rofe, rofe man.' Don't you see, mother, the man had said, ' Does your mother know you're out?' and poor old Schulze"—

But Mrs. Seymour either could not or would not see that this or any other reminiscence on Schulze's part justified Helen in talking and laughing so unrestrainedly with the "new gardener." A different taste in jokes is certainly rather a strain on the affections in domestic life. Nor did the difference between mother and daughter end here. Mrs. Seymour, with all her lavish charity, seldom could see things from any standpoint save one; she was very slow to see below the surface, and she viewed attacks on the general constitution of society with extreme suspicion. Now, Helen had a kind of instinctive mistrust as to the general wisdom of mankind, which in a girl of twenty-two was perhaps rather presumptuous. With all her light-heartedness she had a very keen perception of the mocking irony which underlies so large a section of human life. Then she was very quick to see injustice in the conventional usages of society, and she had a curious misgiving as to the real good worked by many imposing institutions that are supposed to make for the salvation of the human race. In fact, so radical were the differences of temperament between the mother and daughter, that the two were constantly amazed to find what totally opposite conclusions might be drawn from the same premises. So very often, when Mrs. Seymour was not preoccupied with some more than ordinarily grave "case," it occurred to her that Helen was of so impulsive and capricious a disposition that she would one day get into some desperate scrape. When visited with these fears she would gaze mournfully at her daughter. "Mother dear, what *have* I done now?" Helen would ask imploringly.

"It's not what you have done, it's what you *may* do," Mrs. Seymour would answer softly. On this Helen, resisting an inclination to laugh, would say very cheerfully—

"Well mother, to begin with, I won't run away from you."

A graver look if possible came into Mrs. Seymour's face. "Helen, I would be the last one to stand in the way of your settling in life. I hope it is not an idea of my being left lonely that prevents your thinking seriously of Mr. Maskelyne"—

"Mother, dear!" This in an entreating tone, with a very decided colour rising in Helen's cheeks. Then, as her mother looked at her in an enquiring way, evidently expecting a sequel to this exclamation, Helen said, "Who could possibly think of Mr. Maskelyne in any other way than seriously?"

"Oh." This was uttered in a dubious tone. Then Mrs. Seymour with an expression of relief which might have been real or assumed—for the most serious-minded mother is not above a little artifice when urging the merits of an eligible *parti*—"Have you then at last, my dear, decided that your objections are frivolous?"

Then Helen would begin to show a little temper.

"Frivolous, mother. You speak as though I were in the habit of cutting antics like the pantomime clowns, who make and swallow imaginary sausages two feet long."

"Now, Helen!"

"Mother, dear, you're not really cross?"

Such passages at arms as these were by no means rare. It was after a conversation very much on the foregoing lines that mother and daughter drove into town to do some shopping on the forenoon of the day that Madame Pousard had appointed to meet Thornton at Munch's. The carriage was almost opposite the restaurant when Mrs. Seymour saw one of her cases approaching in the person of a draggled-looking woman, with a very bloated red-looking face and an enormous crimson feather in a soiled and tumbled-looking white hat.

"Helen, I want to speak to this woman. Just go into Munch's, and wait for me there. We'll have some lunch before going to Tortollini's."

Helen know that this meant a "case" of a very grave order indeed; and though she inwardly rebelled against being protected in this way like a fragile wreath of Meissen china, she obeyed without a murmur. Mrs. Seymour motioned the woman to the side of the carriage, and was soon lost in earnest conversation. Helen gave a sidelong look, the contrast between her mother—refined and delicate-looking, and leaning back in her luxurious dark green-rep-lined carriage, with its well-groomed horses and solemn coachman—and the reckless woman in her tawdry finery, struck the girl with a sense of painful incongruity, and various reflections rose in her mind which orthodox people might have characterized as unbecoming reflections on the dealings of Providence. But at that moment her attention was attracted by a group of small urchins who were congregated in the gutter within a few feet of Munch's door. One of them an unkempt, barefooted boy, had a good-sized lean grey-looking kitten, which he was engaged in choking with a knotted piece of thick twine, while his companions looked on with admiring grins.

"You horrid little creature," cried Helen, her eyes blazing with wrath, and she snatched the kitten from its tormentor in the twinkling of an eye. The little group of spectators looked on open-mouthed, and the would-be executioner said doggedly, "It ain't yourn." This was certainly true, but who could be so abject as to rescue a long lean kitten from a cruel death, and cast it the next moment into the jaws of the grave? Certainly not Helen. Holding the half-dead creature tenderly in her arms, she ascended the staircase into Munch's "Ladies' Room," grave and stately, with no outward sign of emotion, though her heart palpitated with the thought that her mother would come in presently, fix her eyes on the miserably lean kitten and murmur in a despairing tone, "Oh Helen, what have you been doing again?" For this was exactly one of the episodes that kept alive Mrs. Seymour's apprehensions of what might one day come of Helen's "impulsiveness." To make matters worse the kitten as it revived began to grow restive, and much bigger looking. "What better could happen to it than to be choked," thought Helen, in her revulsion of feeling. Lean to emaciation, and decidedly ragged looking, it certainly was not an animal for which, regarded dispassionately, one would joyfully sacrifice the smiles of an only parent. Virtue, the moralists tell us, is its own reward. Does this mean that the virtuous must be prepared to put up with a broken-windowed attic, or a banker who refuses to look favourably on an overdrawn account? Not invariably; for the encouragement of disinterested self-sacrifice let it be recorded that just as Helen Seymour began to question the wisdom of rescuing a starving kitten from a cruel death, deliverance from her embarrassment came in an entirely unlooked-for way. In order fully to explain this we must go back a little way.

The letter which Charlie Browne drew up at Munch's appeared in the *Guardian* next morning (Saturday) in bold type, and among the *habitues* of that favourite restaurant attracted much notice. Many profoundly respectable matrons who had occasionally gone to the ladies' room for years now began to remember that on many occasions they had had their suspicions as to some of the couples who sometimes wandered into that sanctum. Married ladies, no longer young, whose views on such matters were beginning to crystallize, emphatically declared that if shameless flirtations were to be carried on at Munch's, in the rooms set apart for ladies, they, for their part, must cease to patronise the place. Now, Munch was one of those men whose relations are numbered by the score, and some of them were wealthy, and from a colonial point of view high up in the social scale. Under such circumstances it was inevitable that the comments evoked by the letter signed "Materfamilias" should soon reach him. On the Sunday he dined with his cousin Crunch, who was a financial agent of credit and renown. He had made so much money that he spoke of retiring from business as being quite on the "trapeze." People who knew him intimately said he meant *tapis*. Crunch was in truth a foolish and pompous man, but though his wife turned her face towards Government House when she said her prayers, he had not, as yet at least, turned his back on Munch because of his plebeian occupation. After dinner, as the pair sat over some excellent wine, Crunch said in the pause of an exhaustive conversation regarding debentures and dividends,

"I hope-ah, Munch, that your business will not suffer-ah through the letter-ah that has appeared in the *Guardian*."

The slight affectation of speech which may be observed with Crunch was contracted through his intimacy with private secretaries, &c.

Munch became very red in the face.

"What letter?" he cried, with unconcealed emotion.

"Oh! haven't you seen it-ah?" Crunch produced the *Guardian*, and Munch read Charlie Browne's ultra-virtuous effusion with painful interest, and straightway swallowed it as the indignant protest of one of the many profoundly respectable elderly matrons whose patronage when they came into the city for a day's shopping formed part of his assured annual income.

Poor Munch! It was a bitter moment. "I've kep' my 'ouse most respectable. I've even turned away members of the hopers from *that* room," he said in broken tones, as he stared blankly at the paper after twice perusing the letter.

"Yes, but the tone-ah of society here now is getting very refined-ah," said Crunch, with the air of one who ought to know, and was really an authority on points of social etiquette.

"I'll tell you what," said Munch, fired with a brilliant idea, "after this I'll let no male being into the ladies' room unless he is accompanied or joins a lady of 'igh, or at least of very respectable social position in the room. I don't want strangers and wanderers. I can afford to keep a room for the alight of the place, and I'll do it too."

Munch brought down his fist on the table till the glasses rang.

"Very good idea-ah; very good indeed," said Crunch benignantly.

As Munch was a very loquacious man, and conversed much with such of his customers as had leisure to listen to him, it was generally known on Monday to those who dropped in for 11 o'clock and early lunch that the ladies' room was to be guarded henceforth from vulgar gossip with extraordinary precautions. As many of his male patrons were steeped in that atmosphere of steady conventional decorum, which even British tourists to our colonies find rather depressing, these precautions were looked upon as being "the thing." Thus Thornton, as he stepped into the restaurant a few minutes after 12 on Monday, was at once accosted by Bankem, to whom the proprietor had been explaining how the high-toned refinement of British matrons was henceforth to be jealously guarded in his establishment.

"How'de do, Thornton? Not going to intrude on the sacred privacy of the ladies' room, I suppose? Ha, ha, ha," said Bankem, in the thick jovial voice habitual to him. As Thornton wrote constantly for the *Guardian*, he was of course quite oblivious as to most of the topics that were daily discussed in the open columns of that paper. He thought Bankem's allusion was part of the depressing facetiousness which characterized him, so he answered briefly and passed on. As it wanted ten minutes to the time Mdme. Pousard had appointed him to meet her, he made for the table at which sat Charlie Browne and the three who had been with him the previous Friday when the "Materfamilias" epistle had been concocted. They were in a state of pleasant excitement at the emotion which this production aroused in Munch's breast, and awaited with the utmost eagerness Thornton's movements. But the moment he drew near and nodded to the company assembled, Anthony bounded into the middle of a discussion on the drama, so as to avoid all suspicion.

"You may say what you like about your immortal Shakespeare," he said, fixing an angry eye on Charlie, "but his day is over—unless you cut out the long speeches and give lively dances instead. I went the other night to see "A Midwinter's Tale," or some such antiquity. Everybody made speeches, till I nearly fell to pieces with yawning, and at last an old muff came along a seashore and pretended to find an infant. 'Here's some fun at last,' I thought. I never saw the play before, and of course I knew nothing about it. I hear fellows like Thornton constantly say how divine and witty, and all the rest of it, Shakespeare is; so I naturally thought this supposed brat would turn into a raven and pick off the old chap's nose, or some such witty trick. Nothing of the sort. 'What have we here?' creaked the old fogey, and instead of calling for a policeman or hurrying off to the workhouse with the creature he wandered round with the thing in his arms."

Thornton divined that the young man was putting side on for some reason, and allowed these brilliant criticisms to pass without making any response.

"Which of you fellows has been scandalizing the virtuous mothers of families in the ladies' room?" said the elderly gentleman suddenly; looking solemnly from one to the other of the young men.

What did he mean? They for their part had never had the "cheek" to penetrate beyond the foot of the staircase unless protected by a mother or a sister, "and even then I left my shoes at the door, and sat in a distant corner while I consumed an ice with my eyes fixed on the ground," said Dick. "What is all his jargon about the ladies' room?" asked Thornton. As he spoke he intercepted a meaning look between Charlie and Anthony. "Oh; did you not see this in Saturday's *Guardian*?" and the elderly man took a slip of printed matter out of his pocket-book. It was the letter which he had cut out of the newspaper. Thornton glanced hastily over it. "I suppose this is your idea of a joke," he said: looking at the three young men.

"Well, if I wanted particularly to go into the ladies' room I would think it no joke I can tell you with old Munch goaded to the verge of madness by these old cats of chaperones," said Anthony, without the slightest appearance of self-consciousness. Thornton looked at his watch and found that it was a few minutes after half-past 12. He went up the staircase, poignantly aware that each one of the four men he left at the table followed his movements intently. The first glance round the room showed him that Madame Pousard was not there. "I must wait for her," he thought, but at that moment he heard Munch's heavy elephantine tread coming upstairs. All at once it flashed across him that these young scoundrels downstairs would greet him with brutal merriment if he had to turn on his heels and clear out, because he was not for the nonce under the protection of a lady! He cast a despairing look around. Most of the ladies present were stout and elderly, and seemed to be transacting a very fair fork and knife business for such an early hour, and one or two of them looked at the unchaperoned clandestine male with unmistakeable disapproval. But at a table near where he stood sat a young lady who was too preoccupied to notice entrances and exits. She was with difficulty holding a very lean, long, and disreputable looking kitten, that was making violent efforts to escape. Thornton was distinctly conscious that the first impulse was a genuine wish to serve a young and charming woman, succeeded by the thought—"Here is a chance to escape ignominious expulsion."

"Allow me to relieve you," he said, and there was a mingled kindliness and deference in his manner which prevented the possibility of any imputation of forwardness in addressing a lady to whom he was unknown. Helen, with all her lightheartedness and innate contempt for mere conventionality, would have instinctively recoiled from anything that favoured of presumption. But Thornton looked so unmistakeably a gentleman, and the kitten now that it had revived from its semi-strangulation was so unmistakeably a nuisance, that she looked up with an air of unfeigned relief.

"Ah, thank you, if it is not too much trouble," she said, as Thornton took the kitten and sat down on a chair near her. Munch, entering, saw him conversing with Miss Seymour, and promptly retired.

"It is not a very prepossessing creature, but I found it half strangled by some horrid children in the street," explained Helen gravely.

Thornton thought it looked very much like a kitten he had seen his landlady, Mrs. Dunscome, chasing out of the house a few days previously, and on this most slender foundation he said reflectively, "I wonder if it is the kitten we lost a few days ago." Absolutely no excuse can be made for this bold travesty of the truth except the very commonplace one that the longer Thornton looked at Miss Seymour the more he wanted a pretext for lingering near her.

"Oh, quite likely," said Helen, catching at the idea with joy. Then her conscience smote her for being so very anxious to get rid of the ill-used kitten, and she added, "But I suppose you would recognise it if it were yours?"

"Well, kittens like babies and Chinese are to me exactly alike," answered Thornton, carefully examining the victim, which in his hands had curiously enough become quiet and subdued.

"Is it long since you lost your kitten?" asked Helen politely. Thornton couldn't be positive to a day.

"It seems to know you. What a singular coincidence if it is yours."

"Yes, very," answered Thornton, which considering he never had had a cat or kitten in his life was no exaggeration. But this girl, with her bright speaking face and winning smile, exercised so sudden and potent a charm on him that he was betrayed into a deliberate piece of hypocrisy.

"Now that I look closely at its tail," he said thoughtfully, "I quite recognise it. You see these regular rings of white and dark grey, and the small bit of white at the tip? It's certainly our Tim."

The growth of oral tradition was surely never more startling than this. "Our Tim" had again became restive, and was violently struggling to get away. Failing to do so, he showed symptoms of a resolve to rend the hands that held him.

"I think poor Tim must be very hungry," said Helen compassionately, looking at the kitten's hollow sides. Thornton promptly rang the bell that was on the table close by. "One roast mutton without vegetables," he said to the demure, not to say serious-looking, damsel who answered the summons.

"I suppose he has got much leaner since you lost him," said Helen half apologetically. There was something very dramatic in losing a kitten, and then coming straight upon the person who rescued it from a cruel death a few moments afterwards. Yet the denouement seemed to fall rather flat on the little creature's owner.

"Tortoise-shell cats get lean very quickly, don't you think so?" said Thornton gravely.

"Tortoise-shell!" echoed Helen, opening her eyes very wide. "Tabby, you mean."

"Oh yes, tabby," murmured Thornton, who had the grace to get red in the face at this exposure of his unfathomable ignorance of cats.

"I hardly know how to thank you for rescuing him," he continued, in accents of fervent gratitude.

"Please, *don't* thank me. You can't imagine how mean it makes me feel. Now that you have really found it is your kitten, I don't mind confessing that soon after I snatched the poor little thing from its tormentors repentance set in. 'Rescue a kitten in haste and repent at leisure' was the sort of feeling I had."

"Well, but impartially speaking, it is *not* a pretty animal. Now I think cats, like pictures, can be tolerated only when they have some beauty, unless association gives them an adventitious claim."

"But I suppose before misfortune robbed him of his dinners and soured his temper he was prettier and more amiable," said Helen, smiling; and then she glanced at one of her wrists, which the ungrateful kit had scratched in his early struggles to get away. The sight of this little seam marked with a slender stain of blood made Thornton's heart throb. "A creamy rosebud lined with mother-of pearl," was his mental description of the fair blue-veined wrist which he regarded with so strong an interest. But at that moment the "roast mutton without vegetables" claimed his attention. He cut it up, and the little foundling bolted it with a savage celerity pitiful to see. Helen watched the process with keen interest. She even had a dawning regret that the kit would now be carried off by its rightful owner.

"I suppose they will be quite delighted when you take it home," she said, half wistfully. Was there a wife and family at home? What was the kitten's master's name? These, and one or two other vague questions, rose in Helen's mind. Her conjecture almost made Thornton laugh as he thought of Mrs. Dunscome's sour visage, and the shock of terror with which she would regard a voracious stray kitten let loose on her hearth and pantry. Under cover of being preoccupied with the young animal, Thornton made no reply. There is a line beyond which even a journalist's well-trained imagination refuses to soar. Such a line was the idea of Mrs. Dunscome weeping with joy on the neck of an infant cat, which was capable of dispatching a plate of mutton in an appallingly short time.

Helen glanced at her watch, wondering what could keep her mother so long; and Thornton, with a sinking heart, felt that it was imperative on him to arise, take up his kitten, and walk.

"I am afraid he is very thirsty," he said; and forthwith he ordered a saucer of milk, on which the kitten fell with noisy joy.

"How will you get it home?" said Helen suddenly, and Thornton realized that the bitter moment could not be far distant. The time must come when even a stray kitten can eat no more. As soon as the milk was finished no decent excuse remained for tarrying another moment.

"Oh, I'll get a boy at my office to take it home," said Thornton moodily —the idea of lugging the creature through the streets began to weigh on his mind. As long as this charming girl was looking on with vivid interest the kitten was all very well, but in the absence of such an incitement what did he in cold blood want with any kitten on earth—more especially this one, which had an unmistakable look of the tiger about it?

"Do you think the boy will be kind to it?" said Helen dubiously.

"Do you care for it? In that case I shall not entrust it to Smiley. Now that I think of it, he is not very humane in his disposition."

"But you care for the little thing yourself, don't you?" said Helen wonderingly.

"Yes—oh, yes; but now that he has a taste of roving no doubt he will be very inconstant."

"Does it thieve much?" said Helen reflectively. "Oh Lord, how many million crammers must I tell about this little beast," thought Thornton; but as he did not at once reply, Helen went on—

"We had a kitten once that used to take the goldfish out of the fountains. It was extraordinarily clever with its paws. I do believe it would have knitted if any one had taken its education in hand before thieving became a passion. Ah kitty, now you are beginning to look a little sleeker."

She took up the kitten and stroked it, and the poor little waif, restored by food and drink, began to purr in a fitful sort of way, as if trying to recall the sunny hours of yore when life was secure from ill-usage and starvation.

"No consideration on earth will induce me to cast this kitten off," thought Gabriel, as he watched the fair slender hand stroking the roughened fur. At this juncture enter Mrs. Seymour.

"My dear, I have kept you waiting a long time," she said to her daughter, and Helen blushed up to the eyes with the sudden thought as to how she was to justify herself for consorting with a strange gentleman, and a kitten with a career darkened by reckless Bohemianism. But

Mrs. Seymour was too intimately bound up with charitable organizations and public institutions not to be acquainted to some extent with Gabriel Thornton, whom she saluted with the utmost affability. Thornton was conscious that he was absurdly and most unreasonably pleased to find that he could without a twinge of conscience keep his seat near Helen a little longer.

As it happened he was the one of all others Mrs. Seymour wished to see just at that moment. A frightful grievance in the shape of a landlord's iniquities had just come under her notice. The woman she had spoken to had represented that a sick woman and two children were starving next door to the place she herself occupied.

"I went there at once—that is what kept me so long, Helen," explained Mrs. Seymour, and then she entered on her last "case" *con amore*. The sick woman and her children lived in one of the veriest hovels —earth floor—windows broken, door off the hinges—the daylight apparent through the shingle roof in great patches—yet the landlord had sold every stick of furniture for rent only three days ago. Would not Mr. Thornton write on the subject? Certainly he would be most happy; but it would be indispensable that he should first make full enquiry into the matter. Oh, by all means. Mrs. Seymour could drive him to the spot that minute. And had he lunched? No! nor you, Helen? Oh, I am afraid you must be hungry, child. Well, we had better go; we can drive home in half an hour. Was that Mr. Thornton's cat? "A foundling, no doubt? Poor little thing. Bring it with you; there is plenty of room at Selton." To all this Thornton agreed most joyously, though outwardly his demeanour was calm and staid. Was it possible that in some remote age of the past he had voted Mrs. Seymour a bore of the first magnitude—a fussy philanthropist, whose passion for playing the benefactor to one section of the human race led her constantly into the error of believing worse things of other sections than they deserved? Was it possible that he had often sneaked out of her way at meetings and associations, in terror of being nailed on the spot and entrapped into writing thrilling leaders on behalf of the Aborigines' Blanket Society, the Home for Decayed Loafers, and similar organizations? Looking at Helen as they drove through the soft September air, which was laden with the breath of budding flowers and blossoming trees, the recollection was certainly incredible.

Chapter IV

"Is Mr. Thornton married, mother?" asked Helen a little abruptly, when late in the afternoon, after a most exhaustive conversation (chiefly carried on by Mrs. Seymour) on the subject of cottages for labourers, and kindred topics, Gabriel took his leave, promising to come again at an early date. In the meantime he was to trace the landlord grievance to its lonely lair, and drag it in all its heinousness to the light of day.

"Married?" repeated Mrs. Seymour, with a perplexed air. "Oh, no; I think not. Men like Mr. Thornton hardly ever marry, I should think."

"Oh! why not? What is his claim to celibacy?" asked Helen, a little amused and surprised. As a naturalist constructs the whole economy of an animal he has never seen, from seeing one tiny bone, so people often make very large assumptions on a small social fact. To have a kitten straying from home seemed, in the case of a man somehow, to imply a wife and children—at any rate a wife.

"Well; I should think he has no time for domestic life; he is constantly at meetings and Parliament, and the rest of the time at Clubs, I fancy," answered Mrs. Seymour vaguely.

Helen sat in rather an indolent mood with the kitten on her lap. As Selton Lea was five miles from Gabriel's lodgings, and as he had to go to his office for the rest of the day, Helen had suggested that the kitten should for the time being be left in her charge.

"What a pet you are making of that lean, ragged-looking creature, Helen. Do put it out of the room," said Mrs. Seymour, a little fretfully. It is sad to relate that Helen made no attempt to carry out these instructions. The kitten had, from being a little Ishmaelite constantly on the defensive and terrified if one moved or spoke, become perfectly tame, and persisted in lying on Helen's lap with a curious air of security, which seemed to say, "Here I am, and here I mean to stay."

The next time Gabriel came to Selton he found that the kitten followed Helen like her shadow. It had grown plump and playful, and its fur had become very smooth and showed to perfection its naturally beautiful marking. It now answered to the name of Mushon, which was the rendering given by one of the maids to Monsieur—a title bestowed on it by Helen on account of its increasingly aristocratic appearance. Mushon developed a surprising faculty for begging, standing up on its hind legs for two or three minutes at a time with surprising facility. It also contracted a passion for tea-drinking. The moment that the teatray was brought into the drawing-room, either in the afternoon or after dinner, Mushon mewed ferociously; and finally, when Helen gave it creamed tea in a saucer, it stood up on its hind legs and lapped up the beverage with immense gusto. A certain ferocity in the matter of eating and drinking was the only habit that clung to Mushon of the evil days through which he wandered desolate and oppressed when no man gave him to eat. Thornton came and went, and was daily cognizant of all the growing accomplishments of the gifted Mushon. "I am really getting too fond of your pussy to let you have it back," Helen would say from time to time, and on several occasions Gabriel was on the point of avowing that he was a cheat and an impostor, and had not the smallest claim to the accomplished and fast-growing Mushon. But there was a certain awkwardness in the confession, and it was so delightful to watch Helen fondling the creature that she believed had once been his.

For there can no longer be any concealment of the fact that poor Gabriel was at the last very hard hit. Of course it was not his first love affair by—well, well, what man cares to confess the number of shrines at which he has burnt incense to successive Divinities!—the midnight hours he has given to *her* image, and such dreadful poetry as he was capable of? To count backward from the bright particular star that has at last risen fatefully on the horizon, was indeed an ungrateful task. To linger on the thoughts of Selina with the willowy drooping throat, Rebecca with the shining orbs, Matilda with the Hebe mouth and sweeping lashes. What man dares, except in the inmost recesses of his own heart, count over the appalling procession! Happy is he if in the years to come, when the bright particular star has been plucked from the firmament and sphered by the domestic hearth, his thoughts do not turn with covert regret to some or all of these earlier luminaries.

As for Thornton, he had rapidly reached that exalted frame of mind when even to remember that he had previously fancied himself in love was intolerable. In the midst of his work he would sometimes fall into a profound reverie, going over every little detail of his last visit to Selton; recalling the tones of Helen's voice, her smile, the sudden lighting-up of her face as some mischievous thought came into her mind, or a saucy repartee to her lips. But, alas! with what arch roguery she turned aside any approach to that tender seriousness which is the divine manna of timid love.

How many scores of times did Gabriel rehearse the words in which he might one day dare to tell his love. Thus he would picture Helen among the roses—what a splendid opportunity to say something; ask for a rosebud, and then—Oh! how did those glib novelists always make up scenes and speeches. Did she care for him? A long, long sigh. Presently a vision would arise—an overwhelming vision of Helen installed in some enchanted dwelling as his wife. One moment he dwelt on the word with all the boldness of a yearning lover; the next he was amazed at his undue presumption. But the vision would return again and again. He could fancy her so well glancing over his proofs, and making the most astounding suggestions. He would even laugh aloud sometimes as he fancied the kind of jibes she would gravely insist on dealing to the decorous gravity of daily history as recorded in daily leaders. At the Barbarian Club his place was now often vacant. Yap, Mac., & Co. had become absolutely insufferable to him. There was that all-sufficient complacency about them when they spoke of what they called the "fair sex," which so often marks men of limited intelligence, who have associated only with women of inferior intellect and narrow minds, and this kind of complacency Thornton now found utterly intolerable. His old comrades' stories of love and war and feats on 'change were all equally odious to him.

Of course, things could not go on for ever in this way. The spring was fast merging into summer, and Mrs. Seymour began to speak of going to her house at the sea-side. As that was thirty-five miles out of town the bare thought struck a cold chill to Thornton's heart; it was like an eternal separation to think of one gloomy, horrible week after another passing in endless number without a sight of Helen's face, or the sound of her voice. Several "last parties" were being given in rapid succession at the close of the season, and Gabriel now bitterly regretted that he had so steadfastly in the past refused all invitations to balls and parties. How, how are the mighty fallen. He now often envied Charlie, instead of reading him lectures on the pitiful waste of time involved in going to dances, hops, and balls. At such "scenes of revelry by night" he might have caught glimpses of Helen, and that would have sanctified the most prosaic and commonplace assembly. He did not once mention *her* name to any of his friends, but on one occasion, when Charlie returned to their mutual lodgings about 3 o'clock in the morning, he saw a light burning in Thornton's room, and tapped at the door in passing.

"So you're burning the midnight oil, old man," he said as on entering he found Gabriel seated at his writing-table, in an Oriental-looking dressing-gown smoking a Churchwarden, and enveloped in a cloud of smoke.

"Well, Charlie, you haven't damaged your nose or anything of that sort coming home, have you?"

"Come, I like your style now. Oh, I'd like to make you feel as sneaking as a stage-ghost. You needn't look so mightily amazed."

Charlie threw off his light overcoat, sat down in a capacious easy chair, lit a cigar, which Gabriel handed him, crossed his legs, and stared hard in Thornton's face.

"May I ask you a few questions, Thornton?"

"Good Lord! What has come over the boy? Charlie, if these people, under the guise of hospitality, give you such vile stuff to drink"—

"Now, Gabriel, you shut up! Will you answer me *one* question?"

"Certainly."

"How long have you known Miss Seymour?"

Thornton's face flushed hotly, but he maintained his accent of unconcern.

"You *know*, Charlie, I don't indulge in diaries; they might compromise a lot of you fellows when my biography comes to be written, thus—'The one fault in Gabriel Thornton's otherwise perfect character was the company he sometimes kept, &c.'"

"Oh, confound it Gabriel, do tell me all about this affair. The truth is I am awfully gone on Miss Seymour."

"The deuce you are." Gabriel felt a burning desire to pitch the young man out of his room head foremost.

"Yes, I am. I had her in my mind's eye, Horatio, when I told you some time ago that a fellow got more good of seeing *some* girls for a few hours than he did from his own sex in as many years."

"Ah, that accounts for the unearthly saintliness noticeable about you lately."

"Now, old hoss, there are times when a fellow can stand chaff, and times when he can't. But this is generally your style. I tell you all my affairs—good, bad, and indifferent—and you just listen with an amused kind of a smile, and double a fellow up at the end with some ill-natured attempt at a witticism. You remind me of a German animal I knew once, who used all his spare time in hunting up rare kinds of insects and sticking pins through them in a beastly case of his own manufacture."

"Do you really imagine that you are a *rare* kind of beetle, Charlie?"

"Rare? Ah, no, I'm only *recherché*. But if you're unable to see it, all I can say is don't, don't ask me to bring so select a type of humanity before you, and at the same time enlarge your mind fully to grasp my value. But joking apart, Thornton, as you're such an oyster—a Sphinx—a—dash it—after 3 o'clock in the morning a fellow's stock of original metaphors has a tendency to run out—I'll tell you why I ask. To-night, or rather last night, I had the good fortune to secure two dances with Miss Seymour. After the second dance we had some talk. Miss Seymour said she was thankful the season for party-giving was drawing to a close, and wondered why some original-brained being did not invent some form of evening amusement a little less tiresome. On this I replied, 'Oh, I must speak about this to my friend Thornton. He rails against dances and balls with great vivacity, but I've never heard him propose any substitute.' 'Oh, do you know Mr. Thornton,' said Miss Seymour, turning on me with quite an animated look. In fact, the more I reflect on her expression the less I like it; and, by Jove, Thornton you're blushing. Phew! Well, I thought there must be something in it before you told such astounding lies. 'Come, don't lay your hand upon your sword,' &c. The hour comes to every man when, if he's not a saint nor a fool, he has to lie prodigiously. As most of us are neither, the crisis generally keeps a recording angel at work for several hours. Oh, you're impatient to hear the rest, are you? Well, it's too late to go to bed. Give me a beaker of that lager beer, and another cigar—thanks. In answer to Miss Seymour's naive enquiry, I said, 'Seeing that we have lodged in the same house for two years'—

"More animation. 'Oh, then you would know about the kitten?' 'The kitten?' I murmured. 'Yes, the kitten that strayed away from your place, and that I rescued from an untimely death.' I didn't know whether to laugh at the absurdity of our ever having had a kitten or to weep over your overwhelming mendacity. I did neither, I perilled my soul for your unworthy sake, and—Oh yes, the poor dear little creature! You see I had to confine myself to generalities. At this moment Maskeylene— you know that disgustingly rich grazier, or squatter, or whatever he calls himself—came to claim Miss Seymour for the next dance. Now, I leave it between yourself and your conscience whether you don't owe me a full, clear, and unvarnished tale."

Chapter V

When Allfadir, in the Norse legend, would fain get a draught of Mimr's spring—the fountain of wisdom—he was obliged to leave his eye in pledge. When the day of reckoning comes it is painfully brought home to us that we have, like Allfadir, had to pay heavily for such sips as we were vouchsafed of the wine of life.

Thornton was not given to the habit of dressing up his griefs and disappointments theatrically, and then falling into profound sorrow and pity at his undeserved misfortunes. But he had a habit of going into semi-abstract speculations over his own affairs that sometimes trembled in the balance between sentiment and cynicism. He was struggling mentally with the remains of such a mood as he rode out to Selton two days after the conversation recorded between himself and Charlie. It was late in November, and the near approach of summer was heralded by one of those blighting dismal north winds that intensify and tropically develop the latent pessimism of human nature—a wind that seems laden with remorse and fruitless repining. At its breath the rose withers and the brook dries up; in its presence the shade of trees is quivering and ineffectual. With such a wind blowing the dust whither it listeth, drying up the kindly moisture of the earth, and reducing all herbage to one monotonous whitey-brown, the fiends of unbelief and despair seem fairly let loose. It is difficult to believe that the whole continent of Australia is not a veritable Sahara of waterless sand, excepting a fringe of more favoured land on the seacoast. There are some men and women with a physique so free from the tyrannous dominance of nerves, with so large a fund of activity and cheerfulness, that they are actually unconscious whether the wind blows from the north or from the south, from the east or from the west. But such robust souls are exceptional, and certainly Gabriel Thornton was not one of them. "For the last time" seemed to sound in his ears like a knell as he rode up through the avenue of tall and fragrant bluegums. It was in vain he reminded himself that Mrs. Seymour would return from the seaside in three or four months—the demon of the Australian north wind had taken possession of him, and all was dark and hopeless. Life was a bad dream—man an insignificant atom, borne hither and thither by a resistless fate.

* * *

Mrs. Seymour was not at home, and Thornton was debating with himself whether he would ask for Miss Seymour, when Helen, who was crossing the hall, caught sight of him.

"Oh, Mr. Thornton, how good of you to come to see us in this desperate weather. Yes, mother had to attend a meeting, but you must really wait till she returns, for I know she wants dreadfully to see you!"

There was something in the girl's frank, hearty greeting that made Thornton's heart for a moment beat hopefully, and then black care took possession of him. "It is just her way. No doubt she smiles as sweetly and speaks as kindly to one or two hundred men that she does not give another thought to once they are out of sight."

"Do you know I was just wondering whether it was worth while having tea in for one, two of course it is," said Helen, who, if she noticed that Thornton was unusually gloomy, had a woman's inborn tact not to show it by look or manner.

"I think I would become an infatuated tea drinker if tea were always like this," said Thornton, making an effort to be a little less like the oiled mummy of an Egyptian feast.

"What is the tea like then that you sometimes get?"

"Oh, don't dash the joy of this cup by the question. Perhaps you never drank tea in a boarding-house? Imagine to yourself a very large teapot—plated if your landlady has seen better days—Britannia metal if she has not. If you sit at the far end of the table, and are first served, the compound is thin in the extreme, dashed with a pale-blue fluid, which I believe some nefarious impostor brings round in a small cart in tins early in the morning. I have reason to know, because if I am ever up late at night these tins are smashed up in some mysterious way that makes the neighbourhood resound at the ghastly hour of 6. Oh, I assure you there is absolutely no end to the variations on the noises made by a milk-man—for the pale sky-tinted fluid I speak of is really known as milk. Then, if you are served last, the decoction is more dangerous. There is a bitterness—a gloomy murderous blackness about it then that makes you think of the fair Rosamond and tragic stories of Italian poisoning."

"Ah, you're imposing on my credulity," said Helen, laughing. "If boarding-house tea were really so bad you would not drink it a second time."

"But a little reflection will show you that people go on constantly doing things they hate—drinking liquor they detest—dining with people who bore them to death. The fact is that once people get into the habit of living on after they discover what a monstrous fraud life is they are prepared to put up with anything."

Helen opened her big grey eyes to their widest. "'A monstrous fraud!' Ah, I have it. You're what is nowadays called a *pessimist*. Now I've got a live one I must have an explanation. I have been made to feel quite silly lately with so many of my favourite writers casting the blackest imputations on the world and human life. I have to go out in the sunshine and look at the roses, sometimes to convince myself that the world is really most beautiful. And the same with human nature. I look around among my friends and acquaintances to draw courage from the fact that they would not sell a friend for gold nor assassinate a foe for revenge. And then I sometimes get into a bad habit of thinking about myself, and that is always hateful. I don't expect a bonus from the Almighty for not putting strychnine in my mother's coffee; but I'm not going to be diverted from the point. Tell me do you think really the world is a horrid place to live in?"

"At present I do *not*."

"Bah! don't take refuge in such a subterfuge."

"General allusions must not be made to apply to every moment of one's life."

"No; but why—if I am impertinent, tell me so—is life generally, so perpetually alluded to as if it were a masked leper."

Thornton looked in the girl's face with a troubled look in his eyes. Both were now in deadly earnest.

"No simile within the range of language could overdraw the horror of what life is to many," he replied, slowly.

"Yes, I know, but they are the exception," replied Helen, in a low tone.

"True; but humanity, like a bridge, is as strong as its weakest part, and those who are spared the worst bitternesses of life have they not the doom of their fellows dogging them? We may not be scourged by the Eumenides, but the most fortunate of us are often players in the game who have not seen the trump card. We think it is hearts, but it turns out to be spades—they *are* alike in shape, and we are colour-blind."

There was a pause. "He is not like Mrs. Blodgitt-Spare, who one moment declares that this is a vale of tears and a mocking show, and the next asks you how you like her last dress from Worth's—he really believes it's true," thought Helen. And then the thought was half-formed in her heart that she would like to make him really glad and cast away this bitter belief. At that moment who should bound into the room but Mushon—Mushon no longer lean, nor draggled, nor hungry, but plump, smooth, and most imperious, with an enchanting rose-coloured ribbon round his throat. Seeing cups about he began mewing at the very pitch of his lungs—"a powerful baritone," Helen said as she poured cream and tea into a saucer. Mushon stood up on his hind legs, and sipped away in dreamy content, his two forepaws crossed over his soft breast in a ludicrous way.

"Did you teach him to stand up like that?" asked Thornton, looking on with considerable amusement.

"Oh, I thought you must have taught him," replied Helen. "He began to stand up like this a few days after I took him home."

"I must tell the truth about the little brute," thought Thornton, wincing under the girl's candid eyes.

"Now tell me truly," she said, as Mushon, having finished his tea, jumped upon her lap and composed himself to rest, "would you not like to take him away?"

"No, indeed," said Thornton fervently.

"I pet him a good deal, and he has something of the ways of a comedian about him which in a puss is very diverting, but I don't like to deprive you of him."

"Miss Seymour, I don't know what you'll think of me, but upon my life I never saw the little wretch till the moment I beheld him in your arms at Munch's."

Helen looked up in amazement. "But why?"

The story was told in a few words. Helen's laughter at Munch's determination to keep 'clandestine males' out of the ladies' room was most infectious. And then she became suddenly grave.

"My motive in presuming to accost you," said Gabriel, "was a mixed one. First, it was the desire to escape being ignominiously marched down by old Munch to the edification of the schemers who were downstairs. Then it was the wish to relieve you of the ungrateful Mushon, and then—well—and then"—

Thornton's heart was beating so loudly that he fancied he could hear it, for the impulse came upon him irresistibly to tell all. He felt sure his case was hopeless, but would it not be better for him to accept his fate once and for all than go on in the wretched fashion of the last few weeks—one moment raised by a radiant smile to the pinnacle of hope, the next lost in abject despair.

"I am afraid that you will be angry," he said, with grave simplicity.

All at once Helen became horribly nervous. She thought she was going to laugh and say, "What unique humility," but somehow she did not laugh at all, and there was something disgustingly like a tremor in her voice as she said, "Why should you be afraid?"

"Because I am very presumptuous. Not that I think for one moment. . . . Once you smiled and talked so frankly I would have sworn I knew a thousand kittens to stay a little longer by you. Fate was kinder to me than I deserved, if she never is again. . . . When I rode here this afternoon I had a feeling somehow that it was for the last time."

"Surely not," said Helen, quickly, and then she coloured vividly and stroked Mushon, avoiding Thornton's eyes, which she knew were steadfastly fixed on her face.

Thornton strode to the window and looked out for a moment on the smooth shaven lawn of buffalo grass, which was relieved here and there by clumps of white, pale pink, and scarlet flowering shrubs.

"I can but learn my fate," he thought to himself, but he felt like one who is taking a last look on scenes that have grown very dear to him ere he listens to a sentence which may possibly be banishment for life.

> He either fears his fate too much,
>
> Or his deserts are small,
>
> Who dares not put it to the touch,
>
> And win or lose it all.

"Yes—I certainly fear my fate too much, but"—he turned and stood close beside Helen's chair, and said in a low rapid voice, with many pauses, "Over and over again I have said to myself that it is madness, but I cannot go on like this any longer. No matter at what cost, I must say to you this once I love you. I do not hope in the smallest degree that you love me in return; if you did I would have to warn you that I am quite unworthy of it. But oh, my God! how terrible it is to think of living on and on through all the dreary years that are to come—never to hear the sound of your voice again, nor look on your face. Helen—what? Why do you cry? Oh forgive me if I have pained you. Don't, don't—oh, my darling!"

He stood speechless with dismay, and a throb of wild hope rose in his heart, for the tears were running down the girl's cheeks like rain. In her agitation Helen twisted Mushon's ear rather more than quite accorded with that young autocrat's ideas of what was fitting. He started up, swore vehemently, and ran out of the room. Helen laughed through her tears, and looking up into Thornton's face, she said, "What makes you so dismal? Why should you not hear my voice again?"

"Because it is much better not, unless—unless—Helen tell me. Can it be possible that you love me?"

"I do. Why should I not?" said Helen, rising with a sweet glow in her face, and looking into her lover's eyes with a tender reproach. Woman-like, she could not endure that he, who was in very truth her life's dear lord, should so abase himself before her.

What a strange memorable half-hour followed! What murmurs and tender shrinking caresses, what broken sentences, what amazement and adoration, what an abandonment of happiness—looking neither before nor after—caring neither for yesterday nor to-morrow—but more than content with to-day! If never at any other moment, surely men and women drink the divine nectar of the Immortals when standing on the borderland—peering from the doubt and uncertainty of unconfessed and unadmitted love into the haven where that love becomes a matter of course, and consequently

> "Love took up the glass of Time, and turned it in
> his glowing hands;

Every moment lightly shaken ran itself in golden
    sands.
Love took up the harp of Life, and smote on all
    the chords with might;
Smote the chord of Self, that trembling, passed in
    music out of sight."

Mrs. Archibald Thorndale's Dog

Chapter I

When Lily Herrick became the owner of a very large thoroughbred St. Bernard puppy, nine months old, there were not wanting those among her own set in Paris, who assigned for the circumstance reasons which possessed all the vivacity of direct contradiction.

"It is a visible token of the *ennui* that overtakes one after one's first youth is over," said Mrs. Wm. P. Weston, with the tranquil certainty of a woman who studies dramas, and who must accordingly formulate theories on which to account for the lives of her fellow creatures.

"There is a *naïveté* about young creatures," the lady went on with the historical tone of one who has been engaged in classifying the human species, "which strongly enchains the mind that has grown *blasé* in the forcing atmosphere of Parisian society."

Here Mrs. Wm. P. Weston caught sight of her young son, Wm. P., smudging over a costly series of French photogravures, with the violent tints of a nursery colour box. His mother hastily snatched the portfolio from him, rang for his *bonne*, and dismissed the *naïve* young artist, roaring like a junior Bull of Bashan.

"There is in all young creatures a total absence of moral responsibility and remorse," continued Mrs. Weston, as if nothing had happened to derange the flow of her ideas, "which afford an endless source of amused observation, more especially with young women who have outlived their early illusions. Oh, women always have illusions. They form the justification of their lives."

"Or, at any rate, of their studies," thought her listener. But being a man, he did not say it aloud.

Half an hour later he had the felicity of hearing Miss Caroline Schneider account for Miss Herrick's St. Bernard upon entirely different grounds.

"Lily is nearly 22, but she is still youthful to crudeness in some things, and her *enjouement* over this last acquisition is a case in point. Don't you agree with me, Mr. Bruce?"

Mr. Bruce, who had hardly digested the first explanation offered to him on the authority of one who had long dissected feminine motives through five acts and an epilogue, replied hesitatingly—

"Well, I really don't quite see that."

"Not when people travel as much as Lily and her father do? Really to accept a mischievous puppy; weighing over a hundredweight and talk to him with rapture."

"Does that make the case worse?"

"Mind, it is only what I have heard. I have not seen the Marquise or Lily since my return. Lily seems to be getting rather neglectful of her old friends lately."

Before Mr. Bruce could make any response "Mdlle. 'Errick" was announced by Miss Schneider's natty little Parisian parlor maid, and the young lady herself stood within the *portière* of bronze velvet which enshrouded the double door of the drawingroom.

She looked very young, charming and vivacious in a faultless summer costume—a bonnet and dress touched with a pure pale yellowish green, that suggested an idyll of opening May buds. An extraordinarily large, intelligent looking young St. Bernard stood close beside her.

"Now, Miss Schneider, tell me, would you sooner I just said, How do you do? and retreated with Gustave—or may he come in?"

"Certainly he may, Lily; I am not such a foe to dumb animals as that—"

"Dumb? Dear Miss Schneider, he makes a whole neighborhood resound alike when he is cross or playful. And then do you know the extent and sweep of his tail? No, it is impossible."

"My dear, you are not going to be taboo to me because of any *puppy*," said Miss Schneider, as she kissed Lily on each cheek, with slightly vindictive emphasis on the noun.

"Mr. Bruce, will you kindly see that there are no priceless Sèvres teapots hanging on half-inch ledges in the middle of the room," said Lily. "Thank you. Now, Gustave, you may bring in your tail. Miss Schneider, allow me to present to you my young dog. Gustave Chartreuse—"

"Chartreuse, did you say, Lily?"

Miss Schneider was somewhat hard of hearing, and this infirmity became more pronounced when she was a little alarmed. This was the case at present. For when she fully realised Gustave's colossal proportions, she felt like Queen Sheba on beholding Solomon's splendor, that the half had not been told her, and for the moment there was no more spirit left in her. The apartments she occupied, close to the Champs Elysées, were crammed with the spoils of affluent wanderings in the more classic portions of the old world.

"Yes, Chartreuse," answered Lily. "Gustave was born within a few hours' climb of the monastery. Gustave, stand up till I present you. You must know this is my oldest friend in Paris. Consequently she thinks that if I adore you to-day I will hang you to-morrow!"

"My dear Lily," said Miss Schneider, in a half-shocked tone, while Mr. Bruce vainly tried to repress a smile.

"Gustave has had the happiness of meeting you before, Mr. Bruce; so I hope a second introduction is not necessary. Gustave, speak to Mr. Bruce."

Gustave fawned and made as though he would spring on Mr. Bruce, who being a very tall, slender man, on a slim chair that had its legs gilded and crossed in a fashion that was much more elegant than stable, half rose in some alarm.

"Gustave's tail smashes things like a tornado, but he never bites," said Lily, in her clear, even voice.

Even as she spoke there was a crash, and Miss Schneider, who was very tall and lean, and more than middle aged, was suddenly bent in two, murmuring in broken accents over a little heap of brown potsherds.

"Mr. Bruce, did I not ask you to remove the crockery?" said Lily, reproachfully.

"So I did, Miss Herrick; several vases and cups that were on the lower shelves of the ebony cabinet."

"But then you left this Pompeian relic on a bracket just within the sweep of Gustave's tail. It is 26 inches long, and he always waves it aloft when I ask him to speak to people. Dear Miss Schneider, do let me look at the pattern of these remains, so that I may obtain a facsimile. Oh, I assure you there are ever so many manufactories of Italian curios dating from centuries before the Christian era. It is quite simple; they bury them, and get just the right shade. Papa says we Americans have given an enormous impetus to this sort of thing."

Miss Schneider said something in a constrained voice about a Greek amphora, with its Olympiad, vouched for by Dr. Schliemann.

"I feel sure you should not have allowed us to come in," said Lily, but without very deep concern of voice or manner. "Now, I begin to understand why the Bedouin Arabs are so hospitable. They have no fragile ware; just a dish to hold rice, and a shell of salt. They do have salt, you know, Mr. Bruce; for it is in their creed not to assassinate or rob a pilgrim till he has eaten some at their table."

"Tell me all your news, Lily," said Miss Schneider, after a pause. "I thought I would have heard from you while I was in the Riviera, I was so much later in returning this season."

"But you know, Miss Schneider, how it is. We returned three months ago, and found so many people had eloped and so many things had happened it was useless to try and cope with the news. That is the death of correspondence. If people would only not expect you to tell them things—"

"But how could one carry on correspondence after that fashion," said Mr. Bruce, with the low, slight smile habitual to him.

"Oh! then one might have a chance of speculating on the nice tales that might come to pass, but don't . . . and you, Mr. Bruce? . . . now I cannot tell when I got the notion, let us call it a superstition . . . well, I have one, that you are not a good correspondent."

"How is your father, Lily?" said Miss Schneider, a little dryly.

"Papa, as usual, is devoted to the dreadful scandals of the middle ages. Poor, dear papa! It is a good thing his morals were fixed before he took up with the *noblesse* of the *ancien régime*. Now, Gustave, where would you like to go next?"

Shortly after Miss Herrick went away the wife of the American Minister and her two daughters called on Miss Schneider. They found her bending mournfully over a Japanese tray, strewn with fragments of glittering earthenware.

"My dear Miss Schneider you have had a misfortune," said Mrs. Seaward, her voice and eyes full of sympathy.

"Now Miss Schneider confess this is a memento of Gustave Chartreuse," said the elder of the young ladies, an exceedingly pretty girl dressed in the faultless manner of American Parisiennes.

"We are on his trail all this week," chimed in the other. "It is a second visitation of the Huns. It is like seeing history made. I never before knew how many irreparable things our friends possessed! And Lily calmly takes out a calendar to enter an order for a duplicate! It is a trifle to have your household gods hurled into eternity by a puppy compared to the insinuation that they can be replaced."

"What has made Lily Herrick so callous of late?" said Miss Schneider suddenly.

She had quite dismissed the thought of trying to piece the "tornadoed" vase together. But it was not the bitterness of this discovery which made her speak out. As long as she believed she was unique in being victimised, she would for the sake of her old friendship for Lily's mother have held her peace. But when it transpired that her amphora was but a link in a ghastly sequence of destruction, friendship itself compelled her to seek some clue. To find out why people change for the worse is often to excuse them.

"Well, we are sure she felt Mr. Egerton's death very much," said Mrs. Seaward, lowering her voice.

"The young *attaché*, at the British Embassy, who lost his life in the Bernese Alps?" said Miss Schneider, raising her voice a little in her surprise. "But is it not well known that Lily refused him last winter?"

"Oh yes, but when girls refuse a man that is the very reason that they are filled with compunction when he comes to an untimely end," returned Mrs. Seaward, with deliberation.

On this Miss Schneider fell for a few moments into deep thought. She knew and liked the young man well enough to be able to recall the first time she saw Lily after hearing of his death. No, certainly, there was no trace of sadness—there was rather a more complete detachment than usual from shielding her fellow creatures from blame or ridicule on any score—a more accentuated habit of drawing her own inferences apart from the opinion of others.

"Surely she would be gentler—or wear half mourning or go less into society, if she suffered from remorse," murmured Miss Schneider. "Certainly there are natures that regret renders more misanthropic"—

"But you must not think that Lily set up Gustave Chartreuse purposely to destroy the moral bulwarks of society, Miss Schneider. The dog is Mr. Egerton's dying gift," said the younger Miss Seaward lazily. "Oh yes, he saw the pup in the neighborhood of Chartreuse when it was only three months old, and bought it for Lily. He meant to return that way. He lived two days after his fall, and it was the day before he died that he commissioned Mr. Sydney—who is papa's *précis* writer now, you know— to bring the young St. Bernard to Miss Herrick. He returned only 10 days ago. We have not heard that Lily herself has told anyone—so you need not mention it, unless she does."

"Certainly it looks as if there were something in it," said Mrs. Seaward.

"And yet supposing she were very deeply wounded, why should a girl who has been reared chiefly in Christian countries find pleasure in making libellous statements regarding the art treasures of friends after her dog has destroyed them," said Miss Schneider, in a tone of critical and dispassionate inquiry. To this no one vouchsafed an answer. Nor is it likely any satisfactory reply would be forthcoming had the question been addressed to the culprit herself.

Mr. Bruce had accompanied Miss Herrick from Miss Schneider's, and the two were now in the Rue de Cazan, which, as every one knows, is full of those great commercial new palaces in which wealthy Americans and foreign princes occupy sumptuously furnished *étages* on leases that have a great tendency to be renewed for the remainder of the occupant's life.

It seemed as though this were to form the external outline of Mr. Herrick's history for the rest of his days. Twelve years previously, when acting as private secretary to the then American Minister in Paris, he had taken a flat in the Hôtel de Mévigné in the street named, with his two young orphan daughters and a widowed sister. Mr. Herrick resigned his official appointment nine years before Lily's St. Bernard afforded so much small talk to some of her friends. There was then some thought, and indeed preparation for the return of the family to Boston. But they went to the East instead.

It was there that Mr. Herrick wrote his pamphlet on *Representative Government in Modern France*. In this he dwelt with much emphasis on some social aspects of Government which had hitherto entirely escaped notice. He waited with some impatience for the effect of his utterances in the political world. But he found that those who are immersed in politics are too much engrossed with the interests of their own faction to be anxious for the illumination of truth. One of his countrymen however, a writer of some eminence, reviewed the political pamphlet so enthusiastically and so often, finding it possessed of distinction and historical acumen, that Mr. Herrick could hardly do less than discover that his true calling was literature. He could well afford the vocation, being possessed of ample means. All things considered, it was apparent that his forte lay in historical investigation. As he had never essayed any other, this belief lay beyond the realm of contradictions. Mr. Herrick's decision to be a man of letters fixed his residence in Paris then for the most part of each year. He passed many hours daily in the Bibliothéque reading shelves of antiquated tomes to qualify himself for the final revision of his *Social Statistics of the Middle Ages in France*.

"You see, as soon as papa has got one reign fixed up, he generally finds that some of his authorities have been telling dreadful lies. Then he has to look up some more old chronicles and re-write. So it seems as if I were never to see my native shores any more," Lily said to her companion, as they drew near to her destination.

"I suppose you hardly remember Boston?" said Mr. Bruce.

Yes, Lily remembered it well. It remained in her memory a square, clean looking little place, just as if you had taken it out of a toy box and set it up. Well, perhaps not very little, and not all so very clean looking. But none of those great, drab fronted, weather stained buildings, with iron gratings at the windows, &c., which one gets so familiar with in the old world.

The Hôtel de Mévigné, which Lily and her companion now approached was, though not stamped with the seal of antiquity, a very lofty and many windowed building—built in fact in most respects after the fashion of a great Parisian ancestral house of bygone centuries. The port-cochère stood open; a carriage had just rolled into the court yard. There were parterres of flowers and blossoming shrubs, and a fountain tinkled pleasantly in the midst. The two young people stood near it, watching a few dark feathered sparrows as they chirped and hopped round the rim of the marble basin. "Will you come in?" said Lily, when Mr. Bruce essayed to say farewell; "well, do not be long in paying us a visit, you know the next two months we are always at home on Wednesdays from 8 to 12. Yes, on other evenings Florence and I go out a good deal, and papa lives mostly in the Middle Ages. Poor Papa! he makes so much work for himself by at first believing the histories that give the great people morals; a thing that nature mostly denied them, and which they seemed to get on extremely well without. By the way, Mr. Bruce, can you tell me when morals began to come in?"

"I do not know that they have ever done so universally," returned that gentleman, with his serious smile, and then almost in the same breath, he asked if the Marquise de Lavalle had quite recovered from the effects of the fever. The Marquise de Lavalle was Florence, Lily's only sister, married three years previously to a marquis of the ancient noblesse of France, whose mode of life, it is to be feared, was but too much after that of those historic personages his father-in-law vainly strove to present with decent characters.

"Mr. Bruce is not at all brilliant; he has not even much of the finesse of society," thought Lily, after they parted, and she smiled at the thought that the young man's inquiry after her sister was evidently suggested by the thought that morals were as far from being fully evolved in modern civilisation as clothes had been amongst the ancient Britons.

Chapter II

It turned out that this was not one of the evenings on which the misdemeanors of forgotten sinners claimed Mr. Herrick's society. He brought home to dine, *en famille*, Mr. Archibald Thorndale, a gentleman from South Australia, who was connected with the family by marriage. That is, his uncle had married Mr. Herrick's sister, the widowed lady who had for some time kept house for the Herricks in bygone years. Our frail nature is so constituted that relationship, whether by blood or marriage, does not invariably constitute a bond of affection, nor even of ordinary friendship. But the young man from Australia—he was barely 26—very soon secured for himself a cordial welcome in the Herrick household.

He was a voracious reader, anxious to assimilate fresh knowledge, very receptive to the theories of other people. This ingratiated him with the head of the house. He was good looking, frank and confiding of nature, yet extremely well bred. This formed a passport to the good graces of the Marquise de Lavalle, who had a few months previously returned in an invalided condition from Algiers, where her husband, a colonel of Lancers, was still stationed with his army. The doctors had forbidden her return to Africa, and the marquise and her infant son were settled inmates in her father's house. Archibald Thorndale was a great lover of animals, and soon became a prime favourite with Gustave Chartreuse. It seemed as if this was a recommendation strong enough to form an elective affinity between Lily and her cousin by courtesy.

"Gustave takes to so few people. I sometimes fancy that as he grows older I may have to retire with him into some mountain fastness," she said, plaintively, one afternoon, when the St. Bernard's repugnance to certain visitors was under discussion.

"But by that time I fear our friends' limbs and *bric-à-brac* may he equally demolished," said her father, with an unusual touch of resentment in his voice.

"But don't you think, sir, that gradually his manners may acquire more polish and reserve?" urged Archibald, soothingly.

"It isn't a question of manners as much as of morals," returned Lily, pensively. "Gustave has too strong a sense of virtue. He would like to destroy all that is vicious in art and life. Of course, the thing is impracticable, for what would be left?"

That evening they were all four at the Théâtre Français. The play was *L'Ecole des Femmes*, and the representation had all the refined finish for which that theatre is famous. The discomfiture of the gloomily egotistical Arnolphe; Horace's playful gaiety, his chivalrous devotion to Agnés when in her girlish innocence she had thrown herself on his protection; the mingled timidity and avarice of the servants—all were exquisitely rendered, and left the memory of living transcripts from life, illuminated with that delicately ironical humour which never forsakes Molière.

Horace was personated by a brilliant young actor, whose reading of Agnés's love letter filled the house with amusement and unqualified admiration. To this point in the play the Herricks also yielded unstinted praise. But Archibald Thorndale was less enthusiastic. Agnés was in his estimation a finished coquette. No really innocent girl ever wrote that letter. To this

Lily took entire exception. An animated debate followed. It was continued next day with undiminished vivacity. In the end each was convinced that in some matters the other was beyond the benefit of clergy.

"I see how it is, Mr. Thorndale, though you were born at the Antipodes you are at heart a bigoted Englishman," said Lily at last.

"We are proud to belong to the British race," answered Archibald with a smile. Then after a pause. "But how does that affect our argument?"

"Oh, in every way. English girls are allowed a certain freedom—but on condition that they suspect every man to be a wolf in sheep's clothing. An English Agnés would be impossible—therefore argues the man of British race a French Agnés, a girl who has been brought up in seclusion, and never taught to think evil of anyone, is equally impossible. It is rather ungallant of you, especially as I thought I lately discerned signs of your succumbing to the fascinations of Mlle. de la Fayence."

"Lily, you know better than that," began Archibald with some emotion, on which Lily rose abruptly, saying she had quite forgotten to give Gustave his afternoon broth. For the next few weeks matters went on as before. Thorndale was constantly in the society of the marquise and of Lily, reserving a part of each forenoon for research in the Bibliothèque—sometimes on Mr. Herrick's behalf, sometimes on his own. For though he had come to Paris for a holiday, he did not forget that he was part proprietor of a leading daily newspaper. He had in the past supplied copy on subjects of surprising diversity. It would be expected that he should do so in an abler way after his mind and eyes had been opened by a sojourn in the centre of old world civilisation.

Lily sometimes declared that he was on the verge of turning into an inquisitive man, with a note book. But her personal friends were chiefly interested in seeing that he had turned into a lover with a very definite aim. When in less than three months after his arrival in Paris this aim was compassed the matter awoke the usual amount of incredulity, wonder and comment.

But the brief courtship was speedily followed by a wedding, and a fortnight's honeymoon in Brittany before the happy pair sailed for South Australia.

"Your father will miss you sadly, my dear," Miss Schneider said to the young bride a few days before she was to sail.

"No, Miss Schneider, papa cannot miss any one who does not make social statics for the middle ages in France," returned Lily; "and then Florence will be with him. Even if the marquis returns to Paris—he has applied for transfer from Algiers—all his acres are so heavily encumbered, they can hardly start a *ménage* of their own again. And then of course Archie and I will come back one day. I am shocked to find how far Australia is away from every place. Why we shall have to sail fast for four weeks from Marseilles before we reach Adelaide."

"But, Lily, did you not find out how far away your husband's country was before—before you made your final arrangements?"

"Well, no. You see, Miss Schneider, there are so many other awful considerations you forget the geography. Indeed if you tried to find out about everything the filial arrangements would never get made."

Though Lily had not lost the little sub-mocking strain habitual to her she looked very radiant, and there was a more winsome expression than usual on her face which strongly reminded Miss Schneider of the girl's mother. But how incomprehensibly different the two. Mrs. Herrick had been among the literati of Boston, overflowing with enthusiasm for countless objects, persons and aspirations; while Lily, on the other hand—it seemed to her old friend that the girl had very little enthusiasm about anything, and no sentiment to speak of.

"And yet before a girl marries she must have a fund of both," reflected Miss Schneider, scanning the young bride critically. "Lily is perfectly *fin de siècle*, that is certain; but she could not look so much like her mother if she had not a morsel of heart concealed about her somewhere."

Lily's mother had been very dear to the old lady, and she was one whose friendships were terminated neither by death nor absence. There was a tender inflection in her voice when she spoke again.

"You remind me strongly of your mother today, Lily. I have often wished she had been spared to you a little longer. I am glad you are happily married. You are happy, are you not, Lily?"

"Oh, no one could be kinder to Chartreuse than Archie. He seemed to droop a little before we left Paris, but the breezy coasts of Brittany quite restored him. Now that he is getting older I shall call him Chartreuse."

Lily was speaking a little more rapidly than usual. Chartreuse, hearing his name repeated, got up from his mistress's feet and waved his enormous tail in the slow majestic manner that characterises the motions of large masses.

A slight tinge of colour crept into Miss Schneider's face. She was of a placid, equable disposition; but, now that her memory was crowded with recollections of Lily's mother, it seemed to her as if the girl had abused the privilege which her generation enjoys of treating the most serious subjects with frivolous profanity.

"It may be my growing deafness, but really, my child, I am not sure whether you are speaking of your husband or your dog," she said a little sternly.

"Miss Schneider, you have not quite forgiven Chartreuse that Pompeian pot," said Lily smiling. "Or, at least you have not forgotten it to him. I never could quite distinguish between the two, though Signora Zucca often tried hard to make me. You remember that funny little

Neapolitan governess we had in Florence?"

"My dear, you have had too many funny governesses."

"Oh, no, Miss Schneider, most of them were awful old frumps, who wanted to make one learn about the mummies in Cheops and things. They were hardly ever funny, unless by accident." Miss Schneider reflected that it was not the least use to get vexed at Lily, besides she was to sail away to the under world in a few days. So, after a little pause, she said very kindly—

"My dear Lily, what I mean is that you have been thrown too much on the care of governesses of various nationalities. If your father had only returned to Boston for some years, or at any rate sent you and Florence to school there—"

"It wouldn't have been the least use his doing that, Miss Schneider— we could never have stood the weak tea, bread and butter, with the Boston girls thrown in. We would have got over the gate and run away— perhaps eloped with an Italian music master, with big melancholy eyes and no income."

Lily stopped abruptly, when she saw the unwonted solemnity of her old friend's face. Then she said, in a softer, lower voice.

"Do you think it would have made so much difference if I had been brought up in Boston, Miss Schneider? Perhaps, you think I would have written pretty sympathetic verses, like mother, to dead crows and things. I don't believe it is in me. I hate dead things—crows especially. I dare say I am horrid sometimes—"

"No, Lily, you are never that," said Miss Schneider, with emphasis. "But you have had no native country."

"Except Paris. Don't you think the Bibliothèque is papa's native soil. I am sure he would be an alien anywhere without it?"

"Yes, you are like a native of Paris, and you have lived in Dresden, and Florence and Rome, and part of two or three years in London and Vienna."

"And three winters in the East, and one in Japan."

"And a trip or two to Norway, but always back again to Paris, for the last 12 years."

"But that is not so much because Florence and I love Paris. It's partly because of the dreadful old scandals papa has to look up in the Bibliothèque."

No old scandals in the Bibliothèque could have sufficient vitality for Miss Schneider to make her angry. But an eloquent expression came into her face, which she did not put into words. She merely said—

"But all this doesn't give girls home associations, Lily."

"But it makes a great many places seem like home, isn't that a sort of education for the affections, Miss Schneider?"

In this question Miss Schneider recognised the tag end of one of her former serious little discussions with Lily. But she went on in the same serious kindly tone.

"But with the absence of one's home and country there is a lack of family ties, of the amenities of intercourse with relations, and the discipline of domestic life."

"I think I know what you mean, Miss Schneider. Relations are often an awful bore—one would like to give them away as far as they would go round—and instead, one has to pretend that they are quite sweet and lovely."

Miss Schneider sighed and shook her head. "No, Lily, that is not what I mean. It is that the sweet kindly charities of home life train us to be reticent and forbearing towards one another's infirmities—that they prevent us from looking at people in that detached critical way. There is something very hard and scoffing in the atmosphere of great cities. One catches it up seeing a constant succession of new people—"

"I know your ideal for me, Miss Schneider. You want me to be like one of Mrs. Silas M. Tasker's girls," said Lily suddenly. "They sit round in daisy chains making up legends about each others' small perfections."

"Well, now that you have mentioned them, I cannot help recalling how Eulalie spoke when she first came to see me as a bride."

"What did she say dear?"

Miss Schneider gazed a little doubtfully into the fair young face opposite to her. But it looked so serious, so devoid of malice that she was encouraged to go on.

"Well, Lily; she sat on a low stool at my feet—"

"Just so," said Lily sitting on a white polar bear skin at Miss Schneider's foot.

"And she held my hands in hers—"

"Do give me your hands, Miss Schneider."

The old lady began to doubt the wisdom of her narrative. But she pressed Lily's slender hands in her own, and went on.

"'Oh, Miss Schneider,' she said, 'Ralph is too dear and perfect . . . I do not deserve such happiness. He is too good for me.'"

Miss Schneider felt a tremulous motion against her knees where Lily had in imitation of the model bride hidden her face. The thought darted through her mind that she had at last suceeded in touching that reservoir of emotion which must somehow lurk in the girl's nature.

Inspired by the thought she went on earnestly—

"And you could tell it came straight from her heart, Lily."

"No, dear Miss Schneider; it came straight out of the three volume novel," said Lily, raising her head and laughing outright.

"And after all it is no compliment. I do not know anything that would get upon one's nerves so completely as a man who was too good for one. There is something real mean in the idea."

Poor Miss Schneider was more than taken aback. She was woefully disappointed and a good deal affronted at what she felt to be the girl's callousness. But at that moment Mr. Thorndale was announced, and the young man came in with so triumphantly happy a mien—with such bridegroom radiance pervading his presence—that the old lady felt as if her misgivings must be groundless. He at least belonged to the good old fashioned order of the newly wedded, who perceived no imbecility in believing that his marriage was of the kind which proved him to be the special favourite of heaven.

Could his wife's oldest friend forgive him for taking Lily so far away? He could promise that the first aim of his life would be to make her happy—

"Archie, if you are going into heroics, the proper thing to say is that, 'like a dream my life shall pass away, pass away,'" put in Lily.

Archie smiled fondly at this interruption and went on to tell Lily's "oldest friend" how large a circle of relations he had in his native country, how they would all welcome Lily as one of themselves and how impossible it would be for her to lack affection or society, &c. Lily made a little grimace, and said that at any rate she would have Gustave Chartreuse to fall back upon.

"Is it the old story of one being very much in love and the other just enduring it?" reflected Miss Schneider, after the young pair had taken leave. "I am sorry Archibald has so many relations. Of course, whatever Lily says or does just now is adorable, and no doubt he thinks her most perverse sallies a ruse to hide depths of tenderness and feeling. But is it so? And how long will she remain perfect in the colder light of the days that succeed the honeymoon? To be sure I know nothing of the matter beyond what I read and a little observation. But if a young man is as ardent and blissful a lover two months after marriage as he is after two weeks—well, I don't believe it."

Chapter III

Travelling by sea has changed since Dr. Johnson declared it was like imprisonment, with the chance of being drowned. A trip in a great ocean mail steamer may nowadays be more accurately compared to a sojourn at a watering place with the certainty of a damaged character. There are, doubtless, many travellers whose antecedents effectually secure them against any accident of this kind. And even those who are most wronged by the unceasing tittle-tattle of the idle well fed saloon passengers separated into groups on the deck engaged in tearing each other's reputations into shreds, think little of the matter once the voyage is over. Yet as the essayists and copy books have long informed us, there are exceptions to all general rules. And so the enforced companionship of fellow travellers sometimes gives rise to likes and dislikes which long survive the voyage that engendered them. This turned out to be the case with Mrs. Archibald Thorndale on her voyage to Australia.

During this time there was one individual that attracted and two that repelled her among those with whom she was brought into contact, the three being women. The one she liked was a Mrs. Melville, a widow in rather reduced circumstances, with her only child, a girl aged 8. Mrs. Melville was on her way to South Australia to look after some money that had suddenly ceased to return any income. The investment constituted most of her worldly wealth.

"I cannot find out any particulars from my uncle in law," she explained to Lily. "He just writes a note now and then to say that investments in South Australia are going to the dogs, but he never sends documents to show it."

She was a brave self dependent little woman, yet apt to "get very low," as she phrased it, though well enough inclined to mirth if other people s upplied the material. She was unused to travel, was very shy and reticent, and with her little girl kept apart from the other passengers, making advances of friendship only to Gustave Chartreuse, who took them up with enthusiasm, and gravely paced beside them when they took their daily constitutionals up and down the deck. It was this that first led to the acquaintance between Mrs. Melville and Lily. Afterwards it seemed as if the striking contrast of their past lives, dispositions and circumstances formed a sort of bond. Mrs. Melville would sit by Lily day after day finding unaccustomed enjoyment in her racy, unstudied descriptions of the persons and places she had known. The widow had lived nearly all her life in one of those small stagnant, provincial English towns, in which grey cats, clergymen and spinsters form the most stirring topics of conversation. To her the intercourse of intimate talk, with one whose life had been passed among the leisured classes of the great European capitals, had all the fascination of adventures shorn of their peril.

Nor was the sense of realising a hitherto unknown mode of existence confined to Mrs. Melville. It was a new experience to Lily to come into personal contact with a well born woman, whose history was summed up in trying to make 3d. go as far as 3½d., and whose only permanent recreation in life had been to hunt up the butcher's and baker's overcharges.

"How can people bear to live on in this way, Archie," the said one day, as she thought over the sordid prospects of genteel poverty. "The days crowded with a succession of small disasters—unrelieved even by a great catastrophe—"

"But you find Mrs. Melville much more interesting than my old friend, Lady Keightley, who has £7000 or £8000 a year."

"Oh, but she is such an impossible old thing. Just look at her now with a bunch of puce coloured plumes nodding above her head, like the peacock's feathers of a Chinese ambassador; and that daughter of hers, isn't she exactly like an embryo fish that has prematurely slipped out of the egg, with her round full eyes, and her thin lips always closed?"

"Oh, Lily; you should not talk like that."

"Would you mind lending me a pencil, Archie? Thanks. Now I have the date, 2nd October—just five weeks after we were married—you ceased to be a foolish lover, and with a certain air of marital coldness you very properly told me I 'should not talk like that.' I love to be able to fix dates so lucidly." And with that Lily replaced her small jewel-clasped note book and handed her husband his pencil with a mischievous little nod. The young man murmured some vehement disclaimers. But Lily's manner was so entirely disengaged from any symptom of pique that it speedily became apparent to Thorndale that any show of earnestness in the matter was slightly ridiculous. Still, the time seemed to have come when some serious talk was inevitable.

"I have vainly tried to discover, Lily, why you dislike Lady Keightley so much," said Thorndale, drawing a deck chair nearer to the lounge on which Lily was reclining, a sunshade fixed above her head, while Gustave Chartreuse's colossal form lay prone on the deck, his square massive head nestling against his mistress's hand.

"But how is one to find out such things?" said Lily, slightly raising her eyebrows. "You see our points of view are so hopelessly wide asunder in a thing of this kind. As a little boy you were made to learn Lady Keightley's doggerel by heart, as if it were a cross between Shakespeare and the New Testament. She has evidently been a sort of best idol in your family."

"But, dear, is that any reason why you should dislike and snub her?"

"Do I dislike her? Well, I suppose I do. But surely not because she is a friend of yours. Let me see how it was at the beginning. Gustave, do you know that your mouth grows wider day by day? It is my belief you could swallow a Jonah without winking."

"Lily, may I say it?"

"Oh, I know I should not drop the thread of conversation with you and address Gustave. But consider the temptation. His tail and eyes are so eloquent, and he still adores me. But seriously, Archie, you know I knew nothing of the good old woman the first day she came on deck, and if I disliked her from the first it wasn't because she was your friend. What a figure she was in flowing flowered peignoir, an Indian shawl round her shoulders, her funny little corkscrew curls plastered to her cheeks, on which there was a faint suspicion of rouge, a fan in one hand, a smelling bottle in the other, followed by her daughter carrying three dull looking books, and the maid with three cushions and three shawls. She must have some rooted superstition about the number three. She looked exactly like an extract from some old *Vers de Société*. I turned to ask you who she was, but you had flown to her side all smiles and tears—well, perhaps not tears."

"You absurd child," said Thorndale, laughing, I did not know till that moment Lady Keightley and her daughter were on board. Of course I was delighted to see them, and they were to see me, and were eager to know you."

"Yes, and you hurried back and asked me, in a voice broken with emotion, to come and be 'presented' to Lady Keightley—and please Lily leave Gustave here—Lady Keightley has an antipathy to dogs, especially large ones."

"Yes, Lily, and what did you say in reply? 'And I on my part have an antipathy to old women, especially silly ones.'"

"Yes, but afterwards, when you told me she was your mother's bosom friend, I said I was sorry—and suppose we speak of something else."

"Unless you let me speak of this a little longer, Lily. Thank you. Now don't imagine I want to find fault, dearie."

"But you may, Archie; you may even scold—if you shift the sunshade, so that it protects Chartreuse's head more. Thanks, awfully. And now just give me *Jack*."

Thorndale made a gesture of impatience, but he gave Lily the book, and then paced up and down the deck till Lady Keightley and her daughter also joined the promenaders. Then the young man gave his arm to the lady, and with bent head listened sympathetically and deferentially to her unceasing flow of small talk. The late Sir Thomas Keightley had been a baronet with a small heavily encumbered estate and no income to speak of, till during a tour in Australia he wooed and married the wealthy and literary widow of a wholesale ironmonger. After that event he lived, as the irreverent would phrase it, in clover, till a constitution much the worse for wear, through early excesses and hard living, succumbed to an obstinate attack of jaundice. Since that event Lady Keightley had paid many visits to England. She always returned with the unspoken conviction that titles in the old world were much too common.

Lady Keightley was an incorrigible talker. Let it be said at once that she was selfish, vain and self important, with a mind absolutely sealed against the faintest glimmering of humour. She had written many silly poems and sillier stories. This is too common an offence to be ranked among the more penal failings of mankind. But what rendered the fault more flagrant in Lady Keightley's case was her unmoved and pathetic belief in her own value as an author. She habitually carried about with her a small album inlaid with mother of pearl, in which she had inserted all the notices of the press that had ever appeared regarding what she termed her "works." These notices were subdivided into "shallow" and "intelligent" critiques. Those that praised her literary efforts were placed under the latter category; those that hinted at a defect under the former. Lady Keightley was under the impression that she was distinguished as a writer by a well developed critical faculty and a certain skill in psychological analysis. As any glimmering of either was entirely absent from her books, it will be seen that she was not more belated than the rest of us are in the objects of our special personal vanities. Her first care on making new acquaintances was to let them know she was the widow of a baronet, not a knight; her second was to introduce them to her album full of critiques, and her third to give them the reading of her books in prose and verse. Needless to say, Lily fought shy of reading either.

"This, Mrs. Archibald, is the volume that the reviewers of the better order pronounced to be at once profoundly interesting and serious," said Lady Keightley, the second day after forming Lily's acquaintance, turning over a thin book with a yellow brown cover. "Americans, I know, are great readers. I shall be happy to lend you this."

"Thank you so much, but I never read serious things—not even papa's," answered Lily, who, whatever her other failings might be, was not in the habit of using curling irons instead of dealing in facts.

"How then do you improve your mind?"

"Oh, it just weeds on. I am not sure that it would stand cultivating. Some things would be destroyed if you tried to improve them, you know," said Lily, in a calmly reflective tone. Lady Keightley and her daughter stared, and Archibald, who was present, could not forbear smiling, though he felt more inclined to show his wife that he was displeased at the mock serious way in which she kept his old friend at arm's length . . . He recalled this, and subsequent little encounters of a like nature between his wife and Lady Keightley, as he paced up and down with the latter in the mellow sunshine of the Indian Ocean, while her unfailing stream of self complacent talk flowed on placidly.

How would Lily get on with his numerous relations, especially with his mother? Thorndale was a good son and a dutiful one, but he could not be blind to the truth that his mother, who had been a great heiress, had all her life wielded unusual power, and expected all who came within her orbit to yield her a sure and definite tribute of allegiance. Forecasting the future in the light of what he knew of her uncompromising adherence to her own prepossessions, was Lily likely to yield this? Would she, for instance, out of deference to his mother's feelings, repress what even he himself felt was an undue affection for Gustave Chartreuse? "Animals are all very well, but they must be kept in their own place," had always been a fixed maxim with his mother, and apart from beasts of burden that place in her estimation was well out of sight and hearing. Archibald's eyes followed the direction of his thoughts, and he noticed that his wife had relinquished her book. She seemed to be, as far as he could judge, in a profound reverie. Perhaps—yes, it was possible—that a little winge of remorse had overtaken her for cutting short the little discourse by which he had proposed to broach one or two of the misgivings that from day to day assailed him as they drew nearer to their future home. He resolved that as soon as Lady Keightley set him at liberty he would take advantage of what was evidently a more propitious mood on Lily's part to bring his little connubial monologue to a more effective issue. "After all Lily is such a perfect darling—she will in the end fall in with what I wish," thought Archibald, but even as he reassured himself a morsel of doubt, like a little chilly snake, lodged in his heart.

Had Miss Schneider at that moment been privy to Archibald's thoughts, she might have imagined that the bloom of young love's dream had gone the way of all flesh. But in truth it was not this so much as a recognition of the way in which the crude prosaic realities of life must gradually impinge on the roseate paradise in which for a brief season it had been possible to show them to the door.

No one in a *tête-a-tête* could better cover the delinquencies of a companion engrossed in his own thoughts than Lady Keightley. She took herself and all her small concerns so seriously, taking her listener's interest and acquiescence in all her views so much for granted that nothing beyond an occasional monosyllable was necessary to maintain the illusion of a conversation. But there are limits even to egotistic self-sufficiency and towards the close of their promenade Archibald was startled by hearing Lady Keightley say in a tone of surprise

"Do you really mean that Archibald?"

"Mean what. Lady Keightley? I beg a thousand pardons—but the din of tongues around—"

"I asked you if you thought Lily would refuse to visit your mother without her dog—and you said yes."

"How very absurd," said Archibald with a heightened colour, vexed at his own remissness—vexed too at hearing his half formulated fears put into such bald form.

"You know your dear mother's rooted dislike to treating animals in that—that fashion. And it isn't so much dislike with her; it is principle. Indeed one may say all her dislikes are fixed principles," said Lady Keightley with that sense of moral elation some people derive from their own and their friends' singularity in virtue.

"Oh well, as for that, my wife is sure to do just what is right," said Archibald a little stiffly.

"My dear Archie, I take the privilege of an old ancestral friend," returned Lady Keightley in a plaintive tone. "We who have been for more than half a century spectators of the play of life long to do our little best to smooth matters—to make things easier. It has occurred to me that it might simplify matters if I told your wife, in a friendly way, the objection your mother, in common with myself, has to dogs. But perhaps you have already done so? Fortunately he will be in quarantine for the first few months—only if Lily begins by going to see him too often."

"In quarantine!" echoed Archibald; and then for a little his heart failed him, as he suddenly recollected that there were some stringent rules about landing dogs in South Australia. Nothing had ever happened previously to make him interested in the subject. And now. Yet on a little reflection he was half glad that the matter had so entirely escaped his memory; for ridiculous as it might seem on the first blush, he was not at all sure that Lily might not have made a difficulty about coming to a country where at the outset she must be separated from her St. Bernard.

"I had quite forgotten the matter till this moment," he said slowly. This was a confession which somehow gave Lady Keightley a sensation of pleasure, for she could not doubt that the news would interfere with the serene, and as she mentally termed it "insolent," self-possession of this young American woman. To tell the truth Lady Keightley was so long accustomed to play first fiddle in the only society familiar to her that to find herself, her title and her "works" treated with supreme indifference was an experience bitterly unpalatable. She was a stanch churchwoman, and, as we all know, the first instinct of most orthodox Christians when aggrieved by any one is to visit the offender with pain in mind, body or estate. Lady Keightley belonged to the majority, and she resolved, if possible, to enjoy the triumph of Mrs. Archibald's discomfiture. The readiest way of doing so was under the guise of sympathy.

"Oh, they are very good to dogs in quarantine, Archie. Several of my friends have had dogs there. I'll tell your wife, so that she may not be apprehensive. After all it may get Lily out of the habit of having him so much with her."

"How very good of you. I am afraid Lily will not like to part with Gustave."

They both approached the lounge on which Lily was lying. She was just awakening from sleep, a soft flush mantling her cheeks, her lips slightly parted. Gustave was prone on one side of her. Mrs. Melville, reading Daudet's *Jack* to her daughter, sat on the other. It was no touch of contrition then, but the unconsciousness of peaceful slumber, that had given her an air of pensive reverie!

The passengers were assembling in groups at the port side of the ship talking with more than usual animation. Above the buzz of tongues and laughter, and the click of cricket balls on the starboard side, Archibald heard the shrill call of sea birds; a flock of white gulls were circling in the wake of the vessel. Then the magic word "land" flew from one to the other. The western coast of Australia was full in view. There lay the curved outlines of the shore, with dented little bays and rounded capes and nameless promontories, with a coast line of yellow-red sand in the foreground. Inland stretched serried lines of irregular ranges, clothed with creeping scrub, varied by tall shrubs and occasional trees, the ground showing faint traces of grey, green herbage in the sharp dells and shady gullies that intersected the folds of the rises. A few birds might be seen flying landward. In the far distance a column of pale blue smoke might here and there be seen floating up into the widely vaulted amethyst dome of the sky. These were the sole signs of life apparent to the quickest eye as the ship drew nearer and sailed parallel with the shore.

"Are there no natives—no little villages anywhere?" said Mrs. Melville, with that sinking of the heart which a wide expanse of desert country awakens in those who see it for the first time.

"We have killed all the natives," said Archie, "and the villages have not yet begun."

"Look at your master's country, Chartreuse; tell me will you like it?" said Lily, patting her dog's head as he came to slip his large, cold nose into her hand, while she stood, with a group of others, looking at the shore.

Lady Keightley, who was near, on this brought up the question of quarantine for dogs, and offered her condolences on the enforced separation: "But, of course, you will be able to see him from time to time, Mrs. Archibald. I think it is for five or six months they are detained."

Lily looked at the speaker with slowly dilating eyes. There was no touch of emotion, however, in her voice as she replied, "If Chartreuse has to go into quarantine of course I shall go with him. He is much too sensitive to be left to strangers."

"But, my dear Mrs. Archibald, even children have often to be separated from their mothers."

"But no other young animals are so stupid as children often are. How can they help it, indeed—poor little wretches, look at the parents of most of them. But it is too utterly absurd about this quarantine. Archibald, hadn't we better think of some way of evading this imbecility?" said Lily, turning to her husband, who had at that moment joined them.

The two went apart to discuss the matter, leaving Lady Keightley with a baffled feeling of perplexity and defeat. The only crumb of consolation she gleaned from her abortive effort at annoying Lily was the monstrous proposition she made as to accompanying her dog into quarantine!

Lady Keightley related and reset this incident so often that it became altogether over coloured and dislocated in the way peculiar to words and events torn from their context in an unfriendly spirit. And this feeling was all the more paramount, seeing that Chartreuse was, after all, not separated from his mistress. Thorndale, as has been said, was part proprietor of a leading daily paper; an elder brother, after a few years of Parliamentary life, had recently become Chief Secretary in one of the brief lived Ministries for which South Australia is now renowned. Needless to say that under the circumstances the rules touching the importation of dogs were found susceptible of being essentially modified. Nevertheless, the fact that Mrs. Archibald had been ready to go into quarantine with her St. Bernard made the fortune of many an afternoon tea with Lady Keightley.

"My dear Sarah, I cannot tell you what a turn it gave me when I heard her calmly proposing to separate from her husband, so as to look after that great poodle. And yet I might have been prepared for it. Lady Keightley—my stepdaughter-in-law—knows some American ladies in London who give parties to their dogs, sending invitation cards in their names and letting them eat ortolans off silver plates in company. It just reminds one of things that happened in the decadence of the Roman Empire," and Lady Keightley gave a virtuous little shiver as she trotted out one of the literary phrases so dear to her. "Sarah" was Mrs. Thorndale, Lily's mother-in-law, who listened to all the variations of which the matter was capable, sitting more upright than ever with a tinge of indignation reddening her firm well developed cheeks.

"If any one but you told me of this, Susan, I would not believe it," she would say, in the tone of authoritative deliberation that marked her utterances. Altogether the two were so horrified at the picture they dressed up of such irrational devotion to a dumb animal, that it was evident they cherished a lively expectation of finding ample food for fault finding in Mrs. Archibald's future actions.

Chapter IV

It is not an uncommon circumstance in domestic life to find that the bond of mother and daughter-in-law is one which does not lead to deep mutual affection. It is certain that no son's wife could find acceptance with Mrs. Thorndale unless the younger woman was prepared largely to efface her own individuality. Quite apart from Gustave

Chartreuse it is not likely that Archibald's wife should seriously aim at making herself acceptable on such terms, and from the first the St. Bernard was made a burning question by the mother-in-law.

"I had better tell you candidly, Lily," she said at their second meeting, "I do not like dogs off the chain."

"I am afraid you won't like mine then Mrs. Thorndale, for he is never on the chain, and when his term of home quarantine is over he will accompany me everywhere," answered Lily sweetly.

At this Mrs. Henry and Mrs. Charles Thorndale, who were present, exchanged looks of horror. They were twin sisters, small blonde women, naturally of a facile and clinging disposition, who found it much easier to adopt other people's opinions than to have any of their own. They were not only born but married on the same day, and they had from the first yielded unquestioning adherence to their mother-in-law. Unfortunately, Mrs. Henry's eldest daughter, Mabel, who had already partially developed into a rebel against her grandmother's high handed authority, was also present and Lily's fearless attitude afforded the girl unqualified joy.

"Oh, Aunt Lily, I am so glad you don't give in to grandma," she said the first time after this that the two were alone. "Ma and Aunt Charles are simply like door mats to her—ever so much worse than her own daughters. You know I am the eldest of the grandchildren—17 last birthday, and a year ago if papa and the doctor had not stood by me I would most likely now be dead of a brain fever. You see how fearfully thick my hair is? Fancy what it must have been before it was cropped! Well, I was going in for an examination—Latin and French and German, besides cutting up frogs for physiology. And on top of it all Granny *would* have me do a lot of mythology, Bible history and things twice a week. I began to have *awful* headaches—the kind that make men tie wet towels round them and go into asylums. Then another girl told me I should have my hair cut, and so I just went to Madame Sauvestre's and she cut it off close as you see it. Would you believe it—when Granny first saw me she nearly choked. How dared I be cropped *like a jockey without even consulting her*, and mamma cried and hoped my hair would soon grow."

"And did it," said Lily, smiling.

"Yes, but it soon came off again," said Mabel, nodding her head triumphantly. "When granny made such a fuss I got quite hot and raved a little that night. I called her a spiteful old tabby. It was awful fun to be able to do that and have people tread softly in the room instead of making you hold your tongue. And then the doctor called it incipient brain fever, and said my hair must *not* be allowed to grow; and pa of course said the same. I do think doctors are the dearest and cleverest people of any. It is very jolly now; I don't have to study and my hair must be kept cut."

Mabel was a true daughter of the soil of the unstudious and pleasure loving kind—true as steel to those she liked, but mutinous to a degree against what seemed to her any form of tyranny; lacking in reverence and admiration, and not too scrupulous always as to the ways in which she compassed her own ends. It must be confessed that her crisply curling dark brown hair became her *mignonne* face, her sparkling dark eyes, delicately *rétroussé* nose, and rose red lips, "pouting as if a bee had stung them newly," cut close like a boy's, better than any other style of *coiffure*.

"I should have kept my hair cropped without having incipient brain fever," said Lily, with a moaning smile.

"Ah, yes; but you don't know grandma. Just wait till you see the way she tries to rule us all. She makes one sick of the very name of Thorndale."

Lily had ample opportunities for proving the truth of this. The worthy lady had been born a Thorndale, and married a distant cousin. "She had been all her life remarkable for her robust and invincible belief in the supreme importance of all that related to the Thorndales. An old shoe that had at one time been worn by a long defunct member of the family was in her eyes of far more importance than the living interests of any one who was not connected with her sort. Now a widow of three years standing, and 60 years of age, with eight sons and daughters and 37 grandchildren, and half a million of money entirely at her own disposal, the world was for her divided into Thorndales and Gentiles of the outer court. From the first Mrs. Thorndale felt it incumbent on herself to mould her new daughter-in-law in accordance with her own standard of what was fitting. None of the methods she adopted towards this end were crowned with much success, while some of them were distinctly funny.

"You have so much time on your hands, Lily, and it is so necessary that a young wife should get to understand children," she would say. "Now, to-day I have asked eight or nine of your young relatives to meet you."

Lily might raise her eyebrows and look astonished, but this would not prevent the fond grandmamma from dwelling upon the infantile experiences of her favourite descendants in the second generation. "We all expected that the end had come," she would say in a deep, impressive voice as she went over the crisis of one nursery disease after another.

"But of course it hadn't," Lily said one day, vainly trying to hasten the *dénouement*.

"My dear, why do you say 'Of course?'"

"Oh, no Thorndale ever seems to die," returned Lily, half despairingly.

"With extreme care and proper nursing most children can be kept alive, more especially the Thorndales, who are *all* healthy," returned Mrs. Thorndale severely. "I am thankful to say that, under Providence, my instructions have proved most successful. The great thing is to be prepared for an emergency. Now, suppose you were responsible for the welfare of a child, and noticed one day a slight redness, with a disposition to cough, what conclusion would you come to?"

"That the nurse should keep it in the nursery," answered Lily promptly.

This was the sort of response that Mrs. Thorndale could not endure without invading the limits of polite neutrality, behind which her daughter-in-law entrenched herself.

"A nurse can never take the mother's place, Lily, and I should be extremely sorry to see you delegate the dearest duties of a woman to a base hireling. Nothing could, to my mind, be more odious," she said in a tone of stern reproach. But when Mrs. Thorndale became vehement Mrs. Archibald Thorndale maintained an unconquerable silence. She drew the line at personal recrimination, and this often put the elder woman into a false position, as on the present occasion. She waited for Lily to point out that she could hardly be charged as yet with neglecting her offspring. Seeing that this very valid defence was not made, Mrs. Thorndale after a pause continued—

"Of course I do not say that you will be one of those mothers who put their children out to die with a foster nurse. But there is nothing like training the mind and habits in anticipation of our duties."

Lily was getting supernaturally bored, and rose to go much earlier than she had purposed.

"Is it that you are offended at my trying to be a mother to you, Lily?" said Mrs. Thorndale, in a semi-tragical tone.

"N—o—, but it seems to me that it is unwise to meet trouble half way," answered Lily. Just then Lady Keightley and her daughter were announced, and before Mrs. Thorndale had quite taken in the full scope of this reply her daughter-in-law had gone.

"Now what do you think Mrs. Archibald meant by that?" she said, as the three sat in full conclave over afternoon tea and the conversation recorded. "Was it the misfortune of children dying—"

"Not at all, my dear Sarah, not at all," answered Lady Keightley in emphatic tones. "That is not the creed of fashionable young American ladies of the present day. Oh, they are much wiser than to interfere with their plan of life by undertaking the bliss of maternity, more particularly *une vraie Parisienne*, like Mrs. A. Thorndale."

"Mrs. Archibald Thorndale certainly seems to get into the swim of every possible excitement; I should think she allows herself little or no time for domestic life," said Miss Benson, Lady Keightley's daughter by her first marriage, eager to offer her quota to the sum total of the young wife's imperfections.

Miss Benson's was originally a not unamiable nature. She had been in her youth animated, open to instruction, and interested in subjects apart from the ever renewed rush of common place details, which so often swamp the lives of women of the leisured classes in Australia. But she had been thwarted in the better possibilities of her being. Her mind had been gradually rendered thin and had become impoverished by those untoward accidents of life that sometimes defeat the best development of which human beings are capable. Now, at 37 years of age, she was chiefly remarkable for a taciturnity seldom broken, except to bear witness to the prevalence of the less worthy attributes of her fellow creatures. Envy, and all the minor vices of uncharitableness which flow from it, had unconsciously to herself dominated her views of society. She would have been horrified at the statement put into unvarnished terms. Yet the truth was that to see other women young and pretty, or admired by men for their social gifts, constituted in Miss Benson's estimation a stumbling block which made it easy for her to credit evil concerning them.

Nor must it be forgotten that Mrs. Archibald was one of those women who show to less advantage among their own sex than they intrinsically deserve. The religion of a large proportion of women of the Anglo Saxon race primarily consists in a rigid observance of the smaller *bienséances* of existence. To smile and kiss and say pleasant things when they are really more than indifferent to each other is with such women largely the fulfilment of the law and the prophets. It was precisely in these respects that Lily exemplified to the full the effect of what Mr. Herbert Spencer's disciples call the recognition of the rights and individuality of children. Divested of the embroidery of theorising this means their right to develop the bent of their character unhampered by the repressive influence of their elders. In no country has this method of allowing the young to bring themselves up been so faithfully adhered to as in America. Not so much because the synthetic philosopher is generally followed, but because in that larger, freer atmosphere the "Process of the suns" brings in its train more rapidly that evolution of equality which is gradually transforming society in the old world and the new.

Lily had been allowed full scope in making her own investigations and drawing her own inferences apart from the approval or disapprobation of others. From the first her father acted on the principle that a parent's primary duty is to avoid antagonism with his children. But the discipline of natural consequences, which should have taken the place of parental displeasure or artificial penalties, had been too often borne by servants and governesses. Thus had Lily grown up in cultured independence, a self-governed being—not one governed by others. Among American ladies the type is not rare, and is found by many to possess unique attraction. Its salient characteristics were in Lily's case accentuated by her father's wealth, his residence in European capitals and his bookish inclinations, which led him to mingle largely with people of wide knowledge and literary attainments. No class is more divorced than this from that prostrate worship of Mrs. Grundy which is so comically characteristic of certain sections of the well-to-do classes of Australia, at the present era of its history. Thus, though Lily might out of deference to her mother-in-law learn to keep silent, she could not learn that respect for conventionality that would lead her to say what she did not mean, nor learn to express the sentiments which the generality of people would classify as the proper things to say. She could not lose that impersonal detached way of looking at persons and events which used to strike Miss Schnieder as being rather heartless. Archibald found this attitude of mind on the part of his wife amusing in regard to outsiders, but vexatious with regard to his nearest relatives. He did so on the evening which followed the visit that closed so abruptly. The two had returned from a family dinner party at Thorndale's eldest brother's. It was rather a warm evening, late in August. Lily, on coming home, sank into an armchair, and unbuttoned her gloves with a jaded expression.

"Archie, how many family dinner parties have we been to in the last three months?" she asked suddenly.

The young man, who was sociably inclined and was on thoroughly good terms with all the members of his family, smiled pleasantly, saying by way of reply,—

"There *are* a good many of us, aren't there, Lil?"

"It isn't that there are so many Thorndales, it is that they combine themselves into a mutilated version of eternity. They may have had a beginning, but there is literally no end to them," answered Lily in an accent of mock despair.

"Which of them do you want to do away with, little wife?" asked her husband, smiling.

"The subject is too dangerous. Besides the difficulty for me would be solved by keeping a little more out of their way."

"Well, I thought it was a very pleasant party," said Archibald, a shade of displeasure in his face.

"Oh, Archie, it seemed as if they had given rendezvous to all the bores."

"Remember, Lily, they were all our own family, except the Maskelynes," said Archibald, inferring by his tone that this should settle the matter.

"Yes, and I was not near either of the Maskelynes," replied Lily, with a comical little sigh, which made her husband laugh.

"I was wedged in at dinner time, between George and your uncle James, who talked all the time of the skip-jack and the capricorn beetle and some reptiles that ravage wheat and things. The women talk of nothing but *chiffons* and whooping cough and smashed china, and the men are even duller than their wives."

"But at any rate you got on well with most of them. You like George's wife, Lily," said Archibald in a expostulatory tone.

"Ah yes," answered Lily somewhat doubtfully, and after a pause, "She reminds me a little of a wooden butterfly."

"What can have put such a disagreeable little comparison into your head, Lily."

"Well, I suppose you have known her too long to notice. She is always gushing about things, but she doesn't quite mean it. She praises everyone, and yet drops little disparaging hints about people—like the sting of a wasp in honey—"

"I see what you mean, you small sinner. She makes as though she would fly—but her wings are wooden shams? But Lily, don't you think it would be kinder to overlook people's failings, to act on the golden rule— do unto others you know—"

"Ah how I wish a lot of people would find me so odious that they would not wish to set eyes on me again, or at any rate only at rare intervals, like the flowering aloe. There was your mother to-day—" and then Lily detailed something of what had passed that afternoon. "I wish you had not come away so early," he said at the close with a little anxious fold in his forehead between the eyes.

At this Lily showed a little trace of resentment. Did Archie know what it was to have little impromptu lectures eternally thrown at his head on the measles of 37 babies, with births and christenings thrown in? And if that subject ran dry, it was the Thorndale plate, or the Thorndale nose, or the Thorndale temperament—the Thorndales everlastingly till one was ready to wish—no, she wouldn't say it. She was going to try to be a Christian, and conceal her thoughts. Henceforth no temptation would be strong enough to make her fall into the truth. It became apparent to Archibald that the strained relations between the two might at any moment develop, on his mother's side at least, into active hostility. And in point of fact that is what happened two weeks later.

Mrs. Thorndale and some of her grandchildren came one afternoon to call at Birchlea, the pretty one storied, deep verandahed house, embosomed in trees within a short distance of town, to which Archibald had brought his young wife now close on a year ago. When grandmamma and the party entered the drawingroom, several visitors were present, who were lost in admiration of Chartreuse. They had never before seen so fine a creature.

"He is a true 'consecrate,'" said one gentleman, narrowly examining the white marking which threw the deep orange tawny of the rest of the body into strong relief. A young lady was eager to know what consecrate meant. When she found it was because of a resemblance in the marking to the habit of the Benedictine monks, she thought it was "really too delightful, you know?" Some one asked if it was a descendant of the great Barry. Lily had it vouched on the best authority that Chartreuse's pedigree went back in an unbroken line to the immortal dog of Bernard de Menthon. "Why that was in the tenth century," said a younger sister of Miss Mabel Thorndale's, and then she and her cousins clustered round to look at a dog who was somehow connected with the twilight of history, and who was so extravagantly praised by their elders.

His wonderfully intelligent face, his beautiful ears covered with silky hair, his full chest and great throat and wide lips, his straight, strong legs, his large feet, his full deeply sunk eyes, the haws showing as red as that of a bloodhound—all were points for overflowing admiration. At last one enthusiastic gentleman got a tape measure to make sure of Chartreuse's full length, and found it to be eighty-seven inches. Chorus of wonder and admiration, amidst which the company took their departure.

Mrs. Thorndale sat a grimly silent spectator of this little comedy. Every-one knows how at times, without a breach of politeness on anybody's part, a new comer may be for a little quite out of the swim of what may be going on. This was just then the case with Mrs. Thorndale. Her grand-children had joined the majority, and she sat alone feeling shamefully neglected and overlooked. By the time the other visitors had gone she was almost speechless with wrath.

"I must say, Lily, that a more offensive exhibition of silly devotion to a brute animal I never saw before," she said, the black ostrich plumes in her bonnet quivering with emotion.

"I am very sorry," began Lily.

"No, you are not sorry," retorted her mother-in-law, who, when "put out," was not remarkable for urbanity of manners. "You are sinfully foolish about that dog. You think because you pamper and spoil him everyone else should worship the creature. I object entirely to such proceedings, and I have to request that you will not henceforth bring him near my house. The 'immortal dog' indeed; such terms are little short of blasphemy. Remember, Lily, you are not to bring him," repeated Mrs. Thorndale, determined to drive Lily into some show of anger, feeling that she herself had hopelessly overstepped the limits of courtesy.

"Do you hear that, Chartreuse, you are *not* to come with me to Maplegrove. But I suppose you will soon be going to Seawhaite now, Mrs. Thorndale," answered Lily, softly.

"But you must bring Chartreuse to see us every time you come, Aunt Lily," said young Thorndales, who had remembered the century of Bernard de Menthon, and the other young people followed suit.

Lily could not be induced to descend to personalities, which is one of the traits begotten in some natures by a total exemption from the irritation of fault finding in the days of youth. That this did not endear her just then to Mrs. Thorndale goes without saying. Lily did not of course offend her mother-in-law by taking Chartreuse to her house. But though she went without him the reception she received was so very cold that in a short time her visits became rarer and more rare.

Chapter V

There is probably no form of existence on earth duller than that in which men are exclusively engaged in making money and the women in spending it, except one. That is the existence in which men are exclusively engaged in a vain effort to make money and the women have not got it to spend. Broadly speaking, the Thorndales and their connections fell into the first division. They were all prosperous, and in the course of time expected to be still more so. They were well contented with themselves, and looked rather askance at anyone so unhappily constituted as not to perceive that their plan of life was incapable of improvement. Thus, apart from the rupture between Mrs. Thorndale and her American daughter-in-law, that young lady came gradually to be regarded by her husband's family as a person of dangerously unsound views. One could never be sure that the great landmarks of social respectability would receive proper treatment at her hands. "What guarantee is there for the principles of one who could speak in such a manner?" became one of Mrs. Thorndale's stock exclamations. And then some one was sure to cap the anecdote which called this forth by another still more unpardonable—such as that of the speech Lily made to Sir Wm. Wryneck when he was expatiating to her with bated breath on the incalculable value of the Bimbirrowie Hoarding silver mine.

"Oh, Sir William," she cried, putting up her hands in supplication, "if you knew how I have been haunted by that mine ever since I came to Australia."

"But Mrs. Archibald, do you know how much we owe to that mine," said the knight, prepared to plunge into statistics on the question up to his chin.

"Oh, yes—the sun and the moon and the stars, as well as things that don't go round so generously. But why not make a carved god of the mine and set it on a niche to say prayers to it, instead of always talking about it?" said Lily, gravely.

Although lucky investors in the Bimbirrowie Hoarding Silver Mine paid far more adoration to it than a god on a niche usually receives, it was felt to be very bad taste to sum up the matter so baldly.

Then, instead of feeling reproved by the shocked faces around her, Lily still further horrified Archdeacon Seedling a day or two afterwards on similar lines. The archdeacon was a cheerful, chirping little man, with rosy cheeks and an affluent port wine sort of voice, which was exactly fitted for the more carnal parts of the marriage service, and for saying grace at the lavish boards of wealthy men. The latter was his favourite avocation, and next to that he loved to speak of those who owned such tables. "Yes, I am credibly informed that he owns five hundred original Bimbirrowie Hoarding Silver Mine shares, which means an income of £36,000 a year!" said the archdeacon, in his rich rolling voice. Various sounds of admiring awe were heard.

"Do you think it is quite true, archdeacon, that people can take no money away with them when they die?" said Lily, reflectively.

"My dear young lady!" interjected the archdeacon, with becoming gravity.

"But it does seem a great pity, when money is the only thing many people possess to start them in another life!" pursued Lily.

It was felt that one who could give expression to such sentiments must be darkly tainted with heresy. And the same feeling prevailed among the Thorndale connection with regard to many of Lily's sayings and doings. And so it was that in less than a year after she came to Australia the solemn family meetings still went on, but Archibald's wife was seldom present.

"She is so entirely taken up with the Government House clique," was the accepted explanation from her mother-in-law downward. And though this did not cover the whole ground, yet it was true that an intimate friendship existed between Lily and the Governor's wife. Lady Ida Smiley was a daughter of the Earl of Snowford, who had been the English ambassador in Paris during Mr. Herrick's connection with the American Legation. Lady Ida and Lily's elder sister had been warm friends, and the two families were now connected by marriage, through the house of the De Cazan.

Lady Ida Smiley was of a retiring—almost a shy—disposition. She abhorred crowds and the promiscuous social intercourse inevitably thrust on a woman in her position. She did her best to fulfil its duties, but they often rendered her uncomfortable, not to say unhappy. The Governor, Sir Marmaduke Smiley, was, on the other hand, admirably adapted to play his part as head of a mimic court, being naturally deeply attached to the adulation and fussy importance of the situation. He possessed, too, that robust belief in mere success which made it pleasant for him to consort with those who rose to power in public as well as private life. But he tried in vain to make his wife understand that people who were almost ignored last month should this month become of unique importance because of some funny Parliamentary squabble. To the last, the chameleon-like *nuances* of South Australian politics were beyond her sympathy and comprehension. Lady Ida Smiley was delighted to renew the associations of a happier and more congenial period of life in Lily's society. They had many mutual experiences, having both lived after a somewhat cosmopolitan fashion in the old world. And in Paris they had many mutual friends. Among them was Mr. Algernon Bruce, who was Lady Ida Smiley's first cousin.

It was within a few weeks of Christmas when Lily one morning, having come to spend the day at the Hermitage, the vice-regal seaside residence, to her great surprise found this gentleman at the Gilgal railway station waiting to conduct her to Lady Ida Smiley's pony phaeton. "How do you do, Mrs. Thorndale?" he said, as if they had parted the day before. His voice and manner were as placid as ever. The only change perceptible was the sea voyage tan which overspread his face.

"And I do think there is a more melancholy droop about his eyes and moustache," said Lily reflectively in a *tête-à-tête* with Lady Ida Smiley that afternoon. Lady Ida suggested that he might have been crossed in love. (It may be noted in passing, that in this lady's estimation Australia had been called out of chaos, for the express purpose of forming an asylum at convenient distance from civilisation, for damaged hearts, characters and estates.) He had set out for Australia in so headlong a manner. Lily doubted whether love could ever colour Mr. Bruce's actions. But both ladies agreed it was extremely fortunate he had come just then. They were engaged in rehearsing a pastoral play for representation in the pretty semi-artificial wood that extended round the Hermitage, and the chief shepherd had suddenly been called away by his father's death, leaving Lily, who was the leading shepherdess, desolated at the catastrophe. Mr. Bruce had long enjoyed the reputation of being an excellent amateur actor. He at once consented to be the chief shepherd, and the rehearsals went on vigorously.

The Pastoral was duly rendered four days before Christmas. There was no hot wind running riot like a pampered jade of Asia, and though one blew from the east it was the gentlest of its kind. The sun shone through sylvan groves, and many birds were obliging enough to make themselves heard at a point in the play in which the notes of birds were most becoming. In the foreground there was a large hollow gum tree; behind it a thick grove of Norfolk pines, among which a fountain splashed continuously to mimic running water—a sound so near the one imitated that it would surely take a very hard heart to question the reality. The shepherds were in grey cloaks and picturesque caps, and had the crooks, without which, as we all know, sheep can never be made to grow wool. The shepherdesses were adorned with flowers and ribbons, and all the sparkling finery in which their sex in Dresden china and on the stage, look after flocks and sing madrigals to shepherds. The prompter's voice was not heard more audibly than at other amateur performances. The audience was not disconcerted by finding that "everybody" had been invited, and many of them were genuinely pleased.

Those who were too far off to hear the shepherds and shepherdesses, exchanged smothered confidences regarding their neighbors, and those who were too near the centre to take refuge in this diversion, consoled themselves by reflecting that they gathered much piquant food for conversation later on. Among these was Lady Keightley, who sat in a large arm chair close to the plane tree under which the fortunes of the *dramatis personae* were decided. On one side sat her daughter, on the other the dowager Mrs. Thorndale. Archibald sat behind them most of the time, but was obliged to hurry away before the performance came to an end. The night editor of the paper which he partly owned and helped to conduct had recently been attacked with typhoid fever, and Thorndale, in addition to his usual duties, had undertaken a large share of the missing editor's work.

"My dear Sarah, do you think Archie is looking well?" said Lady Keightley after he had gone away, during the interval that took place after the fourth scene of the last act, when the actors had retired behind the impenetrable bower, overgrown with honeysuckle and passion flowers, which served for a stage screen. Lady Keightley spoke in that bass, half mysterious tone in which women are prepared to make insinuations against their own kind.

"No, Susan, I do not," answered Mrs. Thorndale, with a certain accent of strong moral disapprobation which conveyed the impression that a scapegoat was full in view. But before any more opinions were interchanged the fifth and last scene began.

In this Lily, who was draped in a pale sea green robe garlanded with meadow daisies, her head dress and little sea green shoes adorned with the same flowers, was the cynosure of every eye. She was driven as near despair as the nature of a pastoral play allows; she was the object of a long harangue in iambics by a sullen swain; she had finally to bestow her heart and hand on the faithful leading shepherd. Then the two, followed by all the other shepherds and shepherdesses, retired behind the impenetrable bower, as many of them as had voices singing, and all of them uniting in driving a little flock of sheep before them. These had been lent by the local butcher, and added immensely to the *éclat* of the closing scene.

Mr. Bruce, as the leading shepherd, should have given expression to his joy by playing a merry tune on an oaten pipe. But as his skill in music was limited to taking the part of audience, the oaten pipe had to be omitted, and he whispered his joy instead of rendering it with variations. Gustave Chartreuse took the part of sheep dog, but being now as large as a young calf and so devoted to his mistress that he kept close beside her instead of rounding up the sheep, he did not sustain the character as it is familiar to mankind in nature and tradition. But notwithstanding these and other slight deflections from realistic treatment, all was found to be extremely lifelike.

Indeed Lady Keightley's daughter, who had singled Lily out for special observation throughout the play, was convinced that it gave rise to episodes much too real. Miss Benson did not object on ethical grounds to the Satyr who offered Lily a basket of fruit, nor to the fairies who sang at her from the depths of a laurustinus bush, nor to the various swains whose life's happiness hung on gathering rushes to make rings for her slender fingers. But to see Mr. Algernon Bruce making love to another man's wife in whispers, instead of following the stage directions, surely this was one more evidence of that deep seated corruption of manners and morals, so woefully characteristic of the age! Granted he could not play a merry tune on an oaten pipe, he could at least make a noise, and how much less offensive even harsh sounds would be to well balanced minds than those treacherous advances to that "primrose path of dalliance," which lead so many to destruction. Miss Benson's imagination, like that of many other severely virtuous women, needed but a spark to set it on fire. Already the picture of a ruined home, of two fugitives, flying together rose darkly up before her!

In the meantime the general company were loud in real or simulated applause.

"It was too charming, with the babbling stream, and the song of birds, and the sweet sheep," said that sister in law of Lily's, who had been compared by her to a wooden butterfly.

"Yes, and the actors did their parts beautifully; so different from an ordinary play, where you know everything by heart long ago," replied a young lady, enthusiastically.

"Yes, to be sure, and though some of them forgot their parts, how natural and real the hollow gum tree looked," was the effusive reply.

A group formed round Sir Marmaduke and Lady Ida Smiley, who stood talking to Lily, and one or two more of the performers, while the sides of a gaily striped marquee were slowly raised to the music of a hidden band, disclosing within many tables, loaded with whipped cream and strawberries, very early grapes and late loquats and cherries, iced claret and champagne cup, and delicate marvels of the confectioner's art, &c., &c.

"I want to know, Mrs. Thorndale, what you call your performances —a pastoral drama or a comedy or a tragedy or a morality upon stilts," said Sir Marmaduke, who always set his guests the popular example of indulging in mild jokes.

"Well, not quite a comedy, for the people in it were not mean enough, and the audience did not laugh; and not a tragedy, for none of the shepherds were killed; and yet perhaps some of the audience nearly died of it. Suppose we call it a tragid [sic] comedy," answered Lily.

Before the laugh which this awakened had died away, Mrs. Thorndale was heard in a stage whisper apologising to Lady Ida Smiley for her son's hurried departure. "He is just now so dreadfully overworked—one of the editors of the *Illuminator* being laid up—and I fear Archibald himself is far from well," she said in her solemnly emphatic tones. Lady Ida murmured something indefinitely sympathetic. She could not, for her life, remember whether the *Daily Illuminator* was the newspaper which used to bubble over in hysterics of loyalty on the slightest provocation, or the one that broke out into leaders and letters, darkly hinting at separation from the mother country, on no provocation at all. Lily was close enough to hear what her mother-in-law said.

"'Far from well!' It isn't true. I am sure Archibald is well," she said to herself, with a touch of indignation at the thought that she should not be the first to notice any indisposition on his part. And yet the next morning, as they sat at breakfast, when she scanned her husband's face, as he sipped his coffee and glanced over the columns of the *Illuminator,* she became sure that he was unusually pale . . . Yes, and looking at him sideways, was there not a sharpness in his profile which was foreign to it—at any rate some time back . . . Lily's heart sank unaccountably as she realised that of late she really could not have told whether Archibald looked well or not. She had been so engrossed, first with one thing then with another—last of all with this ridiculous pastoral. It was just a farce with all the fun left out. How absurd of Lady Ida Smiley and Mr. Bruce to be so much taken up with it. But then she herself—had she not thought it charming? She was an ungrateful wretch. She recollected that one of her governesses, a German—Fräulein Kettlitz—had once declared she had no heart . . . "I suppose it is true," thought Lily, as if she were a preacher looking down on a perverse congregation. And yet, could one quite without a heart feel so ill at ease in that organ?

"Good morning, dear." Lily started from her reverie, and then before she could say a word in reply her husband had kissed her on the cheek and hastened out to catch his tram to the city. "He evidently did not expect me to kiss him in return," mused Lily. And then she recalled, as if waking up from a dream, how month by month they had been drifting wider apart; how Archie had grown accustomed to going among his relatives without her; had ceased to remonstrate when she took occasion to keep out of their way; had even taken it as a matter of course that she should somehow get out of spending Christmas day with the family at his eldest brother's. It was true the performance was an appalling ordeal, and her nerves seemed to be playing her false of late. At least she supposed it was her nerves. Perhaps it was nerves that ailed Archie too—but then men did not grow thinner because of nerves. Good heavens! What if he were going to get typhoid fever! Lily rose up suddenly at the thought, as if an adder had stung her. She ordered the pony carriage to be in readiness, and went at once to dress to go into town shopping. That at least was the explanation she fobbed off on her husband, when two hours later she suddenly made her appearance in his private office. Certainly she had given some colour to the statement by buying articles at various shops which might come in useful some day.

"Yes, I have been shopping, and as I passed by I just thought I would look in on you," said Lily, concealing the fact that she had been sniffing the air all the way up the staircase to see if she could detect any malaria therein.

Archibald's face brightened visibly. "Do you want me to do anything for you, Lily?"

"Well, let me see. I think I want to remonstrate with you about the tone of your paper."

"Why you never read it, you little imposer."

Yes, he was certainly thinner than he used to be, and a good deal paler—but how quickly the fagged look had passed out of his face as she chatted with him and went peering into the corners of the editorial sanctum, to make sure, as she said, that he did not keep a jar of cholera or typhoid microbes on the premises.

One person after another knocked at the door, and had to wait for an audience in the ante-room, till Lily felt compelled to hasten her departure. She wanted to make a request, and hardly knew how to do so without any appearance of solemnity or of "goodiness."

"Oh, you poor old boy—is that the best view you have from this den?" she said, pausing by an eastern window as she left the room—"Fifty-five back yards and a hundred chimneys, and some dish cloths drying."

"Oh, but you can catch a glimpse of the sea if you look this way, Lily . . . No, you are not quite tall enough, but just step on this chair."

It happened to be one that had been put in a corner in an invalided condition, so that the moment Lily established a footing on it the chair lurched over and she would have come to grief had not her husband been close beside her. He did not at once release her, and then Lily found it a little easier to make her request.

"Archie, in three days it is Christmas—I can't think of a single thing you have not got in duplicate—"

"What a calumny—Have I got a duplicate of you?"

"Don't be frivolous. The thing is I want to know something you would really like me to do for your sake—"

"You dear darling—"

"No Archie—don't speak as if I were the good little pig that stayed at home. But just tell me—"

"Well, Lily, you know the day before Christmas Eve is my mother's birthday. It is a long time since you have been to see her. I don't say you are to blame, but I find the estrangement rather hard. Spend to-morrow evening with her and stay the night, for I want to come too, and may not get away from the office until late. Then we can go from there to dine at George's house, and what about Chartreuse?" Lily replied that of course he would be left at home.

"Now, dear little woman, isn't this rather a large order I'm giving you?" said Archibald wistfully.

But Lily stoutly denied this. And though that evening and next day she noticed Chartreuse seemed to be rather indisposed she said nothing of the wrench it would cost her to leave him in melancholy solitude to the care of the servants. She wrote her mother-in-law a graceful little note to announce the proposed visit. Mrs. Thorndale wrote a dignified letter in reply, expressing her pleasure at the prospect of seeing her daughter-in-law after so long an interval of little or no intercourse. She was thankful to reflect that this was not owing to any caprice on her part. She was too warm-hearted, too full of solicitude for those connected with her, to bear separation from them without feeling it keenly. Less depth of feeling—a little more coldness—might be a good thing, but she was now too old to cultivate new ways, and she hoped that Lily would be able to put up with her, as she was without any of those breaks in association and interest which were no doubt common enough in *average* families, but had never been the Thorndale policy. She also put upon record her sense of obligation to Providence for the many, *many* blessings the revolving years brought to her. Charlie's wife and small son were going on better than could be expected. This made her *thirty-eighth* grandchild and Charlie's seventh. Fortunately Charlie's wife was one of those exemplary women who found her only happiness in the nursery and by the domestic hearth. Talking of domestic matters, it might not be without interest to Lily to know that the cook and general servant who had been with Mrs. Thorndale for five years had yesterday refused submission in the matter of wearing caps of the kind approved by their mistress. They had gradually made their caps into tiny scraps of ornamental lace. On being commanded to wear some of a proper size and make they had flatly refused and left at a day's notice, forfeiting a week's wages . . . Richard too, was away for the holidays . . . He had not been well of late . . . Still Lily was not to allow anything to stand in the way of her coming. Towards the close of the letter Mrs. Thorndale mentioned that Lady Keightley and her daughter were staying with her for a couple of weeks. Lady Keightley had not been well—neither the hills nor the sea side elsewhere agreed with her, but the beautiful Sherrington air had already done wonders for her, &c., &c.

Lily looked rather melancholy after reading this. It must be confessed that Mrs. Thorndale was not given to strewing roses in the path of one she classified as a culprit, and the picture called up by the contents of her letter was not alluring. Lily disliked Sherrington intensely, her mother-in-law had all the vices of the severely virtuous, and if there was one person she would have avoided meeting more than Lady Keightley it was her daughter. "And I cannot have even you put your nose in my hand so as to keep up my courage, Chartreuse . . . Why do you shake your head so, you prince of darlings? Matilda, I cannot imagine what is the matter with my dog," said Lily, as her maid entered with a basketful of *chiffons*. "William thinks as it's a grass seed, ma'am," replied Matilda. William was the coachman and general factotum of the establishment and credited with unfathomed stores of knowledge in every conceivable direction. Lily consulted him in some alarm as to what a grass seed was. "It's the seed, ma'am, of one of the native grasses which goes on and on till it can't get no further," he said; and then went on to explain that it sometimes got into the ears of animals, and he thought as Shatroose might have one, being given to shake "'is 'ead so very much of late." He further volunteered the information that there was a veterinary surgeon in town who knew a great deal about dogs, and that he would take Shatroose in to him that afternoon, after he had driven his mistress to the railway station. An arrangement to which Lily yielded a grudging consent.

Chapter VI

I t was close on 6 o'clock in the afternoon before Lily got to Seawhaite, her mother-in-law's seaside residence at Sherrington.

The rush of the birthday visitors was over by that time, most of the grandchildren and their mothers having departed. But the birthday flowers, and the birthday cards and presents, and a few special old friends who still lingered, kept up a grateful aroma of rejoicing. Lily's offering was a very elegant Parisian knitting bag of pale blue plush, lined with gold coloured silk, and fitted up with a set of gold knitting pins. This, coupled with Lily's meek submission, met with Mrs. Thorndale's warm approval.

"None of my children have given me anything I like better than this, dear," she said blandly. The occasion was, in fact, one on which her temper showed to the best advantage. To be supreme in her own world, to have felicitations and gifts poured at her feet, to have troops of descendants and friends crowding around her, constituted a situation which met her ideal of what life should be. Not even the shocking ingratitude of her cook and house maid was allowed to interfere with her equanimity that evening. Maria O'Neil was *such* a treasure, so invaluable, and though Jane, the parlor maid, was rather delicate, they would be able to manage very well till the new servants came after New Year's day. It was such a joy to her to see all her family and friends so very attentive and affectionate, and looking so well. Not one of her grandchildren had missed coming that day except Mrs. Charlie and her little new comer, three days old, a splendid baby boy weighing 11½ lb. Neither the nurse nor the doctor had ever seen quite such a fine baby. Indeed all her grandchildren were remarkably good looking and well behaved. Mabel was not quite satisfactory—and that dreadful style of wearing her hair.

"Really deplorable," murmured Lady Keightley, who acted as a sort of high priestess on this auspicious occasion, singling out gifts for renewed and ever repeated admiration, and generally responding to all Mrs. Thorndale's opinions with emphatic seriousness.

"If I had, not in a fashion, turned over a new leaf I would say they were just like two old tabbies purring in each other's faces," reflected Lily, "but I suppose it must end in my letting Mrs. Thorndale be a mother to me. That seems usually to mean being trampled on and bored to extinction from time to time."

Not that Lily really repented having come. Indeed, she experienced an unusual feeling of gladness as she recalled from time to time how Archie had lingered that morning after breakfast, assuring her that she was the best little wife in the world. She had warned him not to imagine she was very good; she could not possibly keep it up. Besides, she had always understood that the very good people died off like flies in a frost, even in tracts, the climate in which they were mostly reared. No, Archie maintained they mostly died off in editor's offices, where one got on a dangerous pinnacle, and twisted one's neck into an arch, and partly dislocated one's neck to look at the sea, and one had a fall instead. Lily found herself smiling covertly over these morning jokes as they all paced up and down the jetty in the rose pink twilight which succeeded an unusually brilliant sunset.

The chief features of Sherrington, apart from the fashion and wealth that congregate there in the summer, are the long, wide jetty, and the weekly arrival and departure of the mail steamers. There was one on this evening stationed at the usual place two miles out from land, waiting for the mails, preparatory to sailing at 11. Already several passengers had arrived with their friends, and the throng of promenaders made way, as a truck was pushed down the jetty from time to time, laden with the trunks and portmanteaux of departing travellers. The day had been oppressively warm, and crowds of people had poured down by the evening trains from the town and suburbs to enjoy the cool of the seaside. Besides this mode of transit numbers had come in vehicles of various kinds and sizes, that were now stationed along the beach, which on both sides far as the eye could reach was dotted with groups of people standing, walking and sitting. As for the jetty, it gradually became so crowded that people could walk only with extreme slowness. But this gave all the more opportunity for conversation, a facility seldom wasted on an Australian crowd, least of all in Sherrington, where the natives of the place had established the custom of taking early possession of the seats ranged along the sides of the jetty in large parties of friends and family groups.

It had been one of Lily's objections to Sherrington as a seaside resort that it was chiefly inhabited by Thorndales. One or two families of them were always staying there. Such was the case now. They flocked round Mrs. Thorndale, and soon found that atmosphere of personal details and domestic history in which her soul delighted. The great subject of excitement on this occasion was a robbery that Geo. Thorndale had sustained in a very mysterious manner. The loss had been discovered only two hours previously. Among other articles of value six table spoons of sterling silver had been abstracted. "Six Thorndale silver spoons! Oh, my dear Amelia, these were part of the plate left by your husband's great-great-aunt Thorndale, with her maiden initials on one side of the handle and her married ones on the other, a practice I have never seen except on some of the Thorndale plate. What are the police about when such infamous things take place! George, do send a telegram to Archibald, so that he may put another paragraph in the *Illuminator* reflecting severely on the negligence of the police. This is the fourth robbery here within a short time. Lily, I trust that you are very, very careful about the plate. The dozen tablespoons marked E.C.T. belonged to your great grandmother-in-law Tamplin. They are sterling silver, but of course not quite so valuable as the Thorndale plate. Yet their loss would be irreparable," &c., &c. Under these circumstances Lily was not loath to be drawn aside by the Maskelynes, with whom she walked to the far end of the jetty, where the fresh sea breezes blew in with refreshing pungency. As they were coming back she suddenly came face to face with her old fellow passenger, Mrs. Melville, with her little girl, grown very tall and thin. They had not met since the day they landed, 14 months previously. They had exchanged a few letters, and then lost sight of each other, as is the way with many intimacies besides those contracted on board ship.

Lily remembered with compunction that it was on her side the correspondence had ceased. It was evident at a first glance that Mrs. Melville's long standing acquaintance with narrow means had now descended to downright penury. Her face, the bonnet she wore, her gloves, her ulster —all proclaimed the fact. Mildred, too, whose dainty little dresses had often excited Lily's admiration, was clad in a hopelessly shabby fashion. "I could so easily have helped her" was the thought that rose up in Lily's mind, and as she looked at the pinched, haggard face of the mother, and the child's wan cheeks, a horrible misgiving arose in her mind that they might have lacked even the necessaries of life. Their clothing was that of a past season, and as she glanced at them in the semi-obscurity of widely sundered gas lamps it suddenly occurred to Lily that their means of livelihood had come to a standstill some months back. As a matter of fact the intuition was in the main correct.

There come periods in some people's lives when want is so close and deft a foe that to have somehow defeated it at all is the sort of victory which is too bitter to bear recalling. Mrs. Melville had hardly passed through the throes of such a time, and every lineament of her face bore eloquent witness to the suffering she had endured.

"I am so glad we have met once more; we are just on our way back to England again," she said, hurriedly, and then she would have talked of something else and passed on. But Lily was not to be put off. She excused herself to the Maskelynes, and turned back with Mrs. Melville and her daughter. It was not yet 8, and passengers were not obliged to be on board the Albion before 10.30.

"We can have some little talk together before you go on board," said Lily, with a little touch of unsteadiness in her voice. The pained poverty stricken aspect of this gently nurtured woman and her little daughter touched her somehow to the verge of tears. She supposed it was those lately discovered nerves of hers that made her feel like making a fool of herself. That these two needed help went without saying. But though Lily had always given a liberal proportion of her pocket money to objects of charity, she had little or no experience in aiding those who, apart from money and position, were her own equals. However, the thing had now to be done.

"Do take my arm, Mrs. Melville, I am sure you have been very ill," she said by way of a beginning. Mrs. Melville took the offered help, and as they went slowly through the crowd, Mildred walking in front of them, Lily became conscious that her companion was in tears. Yes, she was crying—not in the vehement rebellious way in which those unused to sorrow weep; but in the silent unobtrusive manner of one who knows that, though tears may lessen the tension of emotion, they do not take away the cause of grief.

The three made their way to a retired seat near the seaward end of the jetty, and for a little time Mrs. Melville vainly struggled to regain composure.

"You are in trouble—I know you are," said Lily, softly, taking her hand in both her own.

"Oh, I think the worst is over now," said Mrs. Melville, after a little.

. . "It is the sudden change of meeting some one I knew, whose face was full of kindness . . . of hearing the voice of a gentlewoman . . . I have so hungered at times for the sound . . . I felt so dreadfully alone and poor in this great crowd—nearly everyone looking well and prosperous. It is the land of plenty for most, but for me and my fatherless little one it has been a place of bitter need—of destitution even . . . I was feeling bitter and full of despair, asking why we two should miss all the brightness and pleasantness of life and come down to roughness we can ill bear . . . And then you turned with me and made me lean on you . . . I broke down, feeling the hard sting has been a little taken away . . . I cried because I am a little better."

Lily could not well have told what she said in reply. But gradually Mrs. Melville's little story was related. It was one of bitter disappointment and of fraud. Her uncle by marriage—the man in whom her husband had placed implicit trust—had squandered and embezzled the money entrusted to him for investment. Not only so, but he had cajoled her into sending to England for all she could realise of the little patrimony remaining to her, on the plea that a crisis had arisen in his affairs just when she reached the province in which some ready money would enable him to make full restitution of all that had previously been entrusted to him. Of course this also was lost to her. Then came months through which she had kept herself and Mildred in bare existence in a rough little bush township up the north by doing plain needlework by hand. At last she was compelled to appeal to relatives in England for help. But there was some delay, and when a little aid came she had broken down and had for some weeks previously been compelled to apply for Government rations.

"Oh, why didn't you write and tell me?" said Lily, speaking very low, because of a choking sensation in her throat.

"I did say something in a postscript in my last letter," answered Mrs. Melville hesitatingly.

"But surely nothing that would lead me to think—"

"Oh, you do not know how hard it is. And in the end it seemed easier to ask for charity from the country in which all my money was lost than from any one individual. I remember I did write a full account of my affairs to you, and then tore up the letter, and wrote a little hurried one, to which I put a postscript asking you to excuse this miserable little note, as many things too tiresome to inflict on you were distracting me just then."

Lily almost groaned aloud. Her own distractions largely consisted in deciding which social invitations she should accept, and which colours she should wear. But how could she have been so besotted as not to perceive the undercurrent of a letter like this? Mrs. Melville went on to say that the assistance her relatives sent her, along with the proceeds of some clothing and jewellery she had disposed of, was enough to pay her own and Mildred's passage to London third class.

Lily started on hearing this. Then, controlling the impetuous disclaimer that rose to her lips, she quietly asked what the difference was between third and second class for the two of them. On bearing it was £30 she instantly rose and asked Mrs. Melville to remain where she was with Mildred for 10 or 15 minutes, and then, before any remonstrance could be offered, she hurried away.

Lily had a cheque of her husband's for £40 he had given her that morning for the tradespeople's monthly bills. It was in a portmonnaie in the bedroom she occupied of her mother-in-law's house. With this she would pay the difference of fares, and there would be £10 left over as a little gift for Mildred. Fortunately the Albion was the steamer in which Archie had gone to Europe, and the captain and he were fast friends, and had since their return dined with them on two occasions when his boat's stay enabled him to accept their hospitality. She would send him a note with the cheque explaining matters, and introducing Mrs. Melville to him as her friend. Or she might even go to the ship herself; that might be the best plan.

Seawhaite was situated on the sea wall, almost opposite to the jetty. As Lily approached the gate she heard a well known bark. It was that of Chartreuse, whose great form was agitated with gladness from head to tail as he rushed to meet her. Could Archie have brought him down? But, no, he was not to leave the office till nearly 11, and under existing circumstances he would never dream of bringing Chartreuse to his mother's house. In fact Mrs. Thorndale must not see him at all. Explain as one might that his coming was accidental, the mere sight of the tip of the dog's tail would be regarded as synonymous with digging up the war hatchet, and unfurling the red rag, and doing everything else that was of a disgracefully bellicose and undutiful nature.

Gustave Chartreuse had a piece of chain dangling at his wide silver collar. He wagged himself with joy at the sight of his mistress, but when she gazed at him in perplexity there was a strong touch of contrition in his eyes and tail. He clearly felt that the history of his presence was too obvious to be sophisticated by any affectation of innocence. He had seen his mistress get into the Sherrington train, then William had taken him to the veterinary surgeon, conveyed him home and fastened him to one of the verandah posts. In the course of time Chartreuse had snapped his chain, made for the railway station, followed the course of the train, and reached the house which he had oftenest visited beforetime. It was not by any means the first occasion in which he had with unerring sagacity followed up a clue as to his mistress's whereabouts. But never before had his action been fraught with such peril to domestic peace. The one thing clear was that Mrs. Thorndale must not see him. When Archie came he would hit upon some plan. But in the meantime Chartreuse must be hidden. Lily went in by the side gate to consult the servants. The parlor maid had gone to see her mother, and the place was in sole possession of the invaluable Maria. Lily had a strong impression that as she approached the kitchen she heard a man's voice. But when on knocking at the door Maria opened it there was no sight nor sound to verify this conviction. Maria's face was very red and her manner peculiarly effusive. But she found so clever and speedy a way out of the Chartreuse difficulty that Lily was little inclined to be critical

"As for putting the crather into the back yard, 'tis not to be done me darlint Mrs. Archibald, for ye see there's but a span av soil and half an acre av dog. But just at the back gate forninst us there is a row av Mrs. Thorndale's cottages—Thorndale-terrace 'tis called—two av them empty. The keys is hanging in the kitchen here. Shure the sagacious jewel will be happier than any king av them all. The shaints save us, wha-at is the matter wid him shaking his head like a Christian short av his timper?"

Chartreuse sure enough shook his head with great vehemence and moaned under his breath. Lily felt sure he was in great pain, and wondered whether Archibald would ever realise the sacrifice she made in putting her beloved St. Bernard into a deserted house instead of installing him in her own room. She gave him some water to drink, but he would eat no food. Then she went with him into one of the empty cottages, and left him in the sitting room with a rug to lie on. She kept possession of the key of the back gate and back door, intending to visit Chartreuse later on. Then, having secured the cheque, she hurried back to the jetty. Half way between it and Seawhaite she met Mrs. Thorndale and Lady Keightley returning home. Miss Benson was still on the jetty with some friends. "You can return together, Lily, when you have had enough sea air and exercise," said Mrs. Thorndale. "I feel so disturbed at this robbery. I think we ought not to leave our good Maria alone." Lily explained that she had met some friends unexpectedly who were leaving by the Albion, and that she might stay with them rather later than it would suit Miss Benson to be out. But her mother-in-law was so concerned and pre-occupied about the stolen plate, which had two sets of initials, that it is doubtful whether she heard this statement.

A few paces further on Lily met Mr. Bruce. "I have been looking for you everywhere," he cried, with an animation that was very novel to him. "I called at your house this afternoon and found you were at Mrs. Thorndale's. After I got here I went to Seawhaite, and was told you were on the jetty."

"I declare that all this evening I am a mere duplicate of Robinet, a peasant of Lorraine," cried Lily, laughing. "I cannot move 10 yards but something happens."

"Well, I hope your events are as pleasant as mine," answered Mr. Bruce; and before Lily could make any rejoinder he had, with all the frankness of a reticent man when once the ice is broken, plunged into a narrative of an arrested love story. This, after all, was the secret of his "coming like a bomb and departing like a comet," as Lily afterwards expressed it to Lady Ida Smiley. His communication of the affair was rendered more interesting by the fact that the young lady, who first captivated, then accepted, and speedily quarrelled with him, was a young country woman and friend of Lily's—Miss Seaward, elder daughter of the American Minister in Paris. Now, by the intervention of a mutual friend all had been set right, and the cablegram which had reached Mr. Bruce only that morning recalled him to reconciliation and happiness. He had taken his passage by the Albion and would steam away in a couple of hours.

Mr. Bruce, stooping to tell his tale with all the intentness of a happy lover, and Lily listening with due sympathy, passed Miss Benson with a mutual lady friend without seeing either. They looked like two people so much engrossed in each other, that the rest of the world was nowhere. Miss Benson watched them, and felt that her darkest forebodings were more than fulfilled . . . This then was the true explanation of Mrs. Archibald Thorndale's newly found submission and amiability towards her mother-in-law!—An assignation with the shepherd who had whispered his love instead of playing a merry tune on an oaten pipe! The lady turned and stared after the pair with a sternly moral flush rising in her cheeks. She even made an excuse to turn back a little way till they were lost from her gaze in the crowd. What was to be the end of this compromising scene in a new pastoral?

The two who excited these dark suspicions were in the meantime happily oblivious of the reprobation they aroused in Miss Benson's mind.

"This is evidently the date at which things happen in Australia," said Lily, after she had congratulated Mr. Bruce at the close of his confidence. And then she told how she had met Mrs. Melville and her daughter, and how at the last moment their transfer must be managed, from the third to the second class. Mr. Bruce at once undertook to see to this when they should go on board. He would pay the money in gold—he had much more with him than was at all necessary for the voyage—then Mr. Thorndale could remit the amount to him through his bank. He had to go and see about some packages Lady Ida Smiley was sending by him to his mother. They were to come by the half-past 8 train. He would see about them and his luggage at once, and then come to be introduced to Mrs. Melville. They parted within a few paces of that lady and her daughter. When Lily joined them she was struck afresh with keen compunction at the thought of all she might have done for them during the past dreadful months.

"They might have stayed with us," she thought. "Archie would have been so kind and good to them. Mrs. Melville could have made pretty dresses for Mildred and I could have read while she sewed. I would have made her take some of the many, many dresses that keep Matilda shaking them out periodically, and hunting for silver fish. We are just the same size and figure—I don't mean the silver fish and myself, though for the matter of that I feel much meaner than any of them."

"Exactly the same size," repeated Lily to herself, as she glanced at the worn shabby ulster too short and thin to be of much value in preserving a dress or concealing its defects. The hat, too, how narrow it was in the brim, how heavy in the garniture. Mechanically, Lily contrasted it with her own hat—wide brimmed, exquisitely light, trimmed with fine cream Indian muslin and a great double gossamer veil which could be made into two or three for ship board wear. Then she contrasted the dismal little ulster with her own full and gracefully made dust coat in silver grey figured Foulard, elegantly trimmed with guipure and silver grey ribbons and full cream ribbon ruffling at the throat and wrists—in all respects a summer travelling dress rather than a dust coat. The very thing to wear through the Red Sea and stifling canal, when one lay panting in one's chair.

"Have you a deck chair, Mrs. Melville? Then we must go at once and get one . . . I know the very place, quite near the end of the jetty. We shall meet Mr. Bruce, who is to be your fellow passenger." As they threaded their way through the crowd, Lily's mind reverted to a previous train of thought. If she could only array Mrs. Melville in neat, eminently service-able travelling gear like her own . . . At this point in her cogitations a thought darted through Lily's active brain that gave her an exquisite sense of pleasure and relief.

"Mrs. Melville, I am going to ask a favour of you," she said, as they approached the land end of the jetty.

"Of me, dear Mrs. Thorndale?"

"Yes, but you must promise me beforehand to grant it. Oh, it is something you can do for me quite well. I would not ask anything beyond your power."

"Then of course you have only to mention it."

"I want you to exchange your hat and ulster for mine. Oh, but you promised, and you are bound to keep to that. It is so near to Christmas, and there is nothing so nice in the way of a Christmas gift as doing something that another wants you to. Now just try it. Only I guess you have been doing nothing else all your life. But it is quite new to me, and you must encourage me in the practice."

As Mrs. Melville tremulously gave in, they met Mr. Bruce, whose luggage and packages were piled on a truck, which was being taken up the jetty. On examination it was found that Mrs. Melville's modest trunks were in the same truck. They agreed that the luggage should go on by the launch then starting, and that they should go on board an hour later. Then Mr. Bruce accompanied them to make their purchase. Next door to the shop in which they bought the deck chair there was a draper's shop. In the window Lily saw girls' ulsters in Tussore silk. She took Mildred in and fitted her with one, also a wide white hat lightly trimmed. Then they walked back to the beach beyond the light of the jetty, for that little transaction in bartering had now to be effected. Mr. Bruce took Mildred under his charge while the two ladies dropped for a little behind. It was curious to see the transformation that the two articles of apparel wrought in Mrs. Melville's appearance. As for Lily she had as yet been so little wounded by the darts of time or misfortune, that shabby garments merely gave her the look of an heiress, ineffectually trying to seem poor.

When Mrs. Melville murmured at the sight of the mean attire on her friend, Lily at once stopped such reflections by saying that one should not cast up a favour against another. "And seriously dear Mrs. Melville," said Lily in a low voice, "you have taken a few pangs out of my conscience by falling in with this arrangement. When I think of leaving your last letter unanswered,—"

"But you ought not to take the blame. Was it not rather horrid of me not to understand you better? Not to tell you straight how sorely driven I was? You make me feel that we never trust one another quite enough."

"I am sure you had every reason to believe I was a selfish scorpion," said Lily vindictively.

"Mr. Bruce still walked in advance with Mildred, the two chatting like old friends. Silent as he usually was he yet had the art of making children, who were ordinarily quiet, merrily talkative, and of making helpless women realise he was one to be entirely trusted. His look of amazement when the two ladies joined him and Mildred was comical to see.

"Isn't there a tribe of savages somewhere, Mr. Bruce, who swear eternal friendship by exchanging grass cloths with each other! That is what we have done," said Lily laughing. She could hardly keep her eyes off her friend, so delighted was she at the full success of her little scheme.

Then for a short time the four paced up and down the beach, falling into silence as they listened to the waves faintly lapping against the shore with refluent long drawn murmers. The pale light of a young moon disappearing below the western horizon lingered on the sea in which innumerable stars were mirrored in quivering rays. A tinge of colour still tarried wide and high in that legion of the heavens, soft and delicate as the petals of a dog rose. Little boats at anchor were reflected in the uncertain light, so that boat and shadow were scarce distinguishable one from the other. This little space at the lips of the great deep was full of motion and voices and broken lights. In the centre the mail steamer loomed up between the silvery sea and the soft wistful light of the sky, her massive well proportioned form, outlined by the white radiance of the electric light on the dock and through the open port holes. Far away the ocean had strange sad voices—deep calling unto deep with messages too mysterious to be translated into common speech. Inland beyond the little stir of life lay the great woods—darker and more silent, and almost as illimitable as the sea itself. And there between these immensities of land and water many voices chattered the trifles of the passing hour—others spoke low farewells, that were meant for a short space of time, but were claimed by eternity.

Lily parted from her friends on the beach, talking brightly to the last of future meetings and possible adventures. Yet the wide sea and the great ship lying ready for departure—a symbol at once of union and separation, and some other unrevealed influence she could not define—struck chords in Lily's nature that had before lain mute. It seemed as if a new, and hitherto unknown, fount of tenderness had suddenly pulsed into being to make her dimly conscious of the depths and possibilities and infinite pathos of life . . . She watched the travellers till they were lost in the crowd, and then hurried back to Seawhaite, wondering whether Archie would come by the next train, and whether Chartreuse had fallen asleep or was lying awake in pain—and alone.

Chapter VII

There was but a narrow lane between Seawhaite and the row of cottages behind it owned by Mr. Thorndale. Lily went round the back of her mother-in-law's house into this lane, with the intention of going to see how Chartreuse fared. As she approached the cottages she heard his deep bass raised in intermittent howling, and instantly concluded that he must be in an agony of pain. There was a chemist's shop at the end of the lane westward, where it intersected one of the leading streets of Sherrington.

Lily went there in her distress to consult the chemist as to what she could do to relieve her dog. The chemist knew her by sight and entered with much sympathy into the "case." The best thing he could suggest, not knowing what ailed the St. Bernard, was to give her some laudanum to drop into his ear. This might temporarily at least alleviate the pain.

Sherrington was just the right size for the constant and unremitting circulation of social gossip. Mrs. Thorndale was so much of a personage there, that all who knew anything of the family were aware that Mrs. Archibald Thorndale was a young American lady, deemed by her mother-in-law unpardonably eccentric. This was the chemist's mental explanation of the curiously shabby ulster and hat she wore on this occasion. As for Lily, she was so much engrossed in Chartreuse's unhappy situation that she was quite unconscious of anything unusual in her costume. She hurried back through the lane and in at the Seawhaite kitchen entrance to get a candle, so that she might see to doctoring Chartreuse.

Maria was, if possible, redder in the face, more incoherent than before. She speedily got a bedroom candlestick and a box of matches for Lily, and pressed a large piece of plum cake on her for that "darlint and iligant jewel av a dog." When Lily got back into the lane she found that Chartreuse's complainings had entirely ceased. To her surprise the back gate of the yard behind the cottage in which she supposed him to be shut up stood on the latch. She paused at the back door to light her candle.

But before she could put the key in the lock the door was thrown violently open and the flaring light of a bull's eye was flashed into her face. It was held aloft by a policeman, who cried out roughly—

"So we have nobbed your little game this time."

Lily was a courageous woman, but this strange apparition gave her a sudden shock which made her feel cold and sick.

"What do you mean?" she cried faintly.

The policeman offered to take her by the arm, so as to draw her into the cottage. But Lily turned on him haughtily.

"Don't dare to touch me," she said in so stern and authoritative a voice that he instinctively shrank back.

"All right, mum, if you want to gammon the lady just walk in yourself, for we can't oblige you by letting you off after all our trouble," he said, with a low chuckle. Lily divined that she must be entangled in the meshes of some ghastly error, and decided that in order to clear this up she must yield submission. She entered the room, and saw that there was a second policeman in it; also an old man with handcuffs on, who stood leaning against the mantelpiece with a sullen and lowering expression. But there was no trace of Chartreuse.

"Where is my dog—what have you done with him?" said Lily, facing the policeman, who was in sergeant's uniform. He laughed derisively.

"A lady comin' into a empty house at 10 o'clock at night with a candlestick and a bottle o' pizen and a hunk of cake—of course it's her pet spaniel she's after," he said, in evident enjoyment of his own wit.

The effect which Lily's face, voice and manner had produced on him was rapidly counteracted by this inventory of her possessions—also by her hat and ulster. "Poison," in large red letters on the phial of laudanum, which Lily had placed in the bedroom candlestick, formed in the eyes of this penetrating myrmidon of the law an irrefragable proof that she must belong to the criminal classes. As for her face and manner, and something in her voice which had at first startled him—wasn't there adventuresses who took in bishops and governors, and even the higher nobility of England? But at any rate he, Sergeant Chase, knew a little too much of the world to be so easily hoodwinked.

But, to make assurance doubly sure, he turned to the old man in handcuffs.

"Do you know anything of this—this person? Now don't make it harder for yourself by trying to shield any one."

The old man looked up sullenly. Then a wicked gleam came into his eyes. He saw an opportunity for making it warm for the police in another case of mistaken identity.

"Course I do—the very one as nabbed the silver spoons and things—and me, an innocent victim, dragged inter it. You needn't wait for no more pals—there ain't no more."

But the astute police, though fully crediting the first part of his statement, refrained from acting on the latter. From information gleaned by a detective they had reason to believe that another confederate would come to the cottage shortly after midnight. Cheered by the success which had already crowned their efforts, they determined to remain till that time on the chance of adding to their kudos by taking one more criminal red-handed. In the meantime they improved the opportunity by examining the spoils which they had found on the premises when they surprised Jeremiah Dickson, "an old offender," concealing more stolen booty in the place. The six Thorndale table spoons of sterling silver formed part of the spoil.

"Let me ask you, mum, if you know anything of these," said the sergeant, holding them up before Lily.

"They are my brother-in-law's spoons," answered Lily calmly. The police found this a joke of extraordinary merit. They put her down as a "brazen one, and no mistake"—as "a knowing one," and a "cool hand, by Jove!" and opined that she must have come quite lately from Melbourne, or they would have surely seen something of her before this—you bet.

Lily, sitting on an empty kerosene case in a corner of the room, fell into a doze from time to time, with her head resting against the wall.

Startlingly grotesque as her surroundings were, all other feelings became submerged in overwhelming weariness as the time wore on to midnight.

* * *

Some of the inmates of Seawhaite in the meantime were having memorably impressive scenes. It was a quarter past 10 when Miss Benson was escorted to the gate by two elderly lady friends who lived in lodgings a little further up on the sea wall. She met Mrs. Thorndale at the drawing-room door, bedroom candlestick in hand.

"Didn't Lily come back with you? Oh, I suppose she is waiting for Archie to join her on the beach when his train comes in. Good night, my dear. Pray have a glass of wine—the tray is on the table, and your mother has stayed to read a little longer."

"Oh, mother, I could not, I dared not tell her; how are we to break this news to Archibald Thorndale when he comes?" cried Miss Benson, wildly, breaking in upon her mother with an indescribably melodramatic face and voice.

"His wife—his wife has eloped with Lady Ida Smiley's cousin. They have gone off by the Albion. Oh, it is a miserable story."

"Just heaven, is it possible!" cried Lady Keightley, in a low, hoarse voice. She could not forbear the thought that this might somehow be turned into an exciting situation for her next novel. But then came the chilling reflection that the subject might be too *risqué* for the young person. It was Lady Keightley's proudest boast that her works of fiction, so far from raising the blush of shame on the cheek of beauty, were universally chosen for Sunday school libraries and prizes. Still, it might be possible to use an incident so full of thrilling and piquant interest if only the moral reflections before and after were austere and searching enough.

She soon knew all there was to tell—the self absorbed promenade side by side on the jetty, the disappearance of the guilty pair after that from the jetty throng, and then their embarkation together on the last steam launch that took passengers.

"Has she left a letter? If so, it would be on the toilet table," said Lady Keightley, mindful of the dramatic proprieties even in the midst of all the rush of what she would have termed "conflicting emotion."

"It is our duty to see, to make sure of the worst before her husband comes," said Miss Benson, solemnly. And then the two went upstairs, carrying a lighted candle and creeping stealthily past Mrs. Thorndale's door.

No, there was no trace of a letter anywhere to be found. Probably she had posted it. "People do that sometimes, you know," said Miss Benson, peering behind the mirror and the vases on the mantelpiece.

"Perhaps—perhaps she meant to return," said Lady Keightley.

"Would she have compromised herself so hopelessly in that case," urged her daughter. No, they both felt that the widest charity, the most guileless minded, could come to no other conclusion but that Mrs. Archibald Thorndale had crowned her wilful contempt of social standard, her heartless disregard of her husband's relations, her indifference to himself, by outraging morality and decorum and ostracising herself henceforth from the society of all virtuous people.

What a scandal it would be! What a shock to the Thorndale family! What a blow to Lady Ida Smiley! She who was so cold and distant to many of the more highly placed people of the country, though she had, one might say, fallen in love with this young American, and encouraged her insolence by finding all she said so witty and original, and then Mr. Bruce being Lady Ida's own first cousin!

There really was no end to the capacities of the situation, to the lurid light that fell on it from every side. Mother and daughter crept downstairs together after their fruitless search for a letter from the runaway. They were still immersed in the subject, reminding each other of sayings and doings on Lily's part, which clearly pointed to this social and moral shipwreck, when they heard footsteps in the hall. It was Archibald who had come by the 11 o'clock train, and had let himself in by the back way, so as to avoid disturbing the household. His mother always kept early hours, and if Lily kept late ones at Seawhaite it was in the privacy of her own room.

He was therefore a little surprised when he saw the drawingroom door opened and the two ladies come towards him.

"I hope you have not been sitting up for me," he said, as he shook hands with them. "Is Lily here?"

"No, she is not here," answered Miss Benson in a smothered sort of voice, and then she retreated to the further end of the room, leaving her mother to break the terrible tidings.

Lady Keightley had never before had to announce to a man that his wife had eloped with another, but she rose to the dramatic requirements of the position with surprising alacrity.

"My dear boy, prepare yourself," she said in a low voice. Archibald turned pale.

"What is wrong, Lady Keightley? Don't keep me in suspense. Has there been any accident to Lily or my mother?"

"Your—wife—is—gone!"

"Gone where," said Archibald, with a little touch of impatience in his voice.

"Gone by the Albion," said Lady Keightley, in a sepulchral voice.

"Good God. What do you mean? What has happened?"

"Had you no suspicion?"

"I do not understand you, Lady Keightley," said Archibald, sternly, drawing himself up to his full height.

"Oh my poor, dear Archibald," said Lady Keightley in her melo-dramatic tones, but beginning to feel more keenly the "blow that was to shatter his happiness," as she phrased the matter to herself.

"Where is my mother?" said Archibald, shortly. He was in a whirl of bewilderment and consternation, but his first coherent thought was that if Lily had acted in an unaccountable way someone must be strongly to blame.

"Your mother, Archibald, has retired to rest. She knows nothing of this."

"Do you mean that my wife went away without leaving a message—without even telling my mother?"

"Concealment is the refuge of guilt," began Lady Keightley, feeling it necessary to speak more plainly.

"Take care what you say, Lady Keightley," said Archibald, his eyes beginning to flash with wrath.

"Then I will say nothing, but state the bare facts," replied the lady, stiffly. "I was not an eye witness; my daughter was, unfortunately, and no doubt many others. Elizabeth, my love, will you tell Archibald yourself all that you know in the order of occurrence."

Miss Benson came forward slowly, her eyes bent on the ground. Poor a thing as she judged human nature to be in the abstract, no one could say that she was callous to the shame and guilt of a fellow creature.

Archibald listened to what she had to tell like one stunned . . . "In company with Mr. Bruce . . ."

The words seemed to be weaving themselves in red letters all over the room. The perspiration stood in cold drops on his forehead. He became faint and speechless—and when Lady Keightley unlocked the French window of the drawingroom opening on the verandah, he stepped out mechanically, like one walking in his sleep.

The crowd on the bench and jetty had dispersed, the sea lay dark and still under the faint starlight. A great vessel outlined with white light was speeding away westward, leaving a wide, dark column of smoke in her wake. It was the Albion. She would soon be a faint speck on the horizon—then she would be lost to sight. Could it be possible that Lily was on board, that she had been so wilfully indiscreet as to take such a step on the impulse of a moment? Even if she had done so her husband could put no darker interpretation on her action than intolerant impatience of her surroundings. But in the light of voluntary submission to his mother in order to give him pleasure, how could it be possible that Lily should wound him so grievously? His whole heart went out to her in loving trust. Even in the face of overmastering evidence his mind rose in revolt against believing her capable of such cruelty.

"There must be some delusion—some great mistake," he said, hurriedly returning to the room. "If my wife is on the Albion she must have gone to see some friend off and stayed over the time till it was too late for her to return, and so she has been taken on to King George's Sound. Such things have happened before."

He saw the look of pitying incredulity in the face of mother and daughter, and almost hated them. After all Lily had understood them— had with her quick insight gauged their shallow envious natures.

There was a sound of slippered footsteps in the hall.

"Who is here in the drawingroom?" cried Mrs. Thorndale in a shriller less imperative tone than was habitual with her.

Lady Keightley went to the door which stood a little ajar.

"Oh, my dear Susan have you not gone to bed yet? Did you hear nothing? I thought I heard footsteps and voices, and I felt a little nervous about the plate. When I think of those spoons of my great aunt's with the double initials. Is Archie here too—and Lily, where is Lily?

Why, what is the matter with you all?"

Mrs. Thorndale, bedroom candlestick in hand, a portentously respectable peaked nightcap on her head and a loose flannel dressing gown thrown over her, looked little less majestic than she did in her stiff, brocaded silks adjusting the affairs of all the Thorndales and the investments of half a million of money.

Archie stooped to kiss his mother on the forehead, murmured some incoherent words and went out. The walls seemed to close round him and stifle him. He strode down to the jetty where a few stragglers still lingered. He drew his hat over his eyes and hurried on lest any one should recognise and speak to him. But as he passed two men one of them turned and grasped him by the arm.

"I say old fellow, where are you going at such a rate!" It was his brother George. They each spoke with overstrained eagerness of indifferent trifles. Then a dead silence ensued . . . "George has heard it already," thought Archibald—and he wildly thought of putting the matter in a half jocular light—as, "I suppose you have heard that Lily has gone off on a little trip;" or, "No doubt you know that I am a grass widower for a bit;" but his tongue clave to the roof of his mouth. His lips and throat felt as parched as desert sand.

They reached the end of the jetty and stood looking westward. The Albion had dwindled to a tremulous beacon like light on the marge of the horizon.

"I say Archie, has—is there—are you in any trouble?" gasped the elder brother at length.

"Oh, I have been an infernal idiot, making Lily go to places and things," said Archie, breathing hard as he spoke. Of course he intended that his brother should imagine there had been a tremendous shindy, in which he, Archie, had been diabolically to blame. Then George said that

Amelia had heard some cock and bull story from Miss Benson about seeing Lily go off in the last steam launch to the Albion,—and that—but it was absurd—

Then Archibald burst out passionately: "Look here, George, if Lily has done anything that lays her open to reproach, I am the only one to blame, and if I hear anyone say a word against her, if it's a woman I'll tell her straight she's a damned scandalous old cat; if it's a man I'll wring his neck."

George pressed his brother's arm sympathetically and walked back with him to Seawhaite. The ladies were still in the drawingroom. The elder brother joined them, but Archie went up direct to his own room. He turned up the gas and stared blankly round the room. One of Lily's dainty little gossamer laced handkerchiefs lay on the toilet table. A faint breath of wood violets—the only perfume she used—clung to it. He held it to his lips and hid his face from the light.

Chapter VIII

Archibald lay on the bed in his clothes, his face half buried in a pillow, wearing out the tissue of his brain in imagining some set of circumstances that might induce Lily to set out for the old world in so strange and capricious a manner. Then a dull sort of lethargy fell on him in which he seemed to be consciously dreaming . . . There was a patter of four massive paws on the staircase—a cold large nose bumped against the door—then came a light tread—the door handle was turned and two feet and four came quietly into the room.

"Why Archie—are you here? Did you think I was in the dressing room." Archibald started up with a cry. It was true—Lily was there—Chartreuse close beside her, just as when he first saw them.

"Ah, Lily darling, you have come back to me? It was all he could utter just then. Lily had a thousand things to say—a thousand questions to ask, but how is one to speak or even to breathe, held so close in strong arms with kisses rained stormily on one's face and hair.

"Oh, Archie, do let me draw a tiny breath. Why, do you know, that it was I who stole your great-great aunt's silver spoons, with the double initials?"

They laughed in each other's faces; but it was some time before Archibald could sober down to coherent talk, and Lily at intervals made the most astounding statements.

"I have been under arrest for larceny as a bailee and burglary. Archie, aren't you ashamed of yourself, an old married man, to be such a fearful spoon?"

"But, Lily, where have you been all the time? And where— whose extraordinary garment is this you have on? And—surely that is not your hat?"

"Your mother is at this moment demolishing two policemen, and she has discovered that Maria drinks and gives the keys of the Thorndale Terrace cottages to a criminal brother-in-law; otherwise she is still invaluable."

Archie took up the hat that Lily had taken off and looked at it with inquisitive wonder. Gradually he came into possession of the episodes of that eventful evening. Mrs. Melville, Mr. Bruce, Chartreuse, the police blunder all in succession.

"To my other crimes would have been added that of domestic embezzlement," said Lily, looking into her portmonnaie to see that the cheque was safe there; "only Mr. Bruce undertook to see to the transfer, and you can send the amount through a bank."

"You made Mrs. Melville take your dustcoat and hat, Lily, in exchange for her shabby ones; and Mr. Bruce took her under his protection," said Archie, slowly . . . "Oh you angel-hearted child." . . . Tableau.

"But it seems to me your turn for history has come, Archie. When I opened the door and saw you on the bed I made sure you had come in late and didn't know I was missing—fancied that I was in the dressing room. Your mother and Lady Keightley and Miss Benson and your brother George looked like so many midnight conspirators when I came in. They knew I had been either lost or stolen—but did you?"

"I found out when I came you were missing, and oh, Lily, it was horrible."

"What *did* you think, Archie?" said Lily, raising her head from his shoulder and looking at him with big eyes.

"There was not a clue."

"No, but what did you think?"

"That you had gone away."

"Where?"

"In the Albion."

"Oh, you are making fun of me."

"No, Lily; there was a chain of circumstantial evidence—"

"Well, but go on, tell me—"

"You were seen walking with Mr. Bruce—you, presumedly, went with him in the last steam launch—you were gone—"

Lily quickly released herself and sat facing her husband with an unsmiling face.

"Archie, tell me, as true as you are living, did you think that?—did you?"

"Lily, I could think no evil of you. But in the face of such overwhelming evidence, and in your unaccountable absence, I could only try to think how your little disgusts and impatience at people like Lady Keightley and her daughter—"

"Ah, they gathered up the threads to hang me. I begin to see. But did you think I could leave Chartreuse?"

"Why," went on Lily, after an interlude, "it was he, the dear old boy, who delivered me. It was nearly on the stroke of 12, and the police had given up hopes of any other confederate turning up. All at once there came an enormous bump at the door. They opened it at once, each grasping a revolver and a pair of handcuffs. In rushed Chartreuse. He nearly swept the ceiling down with wagging his tail, he was so overjoyed. He had forced his way out somehow, and tracked me into the next house. They looked on his collar, and saw my name engraved on it. I showed them my watch and the jewelled trinkets with the same name, and said if I had really stolen them they had better call in here and have them identified before we went on to the lockup. We knocked at the kitchen door, but Maria was *non compos mentis*. After a pause your brother George opened with three women peering behind him with long beaks and round eyes. "My dear Lily, have you had any accident?" said George, and he kissed me on the forehead, and his voice was quite soft. I am sorry I said his Amelia was like a wooden butterfly. The two police creatures grovelled in the dirt. "Your mother no doubt has given them goblets of wine of Syracuse, and now—tableau—happiness—curtain.""

Lily laughed a little, and rose up, for there were voices and footsteps at the door. Her mother-in-law was eager to see her, and called "Lily" very gently, and Lily responded. All at once she staggered, and everything seemed to swim gracefully out of sight. She did not quite swoon, but the strain of the last hour, and the great fatigue, and her long fast, all told on her. An obstinate fit of giddiness and debility ensued. No one was more concerned at this than Lily's mother-in-law. Even Archie had to retire more or less into the background, when, on the following day— Christmas Eve—she deemed it prudent to summon the family doctor.

He was a round, solemn, fussy little man, who asked questions, as Lily declared, "like a census paper," at the same time nodding with an invincible air of knowing all beforehand. He and Mrs. Thorndale retired into corners and conversed in amicable whispers. After his departure Mrs. Thorndale went about with an up lifted countenance. As she was going into Lily's room Chartreuse suddenly rose up, and the good lady almost stumbled over his colossal form.

"Ah, I am so sorry, Mrs. Thorndale; you are really too good, taking so much trouble. It is too bad that my dog should come in your way like that—"

"Never mind my dear, *his* nose will be put out of joint one of these days!" answered Mrs. Thorndale, with a large benevolent smile, and a mysterious nod which Lily better understood a short time afterwards. But when her husband came in a little later it was of Chartreuse that she persisted in speaking.

"He does only shake his head nor show any symptoms of pain, and yet he has had no laudanum dropped into his ear—only the toe of your mother's shoe—and—and a gruesome prophecy."

"He is all right, the young scamp. He only made you believe he was ill so that you should pet him. But, Lily, what of the prophecy? Have you nothing to tell me?"

"You don't seriously believe my dog would be a hypocrite!" said Lily, getting rather red, but ignoring these timid inquiries.

"Oh, no; it is not a little woman I know who can play the hypocrite and keep secrets."

"Oh, Archie!" Lily's face flushed scarlet, and then there was silence, followed by interludes of low, fond laughter and broken talk of the kind which does not, as a rule, wander beyond those who exchange such confidences.

Hänslein's Disappearance:
A Story of Saxon Switzerland

Chapter I

On a radiant morn, late in May, the garden round the Japanese palace in Dresden was full of the perfume of lilac. Nowhere does this shrub bloom more profusely than in the "Florence of the Elbe"—to use the title that poet Herder bestowed on the charming capital of Saxony and the favourite art-centre of Germany. Luxuriant bushes, loaded with great plumes of the blossom, some pure white, some pale blue as the first timid violet of spring, others a royal purple, and still others—the *lilas de marly*—a sharp red, met Marie Schumann at every turn as she wandered slowly round the garden.

Marie was waiting for her father, who was verifying an obscure date in the history of the Jesuits, in one of the 40 rooms which are stored with the half-million of books that constitute part of the national library. "Father is longer than he expected; perhaps when he found his date it made some of the others suspicious," thought Marie as she glanced at the broad flat gold watch, pale in colour and worn with the service of a round century—a gift on her fourteenth birthday from her mother, who had died before the girl completed her fifteenth year. "It will be just eight years in three days since mother went away," she reflected, her thoughts passing swiftly to that sad epoch as she looked on the face of the faithful old timekeeper that year in year out numbered the hours as with the tireless hand of fate. The memory sobered but did not spoil the gladness that the girl always felt in the presence of flowers and in the hearing of the cuckoo's wandering twofold shout.

She had come to that part of the garden which slopes steeply towards the river, while full in front on the opposite side rise the cupolas of the Hof and Frauen Kirche, the towers of the Royal palace, and the twin spires of the Sophia Kirche. The scene was one familiar to Marie from her earliest childhood, but she stood regarding it now as if as much absorbed by its picturesqueness as a stranger. Around her were groups of nurses, some knitting, some gossiping, a few reading penny stories of love and murder, while their small charges played around or lay with the philosophic calm of Teutonic babies in ample perambulators bulging out with feather coverlets. Most of the nurses were Altenburg peasant women in short voluminous skirts covered by white aprons, on their heads wide Alsatian bows of black silk with enormous streamers of gaily covered ribbon hanging behind, while the short sleeves of their smart bodices left their brawny arms fully exposed. One of these stout brunette complexioned nurses, whose one small charge was fast asleep in its capacious perambulator, gave a quick exclamation on seeing Marie.

"Why, fräulein, I heard you had gone away," she said, bringing her perambulator to a halt, while the long thick stocking she was knitting hung over her left arm. "Jacobis Olga," she went on in a rapid staccato voice, "told me only last night that she saw you and the herr doctor, your father, two days ago in one of the boats going away to a river town in Bohemia, where you had taken a villa for the summer, and I said then— Oh, I wish I had seen the fräulein, if only for a minute to say good bye, and God be with you, and thousand, thousand thanks once more for all you did for me when I was in such trouble. But perhaps then you are not going away after all, fräulein?"

"Yes, Lenda, to-morrow at 10 in the morning," answered Marie. "But we are not going as far as Bohemia, only to Wehlen on the Elbe, in Saxon Switzerland. As for a villa, we have only taken five rooms in one that has a big garden stretching down to the river's brink."

"Ei—ei—but that will be close quarters for you fräulein, after your beautiful place in Christian-street; and Sybilla, of course, goes with you?"

"No, she has taken a place for six months, until we return. I am going to look after the housekeeping myself, and just have a tagelöhnerin[1] to help. You see, Lenda, since father gave up being a director of the historical museum it is no longer necessary for us to live in Dresden."

"Ach so; and wherever he is, the herr doctor can still write learned books about the world before there were any Christians on it. How strange that people can get so much knowledge. It is like finding out the names of the stars that are so far away—one has not enough figures to count the distance."

"Yes, but Wehlen is not so far as that," said Marie smiling. "Some day when you get a holiday you must come to see us. I see father looking for me, so I must say good-bye."

* * *

"Why, Marie, you have somehow managed to give these poor rooms quite a lordly look," said Dr. Schumann two days later, as he stood in the doorway of the sitting-room in which his daughter was busy arranging some china on an old Hanoverian cabinet.

"But do you know, father, I am getting so proud of these rooms that I cannot let you call them poor," answered Marie blithely. "Look at our pretty easy chairs and blue curtains and engravings, and all this fine old china, some of it so precious that mandarins were put to death in the sixteenth century because they ate off that yellow dragon platter, sacred to imperial use alone."

"Yes, child, that is all very well," answered Dr. Schumann. "But

____

[1] A servant by the day.

though you are cunning in making the place look so well, it is poor and cramped, and your life will be poorer than ever before."

"And what about you, father?"

"Oh, as for me, I have my books and my work—so engrossing that I often long for a day of 48 hours. I find myself in a world so deficient in the historic sense that I can never have much time to think of other things."

"Well, and I have a garden full of roses, and June coming on, and cuckoos everywhere, and the Elbe thrown in for nothing," replied Marie. "Look at these wood rafts," she added, drawing back the curtain from the window which looked full upon the river less than three hundred yards away; "what a picture they make floating slowly down. Perhaps you think it is because they are going to sell the wood in Hamburg? But no, they are passing; it is just because I love to watch them; and then look how limpid the river is as it turns towards Vogelgesang. What a charming name for a village—Birdsong—and how pretty the soft cool woods above it look. Just like one of Ruysdael's pictures out of the Dresden Gallery, only this is on such a great scale; and every day it will change a little, but every day it will be so lovely that I shall hardly know which I like most."

"Yes, Marie; that is all very well," answered Dr. Schumann, who, though he smiled in response to Marie's gaiety, yet felt that the time had come for a more serious view of the situation than she was inclined to take. "I know you worship nature and, like other devotees, you find joy in your idolatry. To me nature is little more than the grim power that in one way or another robs us of all that we love, and finally knocks us on the head just like superfluous rabbits. Perhaps that is partly because of my 57 years. But you will not be always twenty-two, and the great disadvantage of coming here is that you will be cut off from the society in which you ought to move. Now wait, Marie, until I finish," said the doctor, holding up an admonitory forefinger in reply to the mutinous expression that had come into Marie's expressive face.

"Your Aunt Bokelmann was talking the matter over with me the night before we left. I agreed with her that you had better stay with them part of each week, say from Friday till Tuesday. You see you have to go in any case on Fridays for your miniature painting, and in your aunt's circles there are always more parties and functions during that part of the week. Your aunt too is kind enough to say that she will see to your party dresses herself, so you need not object on the ground of expense."

"But, father, there are so many other grounds of objection," said Marie in a tone of consternation.

"Not serious ones, my dear."

"Well, isn't it serious that the more Aunt Bokelmann and I are together the less we love each other?"

"Marie, Marie," said Dr. Schumann in a reproving tone.

"But so it is, father. If I express my own opinions, or walk out alone, or read the book I like, or stand up for the people I admire aunt lectures me as if I had broken all the commandments, and then winds up by saying, "But it is your English side, and those years in London, poor child."

"Well, but Marie, you *are* a little impetuous at times, eh?"

"Yes, I know," answered Marie penitently. "Often I make resolutions to be as meek and silent as a saint in an old painted window, but aunt has a way of saying, 'Don't speak like that;' or, 'Don't do such and such a thing—*men don't like it*,' which makes me forget all my good intentions, and then I just sit and watch some of her visitors and think that of all the narrow, bigoted, arrogant people in the world the military people in Germany are the worst. You know she hardly sees anyone but officers and their wives, and since Uncle Woldemar was made a general and they go to Court oftener it gets worse and worse, and now that she has got

Cousin Hedwig engaged to a colonel old enough to be her father, with big red cheeks and a purple nose, and a deep gruff voice, as if he spoke from his gouty toes—"

"Marie do you allow yourself to speak like that?" said Dr. Schumann in a tone of displeasure.

"Yes father, when I find that you want me to leave you so much alone to spend more than half my time with Aunt Bokelmann for the sake of going into society under her wing," replied Marie, her deep soft eyes shining, the peach bloom of her cheeks warmly flushed.

"If aunt only criticised me I would not mind so much," she added. "But ever since you gave up being director of the historical museum she always implies that you are somehow to blame."

"Well, perhaps, I am," answered Dr. Schumann in a dejected tone.

Marie looked at him in surprise.

"It is a secret after a fashion, and I did not see the use of explaining it to you at the time, but I had better tell you now Marie. I had to give up my position because of my article in one of the American magazines on the growth of militarism in Germany. I was allowed to resign; but if I hadn't done so—"

"Oh! What shameful tyranny," cried Marie hotly, "to take your museum from you just because of that article so beautifully written, and not a word in it that isn't true."

"Well, you see, I might all my life have told the truth about the classic ages with impunity," said Dr. Schumann dryly. "But when our own environment and times are as full of interest, one gets tired of living so much in the past, and now that I have begun I fear that I shall go on writing more modern history, and as I can only write of things as they are, I may yet be put to death for putting pepper in a cream tart."

As Dr. Schumann was speaking a loud and abrupt burst of the

mocking sounds peculiar to the laughing jackass came in through the open window.

"Ah, there is my liebes Hänslein," said Marie, looking out, to find that the bird was perched on a pear tree in front of the house. "And there is Fritz, a little below him, silent and gloomy at finding himself in a strange place."

But Fritz did not long remain silent, for no sooner had Hänslein stopped than Fritz burst into a fit of prolonged hooting and jeering, in which his brother at last joined. Then both stopped abruptly and sat after the manner of their kind—motionless as if they were carved in stone.

They were fine, well-grown birds that had been given to Marie when she was in London by a cousin from Australia. They were now nine years old and the heroes of many marvellous tales and hairbreadth adventures. They had looked into the eyes of death in many forms—from the ravages of an alien climate to acute dyspepsia, from suffocation by thieves to an encounter with a Russian blood-hound. But they had survived all, and now as Marie looked at them she suddenly clapped her hands with glee.

"How could I have forgotten this other reason for not going to Aunt Bokelman? It is impossible I should leave Hänslein and Fritz when Sybilla is no longer with us to look after them in my absence."

"Have it your own way then, Mary of Egypt," said Dr. Schumann with an affected air of melancholy. This was a name he had long ago bestowed on his daughter after Ribera's picture in the Dresden gallery. Marie's hair, when unbound, fell around her like a bright soft shower of gold, and this, with the starry radiance of her eyes, gave point to the title. "But then," as she used to say, "I would never kneel joyfully by my open grave, not even for the sake of being put in a prayer-book all over Christendom."

Chapter II

On the following Friday, when Marie went for her painting lesson, she had to explain to her aunt as well as she could how impossible it was that she should stay in Dresden part of each week.

"But when I put the matter before your father he saw it was just the right thing," said Frau von Finckenstein, sternly. "And in fact it is quite arranged. I have had the little spare room in the roof fitted up for you—and where is your luggage?"

"Really papa," said Marie in giving her father an account of the interview, "when aunt said that in her masterful way I felt as if my two trunks, packed and corded, must be waiting round some corner ready for Ottilie and Greta to lug them up stairs into that little room with a tiny window, from which one sees nothing but chimney-tops. . . . How different from the view here, where you look first across the garden getting crowded with roses and carnations, then over the river with long wood rafts or a square red sail creeping into it, and then beyond that, meadows and hills, and villages and shadowy woods."

"That is all very well, Marie," replied her father, "while the place is new to you. But after a few weeks, when the days are as much alike as if they were potatoes, and I am always busy over my writing, you will be sorry that you refused your aunt's offer."

"I bet you four kisses on the eyelids" returned Marie gleefully, "that after six months, when you say to me, 'Now get ready child, we go away to-morrow,' I shall have to confess—'Papa, there is one thing I am unable to pack up and take away from Wehlen—that is my heart'."

"Very well, we shall see," answered Dr. Schumann, smiling, as he settled himself at his pedestal table heaped up with uncut books and magazines, unopened newspapers and pamphlets, with a clear space in the middle on which lay proof-sheets that were in course of being corrected.

Dr. Schumann took up his pen, but Marie put her hand over it, saying—

"Before you begin to work again, father, let me read the time-table I have made for the family."

Dr. Schumann nodded assent, and Marie read—"7 a.m., chocolate; half-past 10, the big breakfast; half-past 1 p.m., dinner; 4 or half past, coffee; from then till 8, walks or excursions; 8 p.m., supper; bed-time according to inclination."

"Good little house-mother, that will do nicely. But I don't know if I can always spare so much time for walks and excursions, you know, Marie."

"That is just why I want you to sign this document, Dr. Schumann, and then I shall see that you keep to it like a Hebrew making bricks without straw," said Marie severely. "You nearly always begin to work at 6 in the morning. By 4 in the afternoon—not counting the time for meals—you have been at work nine hours. Now, if that is not enough time for putting the dates of the world in order, why they must just go on telling fibs."

"But it is not only my historical work on the Jesuits that occupies me just now, Marie. I have another article for the *New York Review* on the anvil, and I am now enlarging the first one to be published as a mono-graph."

"Are you, father?" said Marie, turning very serious. "Oh, I am so glad; I do love that piece of work."

"Because you helped me to correct the English proofs?" said her father smiling.

"A little for that, but mostly because it is so good and shows so plainly how the heaviest burdens fall upon the poorest."

"But do you know that my friends tell me it is dangerous to publish it; that I may in fact be arraigned on a charge of *lése majesté*. It would be much more prudent to eulogise our crushing armaments, far more calcu-lated to *savonnette à vilain*. What do you think, little one?"

"I know you will never write a line you do not believe, even for a red eagle of the first class with ten thousand marks a year added," answered the girl, raising her head proudly.

"Ah, well, if I am to go to prison I must first get on with my work," said Dr. Schumann, once more resuming his pen.

"Yes, and make ready by getting plenty of fresh air four hours daily," returned Marie as she softly closed the study door.

We all know that words spoken in jest sometimes turn to deadly earnest. But for three months to come our historian and his daughter had no real misgiving that this would come to pass in their case. During that period Marie succeeded in keeping her father very strictly to the excur-sion clause of her time-table.

The singular mixture of intense cultivation with wild rocky heights and thick dark woods, which make up Saxon Switzerland, can be no-where seen to greater advantage than in the district round Wehlstädtel, as Wehlen is called in the folk dialect. A savage sea of rocks, with abysses from which the great grey crags rise in splintered-looking masses to per-pendicular heights, overshadowed by tall pines and firs that apparently draw nourishment from the barest stones, make up a scene of such grim desolation that it seems as if the traveller must be infinitely removed from all contact with civilization. But presently a steep footpath that has been made practicable by the art of man goes winding up by woody gulfs and past rocky chasms until a table-land is reached that is formed like a Chinese garden.

All around spreads a smiling friendly landscape that is thickly dot-ted with villages. Charming old villages they are, too, with irregular old house roofs closely clustered together, with overhanging eaves, queer angles and corners, thickly-timbered gable-ends and half-circular little windows comically like eyes, partly buried in the thick red tiles, stained grey and green, and often mended after a primeval fashion that shows they have borne the brunt of many a stern winter. But in the flaming days of June and July there is no suggestion of snowstorms or driving sleet. The fields are full of scarlet poppies and deep blue cornflowers; acres of meadows are tenderly coloured with the soft chrome and pale purple of field pansies—stief-mutterchen the country people call them. In August, when the long twilight begins to shorten, the grey blue silhouettes of the countless mountains which stand out in delicate relief against the darkening sky, begin to be wreathed with a faint vapory mist. This is one of the earliest indications of autumn. Marie first observed this change in the landscape as she and her father were walking across the woody heights that lie between Wehlon and the Bastei. When they got home there were several letters awaiting Dr. Schumann. One of them was a rather portentous looking official missive, which he read with a grave preoccupied expression, while Marie went out into the garden to release Hänslein and Fritz from the cage in which she always left them when she went out.

"I find I shall have to go to Dresden to-morrow on business, Marie," said her father when she came in. "You had better come with me to your aunt's, as it is just possible that I may be detained for some days."

"How can you forget the claims of my family, father?" said Marie in serio-comic reproof. "You know Hänslein will not eat in his cage even if there was anyone here who understood how to feed him; and I cannot leave him at large when I go away. You see he is not a pattern of goodness, like Fritz."

"Then are you always going to be tethered to that sulky bird?" said her father a little crossly.

"No, Väterchen; only for this half-year, while we are economising," answered Marie coaxingly. "When we go back to Dresden in January and Sybilla comes back to us I can trust the two to her as I did before. You know what good care she took of them in September and October last year when we were in Italy and Switzerland."

To this Dr. Schumann made no reply. He was turning over some music that stood on the piano in an abstracted sort of way. Then he looked out through the window as if watching a cargo boat that was slowly sailing by. But all the time it was evident that his thoughts were elsewhere.

"But how will you manage, Marie, if I am away say for a week or two?" he asked abruptly.

"In one way, father, I shall manage very well," answered Marie cheerfully. "There is that box of English novels cousin Rhoda sent me last month. I have hardly read one of them yet. Then there is my painting. I ought to work at that two hours a day more than I do. And then there is my music. Oh, I shall hardly have time for all I ought to do, only, of course, every hour I shall miss you. And why do you think you may have to stay away so long?"

"Sing me one if your songs now, Marie," said her father by way of reply.

And Marie sat down at the piano and sang in her delicious mezzo-soprano—

> Wenn ich ein Vöglein wär,
>
> Und auch zwei Flüglein hätt;
>
> Flög ich zu dir;
>
> Weil's aber nicht Kann sein
>
> Bleib ich allhier.

* * *

"Lizabeth, if you were a girl whose father stayed away four days without writing to you what would you do?" said Marie in a meditative way.

Lizabeth was the old peasant woman who had been engaged by the Schumann's to do the work of their small mènage. She was 72, but looked 10 years older. She had toiled so hard all her life that it seemed as if she had no more capacity for sensation or emotion than a time-worn effigy in an old churchyard. But on such occasions as the present, when Marie had made her sit in an easy chair to drink afternoon coffee in the pretty sitting-room that overlooked the garden and river, the weather-beaten, furrowed old face would look younger, and even a faint smile would brighten it now and then.

"But how can I tell what I would do if I were somebody else, fräulein?" she said in answer to Marie's question in a wondering tone.

"Do you never think of being any one but yourself, Lizabeth?" asked Marie with a note of pity in her voice. "As for me I am always being somebody else—in my thoughts, you know. Sometimes even a bird of passage going away to the valley of the Nile to find the old nest I built last year."

"Ach Gott, it is bad enough to sit down to dinner with my knife and half a loaf of rye bread, but what would it be to fly away from Germany begging your food by the way?"

"I never thought of a swallow being a beggar," answered Marie, laughing. "But, Lizabeth, do you never think of anything wonderful happening?"

"In what way, fräulein?"

"Well, suppose a prince came from Bagdad to see you with 30 camels all loaded with pearls and rubies and gold brocades that would stand alone?"

"If he did not bring a character from the pastor I would have nothing to say to him or his 30 camels, fräulein," answered Lizabeth gravely.

"I never saw a camel except in a Bible," she went on, wondering a little why her answer made Marie laugh so merrily. "An old Bible with many pictures; it belonged to Gustuv Meyer, who lived to be 101. He never went 20 miles away from Hohnstein. He lived on onions and potatoes, and drank rain water, and went to bed when the hens went to roost."

Lizabeth's reminiscences were cut short by a loud resounding knock at the door of the little hall which opened on the staircase. She hastened to answer the summons, and to Marie's amazement in walked her Aunt von Finckenstein, followed by her daughter Hedwig.

"Have you seen father? Has he come back with you?" said Marie eagerly, when the first greetings were over.

"Yes. I have seen your father; he has not come back; he is under arrest for treason to his king and country," replied Frau von Finckenstein, with cold brevity.

"Treason! Is that the word for trying to help the weak and exposing the enormity of our crushing military system," said Marie, with flashing eyes.

The moment she heard the word "arrest" she divined what had taken place. Her father's monograph on the military burdens of Germany had been published two weeks before and been much discussed in the public press. That was why he had been summoned to Dresden and why he was now in confinement. She wondered he had not told her, but then it was his way always to try and save her from worry, and he could not know the worst until after he got to Dresden.

"He has been most leniently dealt with considering his offence," said Frau von Finckenstein sternly. "Only four weeks' strict seclusion, and through our influence with his Gracious Majesty there will be no public scandal. This is your father's message to you, and you had better get ready as soon as possible."

As her aunt spoke she handed Marie a little note which ran as follows:—

"Dear Marie—You see that putting pepper in a cream tart is still a grave crime in our fatherland. So here I am at the — Garrison in charge of my future nephew-in-law for four weeks to come. While I am away you had better stay with your aunt. She will no doubt put up with Häns-lein and Fritz if you ask her prettily. As long as I am here I shall not be allowed to see or write to anyone."

Marie hastily read the words and then looked up as if to speak. But she felt a lump rising in her throat, and as she did not want to cry she kept silent.

"It may be the best thing, after all, that your father should get this severe lesson," said her aunt by way of consolation. "It will teach him prudence and keep him from spoiling all his prospects."

"My father will never devote himself to mere Bildwissenschaff,"[2] said Marie coldly. "As for the despots who are impoverishing the nations for the sake of pre-eminence in the art of human slaughter, they will be exposed more and more every day, no matter how many good men they may unjustly punish."

"As long as you are with me, Marie, you are not to talk treason after this fashion," said Frau von Finckenstein angrily.

"Feeling as we both do, it is impossible that I should become your guest, aunt," replied Marie with equal warmth.

"But, child, it would be so highly unbecoming that you should stay here all alone," said her cousin Hedwig. She was a large blonde young woman of 30, whose phlegmatic temperament, coupled with her mother's rigid discipline, rendered her as colourless as a tame rabbit. But she was good-natured in a polite sort of way, and the turn affairs had taken dis-

---

[2] Studies that aim only at gaining a livelihood.

tressed her. But Marie felt that intercourse with her relatives at this juncture would be intolerable, and in the end she had her own way.

When they were gone she sat down and cried a little, but not for long. She heard Fritz and Hänslein ha-haing at the bottom of the garden, down by the Elbe, which they were fond of haunting for the sake of the young frogs that they gobbled up so rapidly, barely winking an eyelid in the process. And that reminded her that she must put them in their cage before she went across the river to Bärenstein with the daughters of the pastor, who rejoiced in having so much more of her society since Dr. Schumann had gone to Dresden.

"Father is detained and will not be back for four weeks to come," she said to them as they set out. They returned in the gloaming when the soft autumnal mists were creeping along the river and weaving faint wreaths around the mountain heights all round, and the bats were making short broken flights among the myriads of insects that filled the air. Lizabeth met her in the little hall, telling her that Frau Stein had brought a basket of Himbeeren and was just going away. "Tell her to wait a little," answered Marie, and she went to a drawer in the cabinet for her purse. When the hard-working pale-faced little widow was gone and Marie was putting her purse away the thought suddenly came to her like a flash of lightning out of the blue—"How much money have I got?"

She turned her purse out there and then and counted over its contents with painful anxiety. There was one five-mark piece and three half-marks. Then there was a little box in which she kept coppers—10 pfennig pieces. There were 15 of them in all. She went into her father's rooms and searched for any stray coins that might be lying about. In the midst of her perplexity she laughed a little as she thought how she would tell her father that she had picked his pockets in his absence. But though she examined them all carefully and turned over drawers, &c, in his bedroom and study, the total result was only two marks 20 pfennigs. But she was not surprised, for about the middle of the month—it was now the 25th—her father had said that it was lucky she managed to keep house on a few marks daily, as they would be run pretty close until the middle of September, when 400 marks was due to them for the rental of the flat they had let furnished in Christian-street, taking away with them only such items as some table linen, silver, an ancient cabinet, and some choice old porcelain.

So here she was with herself and Lizabeth and two Australian giant kingfishers to keep for four weeks, while all the money she had in the world was a few coppers less than ten shillings!

"If father had only known that I would not go to aunt he would have drawn on his reserve at the Dresdner Bank and sent me enough," she reflected. And then misgivings assailed her lest she had done wrong in refusing to go to Dresden in her father's absence. But the arrangement was intolerable, and still more intolerable the thought of applying to her kinspeople for any assistance.

"Would it be possible to live on this for four weeks?" she thought, hanging over the little heap of silver and copper that had suddenly assumed such paramount importance. She began to divide them into little heaps—so much for milk and eggs, and butter and cream—so much for meat and fruit and vegetables. But in the midst she recollected that the widow Stein was doing some plain needlework, for which she, Marie, purposed paying at least three marks. And there were other claims upon her, too, which she could not bear to thrust aside. For she had not been in Wehlen three months without finding people to whom a little timely help was as the breath of life.

"I must get some more money—but how?" thought Marie, for the first time in her life face to face with the problem which is for so many poor souls the great enigma of existence. Presently her eyes fell on the cabinet on which she had so carefully ranged a choice store of old Chinese porcelain. "The very thing," she said, rising joyfully and taking up the pride of the collection—a small bowl of the Imperial yellow china of the great Ming dynasty—its worth and authenticity assured by the inscription Ta-Ming-Wan-li-nien-tschi, which means "Made during the years of Wan-li (1573-1620)." This unique little dish had been given to her by her father a year before, and he had said half playfully at the time—"Remember, Marie, if you ever want to turn that small incense bowl into hard cash you should get at least 300 marks for it."

"You good old yellow dragon, with five claws," said Marie, apostrophising the strange reptile which adorned the vessel, "to what better use could you ever be put than buying food for an old woman, a young one, and two Australian birds that get hungry every day with incredible regularity?"

Chapter III

"What a lot of money—twelve twenty-mark pieces—and how pretty the red gold looks when one has only a few marks at home!" soliloquised Marie three days later as she was returning from Dresden by the 5 o'clock train in the afternoon.

It was Friday, and she had started an hour earlier than usual, so that before going for her painting lesson she might take the yellow dragon to Herr Zerbst, the great dealer in antiquities, whose shop is in a crowded little street close to the Royal Palace. He had without any parleying offered two hundred and forty marks for the basin after he had examined its texture and inscription carefully with the aid of a microscopical glass. "It is worth more, but the times are bad, and the supply of American millionaires seems to be running short, so I may have to keep it a long time before a customer comes," he said, and Marie thought the sum he named so considerable for a dish so small and a design so very plain, that she did not ask as she intended to do for the sum her father had mentioned. She counted the twelve golden sovereigns over very carefully, and now as she was on her way home she peeped at them in her portmonnaie, with the exultant feeling of one who has transacted a satisfactory bit of business.

As she was crossing over in the ferry-boat—the railway-station is on the opposite bank of the river from Wehlen—she noticed Lizabeth and one of the pastor's daughters walking slowly by the river side, as if in search of some thing that was lost.

"It is Hänslein that is lost; he has gone away," said Lizabeth, as soon as Marie had overtaken them, and then Marie was overcome with regret and remorse, for she now recollected that she had not caged up the birds as was her custom, when she went away for some hours since coming to a strange place. "I saw him last at the edge of the river in Herr Schafer's grass meadow, looking very full in the stomach, and very unfriendly in the face," said Lizabeth. "Half an hour ago Fritz came home by himself; then I came to look for Hänslein, and Fräulein Margareta came with me."

That was all Marie could learn of Hänslein's disappearance until she returned to Rose Villa after sunset, weary and dispirited with a long fruitless search. But when she got back she found Christoph Stein, a derf tändler,[3] and brother-in-law of widow Stein, awaiting her with the news that he had seen a stranger—a tourist—on board of a passenger steamer that was going on to Schandau with the Fräulein's bird in his possession.

"Then my Hänslein is stolen, and I will never see him again!" said Marie, on the verge of tears. It was now the height of the tourist season, and boats often loaded with strangers were passing up and down the Elbe, through Saxon Switzerland every hour or so. Among such hordes

---

[3] Country hawker.

how find out the thief who had laid unconsecrated hands on the pet she had cherished for nine long years? Still, she resolved, besides offering a handsome reward to the police for the recovery of the bird, to go herself to Schandau on the morrow. She was getting ready to undertake this journey at 10 o'clock next morning when Lizabeth came to her door saying in a voice shrill with excitement—

"The gentleman who stole your bird is here, Fräulein, and Hänslein is with him." Marie hurried out, and came face to face with a tall, slight, young man, with dark eyes and moustache, and a sun-bronzed face.

"Marie, how solemn-looking you have grown!" said the newcomer as he held out his hand. Marie stared at him a moment with blank unrecognition; and then her face suddenly glowed like a rise in the sunshine.

"Oh, Bob, it's really you! and such a great tall fellow, with a moustache actually as if you were a hundred years old. So you have come at last, and brought me back my dear, sulky old Hänslein!"

She stooped to caress the runaway, who stood at Bob's feet solemn and unemotional as a sphinx of the desert.

"Are you straight from Brisbane, or did you first go to England? And your mother is with you, of course? How is she? And how in the world did you find Hans? or was it you who stole him?"

"I did not steal him, Schumann's Marie; I took him in the sight of all men as my own," answered the young man, "and before I tell you how that happened I want to know why you stopped writing to us three years ago?"

"But I wrote last; at any rate, to your mother. I am not so sure about you."

It was the old story of a long continued correspondence that gradually died for lack of the fuel of personal intercourse and common interests. Bob Hastings was Marie's second cousin and old playfellow for several years when he and his widowed mother had come to England shortly after Dr. Schumann had been appointed one of the professors of the London University.

"What a jolly little room. What a stunning view you have of the river," said Bob, as they went into the parlour after Hans had been restored to his brother in the garden, where the two burst into sardonic laughter as if the world were on the whole the absurdest planet in the universe. "But I say, Marie," added Bob, looking round, "where is your governor?"

One may imagine the young man's feelings on hearing the tale his cousin had to unfold.

"I'll tell you what, Marie," he said at the close, "you must let me relieve my mind by saying the prayer you invented when the mater took us one autumn to that pretty little farm near Surrey. You don't remember? Well you see you were only a kiddie of five or six at the time. You were going across a little field when all at once an old porker came grunting out of the hedge. "I was awful frightened, mutter," you said afterwards; "but I said a prayer. I said, 'Oh, God, I do hate pigs,'" and that's just what I say now about that cantankerous worm the German Government. Of all the damned—"

"Oh, Bob!"

"Well, Marie, I can't help it. The people of Germany should either make their Government emigrate or else emigrate themselves. Yes, I'll tell you my little yarn. I was on our cattle-station, Winnanilla, in the back blocks, for three years on end, and pretty hard graft it was, what with bad seasons and the visitation of God generally. Then Gerald, my eldest brother, died, poor old boy, and left me a big share of his property. He always went in for sheep, and was the richest of us, though he never married. You know I always said as soon as I had a few coppers to spare I would come and see you. So the mater said she would come too and to let you know, didn't she?"

"I never got a line from her for nearly three years. But why didn't you write yourself, Bob?"

"Well, you see, Molly, when a fellow gets to be 26 he begins to feel a little shy."

"Oh, does he? I shouldn't have thought it," said Marie, laughing.

"No? Then it must be what they call compound reflex action. If you had given me the tips of your fingers, and said, 'How d'you do, Robert?' I would have told you I merely called in as I was passing, or some other thundering lie. But when you gave me your two hands, and smiled like an angel out of the blue—"

"Oh, go on with your story."

"I mean to . . . Well, we took the German boat from Sydney, and there was an old German lady on board that the mater agreed with at once; for, like the mater she has had all the complaints that are known to mankind, as well as a few that she patented on her own account. You may speak of eclective affinities and community of soul. But it seems to me that if people like the same sort of tablespoonfuls out of a bottle, well shaken, three times a day it makes a closer bond than anything else."

"I think you have grown rather disrespectful, Bob. But perhaps that is a symptom of shyness."

"Don't cheek your elders, Molly. The mater was really out of sorts on the voyage, and this old lady assured her that of all the cures in the known world the *mineral-bad* in Schandau was the best. So the mater wanted to go on there at once, but I insisted on staying a few hours in Dresden on the way, so as to look you up. But when I got to your old house in Christian-street, it was in possession of some Americans, who did not know whether you were alive or dead, only that you had left Dresden, and that 'Poppa'—it was a young lady who was speaking to me—paid the rent into some bank. She didn't know the name of the bank, and Poppa was away. So there was nothing for it but to go on with the mater to Schandau, and after settling her at the Kurhaus return to Dresden to go on with my en-quiries, which I did yesterday morning. But when I got to the Bristol there was a telegram from my mother awaiting me that she had sent half an hour after I started, asking me to return at once on most urgent business."

"And you went back by a steamer? But the train would have been so much quicker."

"So it would, but the long journey from Hamburg made me loathe German trains. They have a peculiar stuffiness that hypnotises me, and in a short time makes me feel as if I had vegetated in them since the earliest days of infancy. When I got on board that steamer full of garrulous peo-ple, who seemed as if they had never lost any one belonging to them, black melancholy fell on me. Molly is dead, I thought, or worse, she is married to some German professor who smokes all day and drinks beer the rest of the time. As for Hänslein and Fritz, they have doubtless been sacrificed to science in some way. This is the land of research and thrift.

"Suddenly the steamer stopped at Wehlen. Close to the landing-place I heard the familiar cry of a laughing jack. The moment I saw him I knew it was Hänslein, for there was the scar above the left eye that he got fight-ing with some wild beast of the Ephesus a week or two after I gave him to you, when he was a youngster fresh from the wilds of Queensland.

"Yes, nine years last May I remember I got back from Brisbane with Gerald after being away from England only four months. I had just turned 17, and when I went back to Eton I felt that I was a full-fledged man wasted among imps out of the nursery.

"Well, when I recognised Hans I rushed out and secured him on the impulse of the moment and scrambled back on board as the gangway was sliding back. I thought if Marie is anywhere about and as fond of this old mendicant as she used to be, she will send a policeman in search of the ab-ductor. At any rate she won't budge out of Wehlen until I can see what is up with the mater and then come back. So I left Schandau by the early steamer this morning. At Rathen a crooked little man with a basket got in who would not keep at the second-class end of the boat, but kept crossing the barrier fixing a basilisk gaze on Hans and myself. I found the primitive child of nature regarded me as a thief. But I gave him my forgiveness and a tip when he told me where you lived. And now, Molly, that part of my story is finished."

"And your mother? Was there anything wrong?"

"Only that the *mineral bad* had all at once disagreed with her and she was at death's door. But she would not say so in the telegram for fear that I would take no notice. You see that when any one has been in the jaws of death once a month, or oftener, for a good many years the event gets a little threadbare. But the mater forgot all her ailments this morning in the prospect of seeing you. And how long will it take you to get ready?"

A little over three weeks after this interview Marie was at the Wehlen railway station with her Australian kinsfolk. When the train from Dresden came in sight the mother and son retreated into the background, not wishing to obtrude themselves during the first moments of the meeting between father and daughter. The train stopped, and out hurried Dr. Schumann looking younger and more alert than he had looked for years.

"Do you know, Marie, I have had such a splendid holiday," were his first words.

"That article of mine for the *New Yorker* must be written all over at once. I am so full of ideas that when you touch me I feel them flowing over like electricity out of a cat's back. The new title will be 'The Conditions of Labor in Germany.'"

Marie smiling radiantly, though the tears were thick in her eyes, said softly as she held her father's hands in hers—

"But thou would'st not alone

Be saved my father! alone

Conquer and come to thy goal,

Still thou turned'st and still

Gavest the weary thy hand."

Teresa's Betrothal:
A Tale of the Coral Fishery

Chapter I

"Yes, last year was bad for us, but this season will be worse," said Lucia Biondi, while her knitting needles clicked sharply as she knitted with surprising rapidity in the Italian fashion—that is with one of the needles stuck into a wooden sheath fixed in her waist-band—as she worked off the stitches with the other needles.

Her daughter Teresa, sitting on the door-step, was also knitting in the same rapid manner; she lifted her eyes for a moment when her mother spoke, but she made no reply.

"Instead of adding to the little store in the Banca di Risparmio," went on Lucia, "we shall before the winter is over have to draw some out."

"But now that father is getting well again things will go better," said the daughter after a short silence, broken only by the click of her own and her mother's needles. Each was engaged in closing a long, stout, masculine stocking of the knickerbocker kind.

On a massive old walnut table in the middle of the room three pairs of the same kind were completed, and lying on a large napkin of coarse homespun linen of snowy whiteness.

"Yes, your father is getting stronger," said the mother slowly, her brow puckered with care, "but his malaria during the greater part of the harvest was a grand misfortune, and he still needs strong, nourishing food; our bread soup and mezzo-vino are not enough for him, and the good red wine that cost only 30 centesimi when I was a girl is now 70 centesimi the fiasco. That is why I thought it so kind of Antonio. Oh, I did not tell you.

Well, when I met him this morning he said when he kills his baracchio on Wednesday he will send us half a quarter."

At the mention of Antonio's name the girl's face visibly hardened. "Antonio had better keep his veal to himself, we are not such beggars that we need take charity from him," she said, knitting with such excited haste that she dropped a stitch or two, and bent more intently over her work to repair the mischief.

"Pride out of place is like a fire of straw; it makes a flame but boils no water," said the mother severely. "We need friends, and when we find them, we should thank God and the saints instead of using our tongues like a wasp. It is not only your father's long illness that makes us so poor, but everything has failed us more or less—from the grapes to the artichokes, from the hens to the silkworms, and all the time the taxes are going up like a river in flood. If their excellencies could help us, they would, but the House of Contarini has been in the hands of the Hebrews for generations, like sheep at shearing time."

While Lucia spoke she was knitting all the time very rapidly, until she had come to the actual closing of the stocking toes, when the nature of her operation made her movements more slow. Teresa, who was keeping time with her mother, glancing now and then to see how near she was to the finish, rose as the latter ceased speaking. The girl seemed impatient of more details as to the poverty of the family, and went out into the intensely-cultivated field that surrounded the cottage. She returned in a few minutes saying she had finished, and gave her mother the completed stocking.

"They are good," said Lucia, stretching her own and Teresa's handiwork to their fullest extent as she spoke, "and now you had better take them to the Palazzo, and be sure you tell uncle 'Menico that you want to see the Marchesa herself, and not the Contessa, who always looks for faults, and has a tongue like a pair of scissors . . . Well, now, Teresa, it is November, and you know the winter is the step-mother of the poor. If by any chance, you meet Antonio."

"If I do I shall cross over to the other side," replied the girl hotly; "I know very well, mother, why you go on so about our poverty. But if Antonio had all the wool of Foggia, and all the wheat of Tuscany, and if I had to beg a crust of black bread on the highway, I will never be his sposa."

Without waiting to hear what her mother might say in reply, Teresa hurried up the steep stone stairs that led to the upper part of the cottage, which was one of three rooms. The kitchen in which Lucia stood folding up the stockings was the centre and chief part of the dwelling. From the low raftered ceiling hung some small hams and scores of bunches of grapes, the latter proclaiming that the vintage was well over. Along one side of the room high up ran a wooden shelf, on which were some loaves made of "Gran Turco" (Indian corn), and several small round cheeses made of ewe's milk, known as "formaggio di pecora." A loom stood by the window, and in the recess between it and the fireplace hung cooking utensils of copper, that gleamed without a speck to dim their lustre.

A small fire smouldered on the open hearth, over which a large iron pot was suspended on a stout hook and chain. A walnut bench with a straight carved back, two or three chairs, and cane stools, a small bed under the stairs, and a large walnut sideboard of antique design, constituted the principal contents of the room. The latter piece of furniture was an heirloom, for which a fashionable dealer in bric-a-brac would have given a handsome sum of money. But though Lucia was not free from avarice, it is more than likely that she would have withstood the temptation, for she belonged to a stock of contadini who were accustomed to hold by their ancestral possessions from one generation to another.

It was indeed owing to her high spirit that Lucia's own family now occupied a status midway between peasant proprietors and day laborers. After her marriage twenty years before, she had found it intolerable to live with the Biondis in an establishment where her husband was the youngest of five brothers, all married and living together with a determined old mother, who ruled the household with a rod of iron. On leaving the parental roof Lucia and her husband leased the cottage they now occupied with rather less than an acre of land. However, though there were five of them to keep for the last fifteen years—father, mother, and three children, of whom Teresa, aged 19, was the eldest—the produce of this patch of ground, eked out with working for others, enabled them not only to make both ends meet, but also to deposit a little in the Banca di Risparmio (savings bank) from year to year. But of late, as may have been gathered from Lucia's discourse, reverses had overtaken them, and this, with other reasons, made the mother anxious that Teresa should look with favour on Antonio Vanucci, the prosperous middle-aged widower, who had proposed himself as a son-in-law to Lucia a few weeks ago.

"But no, it is clear she will not listen to him," the latter reflected, as her daughter disappeared up the little staircase. "I cannot force the cards. Ah, Dio mio, Dio mio, how girls seem to be sent into the world to do the wrong thing. It is as I feared—her heart is set on that young birbone Carlo Sperani, who went into the army a pious country boy, and came back from Africa, after three years, a hot tempered soldier, who used his knife on a Christian instead of cutting up pigs. I wish he had been caught and put into prison; but who knows? That might only have made her more in love with him than before. Apoplexy on the evil spirits that make things go so contrary."

Lucia's despondent train of thought was interrupted by Teresa's return ready to go out. Though her costume—a red and blue skirt, turned up over a full white petticoat, a narrow bright apron, and a gay kerchief on her shoulders—was not indicative of the fine instinct for colour, once innate in her race, yet the vivid tints enhanced her good looks. Her glossy black hair, crisply waved, her straight profile, sparkling dark eyes, the dusky carnation of her cheeks, and slim, graceful figure made her a most attractive looking girl. Lucia's eyes rested on her with an expression of pride, though she still maintained an air of displeasure as she gave Teresa the stockings neatly folded in the linen napkin, saying as she did so, "When the Marchesa asks after your father, tell her that, though he is with Beppo, finishing the vintage at Antonio Vanucci's, he is not at all well. If you call at your Aunt Gina's shop, tell your sister that if she is wanted she can stay a few days longer. And tell your uncle Menico that he is to be sure to come and eat a grain of rice with us on Sunday."

A few minutes after Teresa left her home, the Angelus bells began to ring in her native town of Estvecchio, and the sound was taken up by the villages around, until the air was charged for a little time with the varied cadences of bells, far off and near at hand, some softly muffled, others clear and loud, but all mellowed by much use for many long years. Teresa murmured an Ave Maria, and as she did so, her eyes strayed towards the Adriatic, whose grey-blue waters, seen through the softly undulating hills, made the eastern horizon luminous. For Estvecchio is near the southern border of that region which lies between the Adriatic and the Sibylline range of the Apennines.

It is a country that even with the primitive modes of agriculture which still largely prevail, brings forth wheat and maize, grapes and olives in abundance. Chestnut, mulberry, and walnut trees grow everywhere; silkworms are reared by gentle and simple alike. Great dove coloured oxen draw quaint old waggons among the harvest fields and along the highways with the tranquil bearing of creatures that are as yet remote from the vulgar hurry of modern life.

The Biondi cottage stood at the eastern extremity of Estvecchio, which is one of those feudal looking places, whose massive walls and many towers crumbling into decay carry one straight into the middle ages. But they had no railways and daily mails in mediaeval times, and now Estvecchio can boast of both these emblems of progress. The post-office, it is true, is in what was once an old convent, but the street side has a smart new front that in part redeems the building from being hopelessly picturesque. It faces the Piazza Garibaldi, and along the lower story there is a colonnade, which is a great resort for idlers at all times and seasons. But Teresa, who went some distance out of her way to call at the post-office, did not pause among the idlers, nor look to the right hand, or to the left, as she went direct to the Poste Restante window and asked if there was a letter for her. When after a few moments, the official returned with one, the girl's cheeks flamed like a pomegranate blossom.

"Happy news to you," said a young man of her acquaintance as she was turning away. Teresa nodded and smiled by way of answer, and then crossed the piazza to the Via Pio Cinque, the half-deserted street in which the Palazzo was situated. Here she opened her letter, and read it as she walked slowly on.

"Carissima—I am safe and well away here in the mountains among friends. My trouble is that I cannot count the days or months until we meet. A comrade here, his name is Tista Lomelli, is going to the coral fishing at Easter, and I am going with him. Tista was there last year, and he is going this season in the same boat. We shall be away on the coast of Barbary from April to the end of September. I shall come back with 300 lire, we shall have a handsome wedding, and my good old uncle and aunt will be glad to give us a roof and a welcome. My uncle will have to hire a man while I am away. Before I got here I heard that villain Giorgio was on the piazza as well as ever in less than a fortnight, and yet for that scratch given to him because he drew his knife against a man who was too weak to take his own part, I must hide away like a church thief. That is what comes of having a Sindaco who knows no more of justice than a pig does of sculpture. Sometimes I feel as if I could cry with four eyes through anger. But do not be afraid, Carina, I promised you that night before I ran away that I would give up being a passionate man, and may I live the life of an ass and die the death of a dog if I am not faithful to you in all things till the day of my death."

The tears were thick in Teresa's eyes when she got to the end of this letter. "The coast of Barbary," she said half aloud with a confused remembrance of legends concerning ferocious Moors and Christian captives heavily chained in dungeons, without a ray of light. And when would she see Carlo—if ever again? Her heart sank, and the tears fairly overflowed until she was obliged to wipe them away with the corner of her apron. Then she said to herself sternly that it was a disgrace to cry in public. "Carlo is brave and he loves me," she thought, and the certainty of this revived her spirits and brought back her courage. She carefully dried her eyes and furtively kissing the letter thrust it into her bosom.

For she was now drawing near to what was always known in Estvecchio as "The Palazzo," though the mansion was far from being the sole building in the town to which the title was allowed. But this one belonged to the Contarini, who had been the great people of the place for many centuries, being in point of fact, one of the sixty patrician families inscribed on the tables of the Capitol. The Contarini had in the days of their power ruled a province; given princes to the church, counsellors to kings, ambassadors to foreign Powers, and led armies to battle. But gradually they had dwindled in wealth and importance. Filippo Contarini, the present head of the sept, was still marchese of the Holy Empire, Baron of Coromila, and Chevalier of the Order of Constantine. But his only remaining estate running up to the eastern walls of the city, and on which the Biondi cottage was situated, had come to him so heavily mortgaged, that it seemed only a question of time when it should pass into the hands of strangers. The castle of Coromila, 30 miles away, was now a grey mouldering pile, with broken towers and dismantled chambers, in the midst of a malaria-haunted plain that was a marsh in winter and a sea of dust in summer.

By comparison to this "The Palazzo," in Estvecchio, was a cheerful building. A wide flight of marble steps led from the street to the huge nail-studded door, above which extended balconies and rows of tall grated windows. Teresa rang a bell at a postern door, and was admitted by an old retainer, who greeted her affectionately, being the Uncle Menico (Dominic), to whom Lucia had sent a message. He was the uncle of Teresa's father, and for many years butler at "The Palazzo," having been born and reared in the service of the family. He was a small, thin old man, in a very shabby undress uniform. But to-day his eyes were shining, and his cheeks were flushed with unwonted excitement. Menico had never married, and Teresa, who was his figlioccia (god-daughter) had always been a special favourite with him. He led her to his little office-room in the basement storey, saying, "I thought you would be here to-day, carina. The Marchesa has been very much engaged since yesterday afternoon, but she will see you. This is a great time for us, and I will tell you what has happened, but you must speak of it only to your father and mother, until their excellencies tell the news themselves. You know the beautiful American lady that Don Capitano Luglio married?"

"Oh, yes, the one who was here last June with a Bambino as lovely as an angel."

"Well, her father is dead, and has left her more money than two Jew bankers could count from sunrise to sunset. The first thing the Donna

Beatrice is going to do with her millions is to redeem the Contarini estates. The news reached us only yesterday. And that is not all; the Capitano is ordered with his regiment to Genoa, and they are coming here on their way from Naples. Put these few biscotti into your pocket, my child, and go and wait in the Serpentine corridor, I will tell the Marchesa you are there."

Teresa crossed the wide mosaic-paved hall and ascended the great white marble staircase to that part of the second story that her uncle indicated. It was a corridor that ran between the state rooms and some of those in daily use. The former were for the most part great lofty saloons with polished carpetless floors, and no furniture more modern than that of the last century. But there were some beautiful old pictures on the walls; among them a sweet-faced Madonna and child by Perugino. Teresa, who knew every room and nook of the palace from childhood, stole in passing into the room in which the painting hung. A few years before she had been in some girlish grief one day when she sat at "The Palazzo" and had prayed to this Madonna for help, and what she prayed for had come to pass. In the old days the trouble had been her mother's refusal to let her take part in a carnival procession. But now her sorrow was a part of that poignant tragedy that underlies all human affairs. She was in terror of lifelong separation from her lover—of deadly peril for him by land and sea.

"Oh, Madonna, mia, madre di misericordia, abbiate pieta di me," she cried, sinking on her knees before the Madonna. Sobs choked her utterance, while the tears that she had so forcibly checked, ran down her face like summer rain. She was startled by a low exclamation near her, and starting up she stood face to face with the Marchesa.

"My poor child, you are in some trouble; what is it?" said the Marchesa softly. Teresa's first impulse was to tell her whole story. But she was restrained by that practical fibre which is seldom absent from the nature of Italians, even when they seem most ardent. She knew that in the few months that had elapsed since Carlo returned, after serving his time in the army, he had in one way or another gained the reputation of being rather reckless, and she reflected rapidly that the Marchesa would be more likely to serve her if she knew nothing of the attachment between herself and the young man. So she compromised matters by saying that she was in trouble because her mother wanted her to be Antonio Vanucci's spouse.

"My mother, I know, is uneasy, because my father's health is not good, and the season is bad; I do want to help them, excellency, but not in that way," she said in conclusion.

"And so you asked the Madonna to help you, poverina? and so she will, child," said the Marchesa kindly. "Come into my salotto for a little," she added, leading the way into the serpentine corridor, so called from the marble with which it was wainscoted. As they passed through it the folding doors of one of the staterooms stood open and the sound of voices was heard within.

"They are getting it ready for Captain Luglio and his wife, they are to be with us to-morrow," said the Marchesa in a voice of quiet gladness. She entered the room for a few minutes, giving some directions to the two maids who were at work there, and Teresa looked in at the door, admiring the tapestried and panelled walls, the beds canopied and curtained with faded silk brocade, the sheets and pillow-slips trimmed with fine Venetian lace and embroidered with the family arms.

"They cannot stay long with us," said the Marchesa, as she came out and went on to her salotto, a little sitting-room on the opposite side of the corridor. "But the Donna Beatrice, my daughter-in-law, has written to ask whether there is a good healthy young girl among our coloni that

I could recommend, and let her have as an assistant nurse. Mariuccia is not as young as she was, and the dear Bambino is beginning to run about like a cicala."

"Oh, excellency, would I do? I am so strong, and I love the beautiful Bambino with all my heart; could I go with them to Genoa?"

"You are the very one that I should like to recommend if your mother would let you go so far," answered the Marchesa, smiling. "The Donna Beatrice is kindness itself, and she will pay you well; so you see, Teresina, it is a good thing to go to the Madonna with your trouble," added the Marchesa, as she noted the eager joy of the girl's face.

"Oh, I am sure my mother will let me go, excellency. I will tell her as soon as I get home, and these are the stockings for the signore; we finished them this afternoon."

As she spoke Teresa presented the bundle of stockings, which were part of the rent paid annually in kind by the Biondis for the cottage and land they occupied.

The Marchesa looked at them and praised their quality and work-manship. "No others wear so well for hunting," she said as she touched a bell-rope. When Menico appeared, in response to this summons, she directed him to give Teresa a fiasco of Vin Santo for her father, and sent a message to Lucia that she was to come to the Palazzo on the morrow.

It was some time after dark when Teresa got home. The tall earthen-ware lamp, with two wicks in a boat-shaped cup, half full of oil, was alight, and the father and mother and Beppo (Guiseppe), a tall, slender lad of 17, were seated at supper. Teresa placed the fiasco on the table, and delivered the Marchesa's message regarding the same. Her father, a dark, grave man, with silvering hair, called for glasses, and pouring some wine out for each, raised his own, saying, "To the health of her excellency." Teresa sipped some wine and water, being too much excited to touch the dish of smoking polenta that her mother placed before her until she had told the story of the sudden wealth of the Contarini family.

"And so the American heretic of no birth is going to build up the fortunes of the house once more," said the father, meditatively.

"Ah, but yes, the good red gold of the Signora Marchesina will make up to the family for her not having forefathers from the time of the flood," said Lucia, who had received the news with the keenest interest. "And besides," she added as she rose from the table, "the Donna Beatrice is turning a good Christian. Ever since the Bambino was born they say she goes to mass."

"And now she wants an assistant nurse for him," said Teresa, speaking to her mother in a low quiet voice; "a strong young girl of good character that the Marchesa could recommend."

"Who told you that?" asked Lucia with vivid interest.

"The Marchesa herself."

"Has she yet fixed on a girl?"

"If you are willing, she will recommend me," replied Teresa in a voice that was low, because of her extreme agitation, though outwardly she maintained an unmoved demeanor, being anxious that her mother should have no inkling of the fact that to go to Genoa and be there at Easter was the dearest wish of her heart.

"Eh, but that is kind of her excellency," said Lucia slowly, and then, after a thoughtful pause, turning to her husband, she said, "Our Teresina is a prudent girl, and the donna would be good to her; what better could happen to us in this hard season?"

Tommaso Biondi, who was filling a small black clay pipe, made no reply for a few moments. Pressing the dry, light-coloured tobacco into the bowl, he placed a small coal off the hearth in it, and smoked at the cane stem until a spiral column of smoke floated around him. Then, looking full at his daughter, he said, "What does Teresina think of going so far away?"

"I would like to go," answered Teresa, in the same quiet voice in which she had spoken before.

An hour later Teresa sat in the little chamber which she usually shared with her younger sister Giulia, who was now staying for a few days with an aunt, whose husband had a drogheria (druggist and grocery shop) in the town. The room was also used for storing things in it, and the winter supply of potatoes, maize, tomatoes, and lupins, were ranged in piles at one end. Before the little square window there was a tiny and rather shaky wooden balcony, in which were hung on big nails, red peppers, black melons, and yellowish-grey cantaloupes, as these things keep better in the open air.

Teresa stood at the tall walnut chest in which the best clothes of the family were kept, writing a letter to Carlo, telling him how she was going to Genoa in a few days, and would be there when he came at Easter. It took her a long time to write this letter, for though she had been as long as Carlo at the communal school, she did not write nearly as well as he did, for he had been further taught in the army. "It is like the scratching of a fowl," she thought as she surveyed her rather blotted epistle. But the piece of taper she had saved for more than four weeks so that she might write to Carlo when she had heard from him, was burning low, and so she had to finish rather abruptly.

Chapter II

"Easter came early that year. So from the day of Giovanni di Dio—that is, from the 8th of March—Teresa began to look for Carlo in Genoa. Early in December, he had made his way to the state that is still known in Italy as the patrimony of St. Peter, and had taken service as a sailor in a felucca, trading between Civita Vecchia and Naples. So he would come by sea from the former port, on some day between the 6th of March and Holy Thursday, fourteen days later.

Several letters had passed between the two during the months that had elapsed since Teresa left her home. From the first day that she had seen the wealth and beauty and great commerce of Genoa, she had cherished the wish that Carlo should seek work there, instead of entering on such a perilous undertaking as this was. She had picked up a good deal of information regarding the matter; for Pietro, the coachman, had a brother who was once in the trade, and his sufferings were those of purgatory—bad food and cruelly hard work under a padrone, who had the nature of a demon. To which Carlo had replied, that Teresa must pay no heed to such pappolate (stupid stories), and who was Pietro that she should be talking to him about their private affairs?

"Pietro is my very good friend," replied Teresa, promptly, "and so is Concetta, his wife, who lives in a little street behind the Via Balbi, a stone's throw from our palazzo. They have one little girl four years old, who often comes with me and Mariuccia, when we take the Bambino out in his little carriage, lined with blue velvet. Pietro and Concetta say you must come to their place as soon as you land. The address is Vico Senatega, No. 27, and the fourth story. Concetta is a sarta (tailoress), and sometimes earns more money than Pietro, by making costumes for marionettes. She is a Tuscan, and was maid to Donna Beatrice for years before either was married. The Donna is very fond of her, and allows me to go to her two or three—sometimes four—evenings, each week, for when the Bambino is asleep there is nothing for me to do, and Mariuccia is always there if he wakes, but he hardly ever does till morning. In this way I am beginning to be quick with my needle; in one hour I can sometimes dress a general, a princess, and a pulcinello, for it is only the outside bits of satin and stuff; there is nothing under. I can run from the back gate of our palazzo to Concetta's while I count 50. That is why you must come there as soon as you land; for if it is at night, when Pietro is at home—and he is nearly always at home after 7 during Lent—he will come and tell me, and if it is in the daytime Concetta will come."

It was neither Pietro nor his wife, however, who brought the news of Carlo's arrival. It was Nina, their four-year-old little daughter, who came late in the afternoon of the Tuesday before Holy Thursday to say that mamma wanted to see Teresina, if she could be spared. Teresa and Mariuccia had just returned from the Giardino Acquasola, where they had been for a couple of hours in the balmy air of early spring, with the young heir of the ancient house of Contarini, and the grandson of the late Joshua B. Briggs, late pork butcher of Chicago. Donna Beatrice, only child of the latter, came into the day nursery a few minutes after the message reached Teresa; and in reply to the girl's timid request, at once gave her leave to go to Concetta for two hours.

"Has anyone come to see me, Nannina?" asked Teresa, as they were crossing the courtyard to the postern-gate that opened on the Vico Senatega.

"There is a strange signor, and as soon as he came mamma sent me for you," said Nana. This left no doubt in Teresa's mind as to who the visitor was, so when she came to No. 27 she rang lustily at the door, and when it was opened from above in the fashion of tenement dwellings in Italy, she called to Nana to close the door, and rushed up the long, steep stairs with the swiftness of a fawn. And there, half-way, was Carlo, tall and bronzed, with brilliant eyes and flushed cheeks, holding out his hands to her, and on seeing this the blood rushed hotly over her face. Then there was a silence, broken by low words of endearment, until Nana, whose tiny feet would not carry her very fast upstairs, joined the two, and looking from one to the other, said gravely—

"Is that your uncle come to see you, 'Rina?" for Nana's experience did not as yet travel beyond the range of blood relations. At this enquiry the two laughed merrily, and when Concetta heard the joke she joined in their mirth. She had the table spread very invitingly, with a snowy linen cloth, on which was ranged a pretty little coffee service, a wedding gift from Donna Beatrice, and a large pan-forte cake, brought by Carlo.

"Madonna, santissima, what a long time it is since we parted," he said, looking at Teresa, as if he could not take his eyes away from her face.

"And no sooner are you here than you will be gone again," said Teresa, who even in the first joy of meeting could not help counting the days until her betrothed should set sail for that African coast, where wild storms and all kinds of hardships might await him. "Could you not stay here and get work for a few months, and then go back to your uncle Carlino?" she said timidly resting her fingers on his sinewy brown hand.

"But to talk like that is folly, Teresina," he replied, knitting his brows, "a bargain is a bargain, and not to be made on Monday and broken on Tuesday. Tista, the son of Lomelli, said to me early last November, after I got to Altacqua, where his family gave me a hearty welcome, and food and shelter, 'Will you come with me to the coral fishing on the Barbary coast? I was there last year, and came back with two hundred and fifty lire. If I get as much this season, Leila, the daughter of Matteo, the carabiniere, will marry me before the day of San Bastiano.' And I said to him, 'Good; I, too, want to give a wedding feast before the Day of San Bastiano, and I will not return to my uncle empty-handed, after putting him to the cost of a hired man for so long.' I could get work in Genoa. Yes, but what is earned to-day is gone to-morrow. Even if you sleep in a basso (cellar-room) it costs so much each week, and whether it is Saturday or Sunday your soldi are always melting away. But there, far at sea, it is quite another thing."

"What Carlo says is true," chimed in Concetta, "better give the wool than the sheep, as we say. But now come to the table and eat and drink together, and thank God and your patron saints, that you are both so young and strong."

When they had drunk coffee and eaten of the panforte, Concetta and Nana went out to do some marketing, and then the lovers talked together more confidentially. Carlo took a little red box out of his breast pocket, and told Teresa to open it, and when she did so she gave a cry of delight, for it contained a pretty set of coral ornaments, and a chased silver ring with a little coral heart set in the centre. When Teresa replaced the small earnings she usually wore by the long, graceful coral ones, arranged the coral pins in her glossy hair, and clasped the necklet round her throat, she looked at herself in the hand-mirror that lay in Concetta's work-basket, and laughed with pleasure, saying, "Madonna mia, but this is such a good day, I must not complain of anything for a year to come."

"In less than a year we shall be married," said Carlo, as he slipped the little silver ring on the third finger of Teresa's right hand. "By the time I come back," he went on, "that foolish affair with Giorgio will be quite forgotten, and our wedding must be between the Nativity and the day of San Sebastin, the 25th of January, and no one can say it had better be otherwise."

"But, Carlino, I think I had better not tell my mother until you come back," said Teresa hesitatingly.

"But why, carina?"

"I will tell you," answered Teresa, "the Donna Beatrice is going to make the villeggiatura at Estvecchio this summer. If my mother knew that we are fidanzate, and you still far away without land or money, she would be full of gloom, and each time she saw me she would say a new proverb made by old people, who are wise but have a hard heart. She would say "Far from the eye and far from the heart," or "The proud go away on horseback and come on foot," or "Hope is the cat that licks the hand and scratches the back."

"But, Teresina," interrupted Carlo laughing, "if you say all those hard old things it is the same as if your mother said them."

"No, because when you are here I don't believe them," said Teresa promptly, "but when you are on the wild sea and I hear nothing of you for weeks and weeks, for you are to be away so long."

"Our signed agreement is from the 25th of March to the 29th of September," replied Carlo, "but don't think of that just now, think only of the seven long whole days on which we can see each other before I sail."

"From the Annunciation of the blessed Madonna to the festa of San Michele, ah, it is a long time," murmured Teresa, and seeing the shade of sadness that had fallen on her face Carlo comforted her in lover fashion.

"But, my heart, I will tell the Donna that we are betrothed," said Teresa, after a little silence. "For she is of the kindest, and if she knows we shall have more time together while you are here."

Teresa was not in error in saying that the Donna Beatrice was of the "kindest." When she heard the girl's story she had an interview with Carlo, and was so much pleased with his appearance and bearing, and the candid account he gave of the affair that got him into trouble, that she became his partisan on the spot.

"My little boy will cry his eyes out when Teresina leaves him," she said, "but you must have your wedding as soon as you return, and may you have good luck and fair winds all the months you are away."

In the meantime Teresa was spared from her duties for a part of each day, until the date of Carlo's departure. During these days the pair went up and down the city, among the streets and squares, palaces and churches, that rise in a semi-circle from the shore like the seats of a great amphitheatre. On Venerdi Santo (Holy Friday) they went to San Lorenzo and knelt side by side among the vast crowd that thronged the great Cathedral, while the offices of the Tenebrae were sung. And when the darkness gradually deepened, while the lights were extinguished, Teresa let fall the tears that were often ready to come when she kept a smiling face. When they were going out she led the way to a side-chapel, whose altarpiece, like all the other paintings on that day, was draped in black.

"It is a beautiful Madonna with the Bambino in her arms," she whispered, "and all the time you are away, Carlo, I will come here and pray for your safe return."

Then she dropped on her knees in front of the altar, and Carlo, whose usually buoyant spirits were affected by the solemn gloom that pervaded the city in memory of our Lord's crucifixion, also knelt down and devoutly repeated a prayer, beginning, "O, madre mia, dolcissima, non permette ch'io perda Dio." (O, my sweetest mother, do not permit that I shall lose God.)

On the next day they went down to the harbour, and watched some great ocean steamers going out, and others coming in, and when they looked at the far heights of the Apennines away to the north, they recalled the days of their childhood, in their quiet homes beyond these mountains, and talked wistfully of the day when Carlo's boat should safely sail into port.

But Easter Monday was so joyful—bells ringing, flowers everywhere, and the streets crowded with holiday-makers—that when Teresa joined Carlo and the Pietro family they both forgot for a time that their parting was so near. They walked for a time in the spacious Acquaverde, where the band was playing, and in the evening they went to the theatre Paganini, where they enjoyed Goldoni's "La Locandiera," from the moment that the curtain rose until it fell amid deafening applause.

On the day after that the coral fishing fleet sailed away from Sestri Ponente, Teresa had the whole day to herself, and went with Carlo, Concetta, and Nana by the 7 o'clock train to the little town, which is about five miles to the west of Genoa. They went at this early hour so as to be present at the blessing of the boats, when the priests and acolytes went in procession from one boat to the other, sprinkling them with holy water and intoning prayers for their safety in storm and calm. The fleet numbered 16, and were all owned by a wealthy firm of Genoa, who equipped the boats and sent them, some to Sardinia, some to Corsica, and others to Senacca, the great coral banks off the southern coast of Italy, where of late years so much coral has been fished. Five were going to Barbary, or the Algerian coast, and of these Carlo's boat was the largest. This contingent, for some reason connected with consular papers, was, contrary to expectation, prevented from sailing until the afternoon.

"That gives us four more hours together," said Carlo, on learning this; "we could take a turn to the Pallavicini grounds."

But Teresa was too much interested in the departure of the boats, and Concetta agreed with her that it was better to remain at Sestri. So they watched the barques, one after the other lifting anchor, while groups of friends and relations—a large proportion of them women and children—stood on the shore, throwing handfuls of salt water and sand, as each vessel glided away, and crying out, "May she fish in safety, and return full;" "May the Madonna be with her day and night;" "May she sail like a barque of the angels, and come back with rose-red coral."

There were mothers and wives and sweethearts who tried in vain to keep back their tears, but they all tried to smile as they uttered their wishes for "bon auguri" (good luck), because to weep when speaking these would have been an evil omen. It was a pretty sight to see the boats, as they scattered over the azure waves of the Mediterranean, some with snowy sails, some a pale yellow, others a vivid red, striped with black; while many were adorned with moon faces, star-fish, sea-serpents, mermaids, and other mythological monsters of the sea.

"Now shall I sing 'Sul balcon della mia bella,' little one? for you are looking too serious," said Carlo as Teresa stood in a prolonged silence, with her eyes riveted on the retreating fleet.

"I was saying a prayer for all of them," she said simply.

"Ah, yes, there will be women thinking of these fishers day and night, but will they all return?" said Concetta softly.

"Perhaps not, but don't begin to bury us while we are still warm in the sunshine of the spring," said Carlo, in his blithe, melodious voice. "Come and look at my boat. L'Allodola (the lark), she is close to the wharf there; you can step on board without any trouble, there will be hardly anyone on board for an hour or two."

L'Allodola was a little schooner of seventeen tons, with a crew all told of nine men and one boy. There were a few of the fishermen on board, among them Carlo's friend Gianbattista, or Tistalomelli. He knew that Teresa was his friend's fidanzata, and greeted her like an old acquaintance. He went with them over the boat and explained that the great piles of hemp which were heaped on the deck were for making the coral-nets, which were strong of texture, with wide meshes. He showed them the fishing machine, which consisted of two strong beams of hard wood, fastened together with metal clasps, in the form of a cross, with a stone of about 70 pounds fixed at the centre. The nets, four in number, each 18 yards long and one wide, are fastened to the arms. When the boat reaches a coral bank, the machine is lowered and moved up and down against the submarine rocks, by means of a capstan, turned by the whole of the boat's crew, except the padrone, who directs the movements of the operations by means of a second rope, which is attached to the chief one, some feet above the point where the latter is secured to the centre of the cross. The coral branches are caught in the meshes of the nets, and remain hanging in them, until with great straining and tugging, the crew draw the nets on deck.

"If the coral is jet-black or the colour of the heart of a rose," said Tista, "there is great rejoicing, and perhaps a handful of macaroni is put into the soup that evening."

"And when you do not have good fortune, what do you have in your soup?" asked Teresa.

"Garlic and pepperoni boiled in water with some olive oil put to it. This is where we make our soup," said Tista, opening the door of a galley as he spoke, and showing them a stove with an open hearth on top with a great iron pot hanging above it. "We break these up and pour the soup over them," he added, holding up a large and very coarse kind of sea biscuit as he spoke.

"And no meat or coffee or erba or polenta?" said Teresa.

Tista smiled and shrugged his shoulders. "When the weather is bad," he said, "we do not make even pepperoni soup; we just spread a little oil on the biscuits and take a draught of water, and sometimes the water is such that we must take it through our closed teeth, so as not to swallow too many of the strange creatures that God has made."

"But L'Allodola is a splendid boat, and always has good luck," interrupted Carlo, who was not anxious that his betrothed should hear too much of the prospective hardships of his lot.

"Body of Bacchus, don't say that," ejaculated a grizzled fisherman, who overheard the young man's boast; and as the old fellow spoke, he made the sign of the horns with his fingers to ward off the evil eye. "We have a new padrone this trip, a Sicilian, and there he comes," he added, pointing to a short thick-set man with a very dark flushed face, who was coming along the wharf, and came on board, followed by two or three of the crew.

"We had better leave now," whispered Concetta, and Carlo invited Tista to come and dine with them. As the little party left the boat, the padrone's glittering black eyes rested with bold admiration on Teresa's face. She afterwards remembered that she could not help shuddering when she met his eyes.

They went to an osteria facing the sea, where they had dinner, and gave alms to a wandering musician, who played the mandoline and sang a mournful love-song in a pathetic baritone that brought the tears into the eyes of all the rest, while Teresa sat smiling and dry-eyed, feeling that if she allowed herself the smallest emotion she would be overwhelmed with a storm of weeping. The skipper's face was like an evil dream to her: and the sight of the poor, rough, little ship, with all that Tista had said lay heavy on her heart. "But the Madonna has helped me so often, and now this is the greatest thing of all that Carlo should come safe back; no, she will not forsake me," she thought, while outwardly she smiled when Carlo caught up a strain of the love song and pledged her in a glass of old Chianti.

After dinner the two strolled away, apart for a little time. "Carlino, promise me that you will not quarrel with that Sicilian padrone," said Teresa, as they paused where L'Allodola and her companions lay full before them.

"Of course not, carina. Where the mule has fallen once he does not stumble again."

"But it may be very hard for you," said the girl gravely. "Say a little prayer every day, even if it is only Gesu, Ave Maria, gloria. I will have plenty of time, and I will say longer prayers for you every day."

Carlo, whose voice was far from being steady, made the required promise with solemn gravity. An hour or two later L'Allodola and her sister barks sailed away towards the east.

Chapter III

About a month after Carlo left Teresa got a letter posted from the Algerian port at which they had landed to pay the tax levied by the French Government for fishing in these waters. "We had fine weather," he wrote, "and made our nets on the voyage. Tista has not been well; he and the Padrone had angry words more than once. The last Padrone of L'Allodola was a good man, but this one is very different and hardly anyone likes him. To me also he spoke with much insolence twice; but I remembered my promise to you and answered not back. And to Tista I gave good advice, and said to him one of your mother's proverbs, "He who wants eggs must bear with the cackling of the hens."

"The Algerian reefs we fish are divided into ten portions and only one is fished each year, as it takes ten years for the coral to grow. The reefs we are going to this year are famous for their good coral, and they say we are likely to have a good season. The food is not so bad; after supper we often tell tales to each other and sing. One of us plays the guitar, and the song I like best I have learned and will sing to you when I come back. Here it is—

> 'Palomba che per l'aria va a volare,
>
> Ferma che voglio dirti due parole,
>
> Voglio cavà una penna a le tue ale,
>
> Voglio scrive una lettera al mio amore,
>
> Tutta di sangue la voglio stampare,
>
> Per sigillo le metto lo mio core;
>
> E finita de scrive e sigillare,

Palomba, portacella a lo mio amore,

E se lo trovi in letto a riposare,

O Palomba riposati tu ancore.'"

"A vessel will come to us with fresh water, ropes, and provisions at the end of July. You can send me a letter by that to the care of the Genoa firm; it will be the only time I can hear from you, but I may get a chance now and then to send you a line by a passing boat."

Teresa read this letter until she knew it by heart. Before the time came for her to write she went with her mistress to Estvecchio for part of the summer. She was overjoyed when she saw once more the cathedral dome and the towers and campanili of her birthplace, as the train rushed towards it on the golden afternoon of a cloudless day of mid-June. She had thought Genoa so splendid, with its grand churches and marble palaces, its harbour thronged with ships, and its streets crowded with men and women. But how much lovelier she now found this quiet old city, set in a table-land where corn and olives and chestnuts were ripening day by day; where all the fields and lanes were trellised with a network of vine leaves; where the Sibylline hills rose in wooded beauty on one side, and the Adriatic, with the azures of the Madonna's robe, glowed on the other. Her absence for seven months from her own country and people made everything so dear to Teresa that when she saw the women spinning with their distaffs at the doors, and caught sight of the roughly-made country carts with wheels of one solid piece of wood and a curved shaft rising above the heads of the great dove-coloured oxen, who drew their load with such unmoved calm, she could have wept for joy to think that she and Carlo would spend their lives where every sight and sound was as familiar as an Ave Maria.

And when on the evening of her arrival she hastened home with leave to stay all night and found her mother spinning, her father and

Beppo just come in from working among the vines, and Giulia—who was shooting up into quite a tall girl—getting ready the evening meal, she laughed and cried in turn as they all crowded around her. And what joy it was to see their delight, at the little gift she had bought for each—a shining leather purse for her mother, knowing that the old one had long been without a clasp and had to be fastened with a string, and in this new one she had put a crisp two-lire note; for her father a white clay pipe and a few ounces of tobacco; for Beppo, a crimson necktie; and for Giulia a blue and white scarf.

"But, Teresina, it seems to me that your face has grown a little sadder when you are not laughing or talking," said the father, looking at Teresa attentively as they sat at supper, "are you sure that you are happy and that they are all quite good to you?"

"Oh, yes, father, they are all as kind to me as May weather," answered Teresa eagerly, "but one gets older," she hesitated and then all at once she felt it impossible to keep her great news any longer a secret from her family. So she told her story to them all, as they sat there in the mellow rays of the tall old earthenware lamp, that cast as much shadow as it gave illumination.

"And so he is away in the wilds of the sea, at the coral fishing—poverina, poverina," said her father softly.

"But he is quite well, see what he has written to me," said the girl, taking her one love-letter out of her bosom. "He will come back whole and well on the festa of San Michele," she said, as she smoothed out the letter, which was getting well worn with being so much read and carried about, and her eyes were shining with confident hope as she thought of her many prayers to the blessed Madonna in San Lorenzo.

"Well, Teresa, if in time to come you cannot digest your food by day nor sleep at night because of the choice you have made, remember that I did my best to give you a home, that has busy fields in summer and full barns in winter," said Lucia, but speaking as if more in sorrow than in anger.

"Mother, you are not much displeased with Carlo and me," said Teresa aside to her mother, when it was getting near their early bedtime.

"It is no use trying to stay with the devil and with holy water at the same time," said Lucia, with a half smile. Then she opened one of the deep drawers of the ancient sideboard and began to turn over the house-linen that would be part of Teresa's corredo (trousseau) when she married.

"There are ten tablecloths, six for common use and four finer ones, a dozen and a half table napkins, a dozen pillow-slips, and seven sheets," she said as she touched them in turn, each set tied with a length of blue tape. Teresa and her sister had helped to spin and weave these, as well as a similar portion for Giulia, during the long winter evenings from the time that they were eight or nine years of age.

"To make a marriage without a roof to your head would be but trying to grow grapes in the summer of San Martino, which lasts only three days and a bit," said the mother, as Teresa was going up the steep little stairs to bed. "The question is will Poldo and his wife find room for the two of you at their table."

Poldo (Leopoldo) was one of the coloni of the Pucci estate and village, four miles from Estvecchio. Poldo had two sons of his own, but they had emigrated to Brazil many years before, and Carlo, who was an orphan— the only child of Poldo's brother—had from the age of nine been brought up by his uncle like a son of the house. Teresa knew that Poldo was ready to welcome her as his nephew's sposa, but her mother had a way of dashing her hopes, which made the girl afraid of ominous prophecies, and so she kept silent on the point. But the matter was set at rest, even to Lucia's foreboding mind, on the following Sunday, which happened to be the festival of St. John the Baptist. He was the patron saint of the city, and there were to be illuminations and merrymaking in the evening.

Among those who came in one of the high, light-going little vehicles called bagheri, which are a cross between a gig and a spring-cart, were Poldo Sperani and his wife Annunziata. They met the Biondi family in the piazza in front of the cathedral, and straightway Annunziata, who was a portly, good-natured looking old woman, dressed in her best black silk skirt and velvet bodice, with great gold rings in her ears and a handsome string of pearls round her throat, took Teresa in her arms and imprinted a baciozzo (hearty kiss) on each cheek.

"Ah, you are the girl who is to be our Carlino's sposa," she said, in a caressing voice. Then following her husband's example, she greeted the parent Biondis, saying as she did so, "You know they are fidanzate, these two, Carlo and Teresa, and they must have a wedding as soon as he comes back," she said, with intentional emphasis to Lucia, for though they had never been intimate, and seldom met, she was aware that Lucia's goodwill had been entirely in favour of the prosperous Antonio Vanucci.

"Yes, young ones are often anxious to build a nest even when they have not got a bit of stick or a scrap of wool to make it with," said Lucia coldly.

"Diamine, but why should they build a nest when the old one is all ready to take them in?" said Poldo, with some warmth.

"Well, at the carnival we know who has the fat pullet; if they are welcome in the old nest it goes well," said Lucia urbanely.

"And when the bambini begin to come the old ones will take care that it is not macaroni to-day and hunger to-morrow," said Poldo, with a jovial laugh.

Teresa was very happy that day, and all through the chanting and marching, the chiming of bells, and swinging of incense, and fluttering of banners borne in processions; and later, through the crowds of town and country people, eating and laughing, gossiping and lounging about, as they waited till the illuminations should begin and every window would have its own cresset of light, the thought uppermost in her mind was "Carlo will be back in three months, and then like the people in the old stories, we shall live in peace ever afterwards."

Chapter IV

A week after the day of St. John, Teresa got a second letter from Carlo that made her very anxious. It was written at the coral bank where they were fishing and had been brought by one of the boats that had been damaged in a storm and had to put in at Tunis for repair. The season, so far, had been good. The work was hard—they began at daylight and went on till dark, with few and short stoppages; the sun was of Africa, and the only change they had in their food was that sometimes they had less of it one week than another. But nothing would have been too hard, if it were not for having a Padrone who was only fit to be food for carrion crows. Here there came a line or two that had been afterwards carefully blotted out. Then the letter went on "But a third of the time is over, and the road is never so long when we know where it ends.

"When things are at the worst I touch your likeness in my pocket and think of my promise to you, and so the days pass into a month, and each month there are fifty lire earned for you and for our wedding, and then there will be long years to come when I shall sit by the fire on winter nights and tell you of all that happened when I was a coral fisher . . . One of the fishers is a Neapolitan, and he says that wherever the Padrone is present, though he may be alone, there you will always find one scoundrel and two assassins. He has a saying that perhaps your mother knows, but I never heard it before: 'Riches are got with anguish, possessed with fear, enjoyed with sin, and given up with grief.' So, carina, maybe it is as well that you and I will never have riches."

The night that she got this letter Teresa had a strange dream. She saw L'Allodola as plainly as if she were wide-awake. The sea all round it was as calm as a lake and there was a great yellow moon shining over the sea and the ship. She seemed to be looking at the boat as if from a little distance, and at first she could see no one on board. But as she looked two men rose up stealthily and walked softly to the side of the ship. She could not see their faces, but she knew that the two men were Carlo and Gianbattista. She wanted them to see her, but she could not utter a sound, and they never turned their heads nor looked from one side to the other. They stood motionless for a moment, and then Carlo got over the side of the ship and plunged into the sea, and Tista followed him. She stood stupefied for a moment, as if she had been heavily struck. Then she gave a great cry and she found herself sobbing out aloud, with Mariuccia hurrying from the night nursery in which she slept with the bambino into her (Teresa's) little room, which opened into the latter one and was separated from it only by the heavy portiere across the open doorway.

"Body of thy soul, child, what is the matter?" cried the old nurse, in great alarm, holding the little night lamp she had snatched up so that she could see the girl's face.

It was as pale as death and her breath came convulsively.

"Oh, Carlo, Carlo, he went into the sea, and Tista went in after him: I saw them—I saw them," she said wildly.

Then she flung herself on her knees at the foot of her bed, where a coloured earthenware figure of the Madonna hung with the Child in her arms, with a tiny basin of holy water at the foot.

"Oh, blessed Mother, but thou hast not let him perish," she said, weeping unrestrainedly for a few minutes.

"Santa Maria, but this is folly—you have a dream—an idle fable of sleep, and you take it like the Gospel of St. John," said Mariuccia half angrily, when Teresa, calmed by the burst of weeping, rose from her knees and told her dream. But though she tried to make light of the girl's vision Mariuccia dipped her finger in the holy water and made the sign of the cross.

"It may be, excellency, that the girl ate too much fruit or it may be that the dream was no dream, but a revelation. Such things have been, Eccolo," said Mariuccia next morning to her mistress after she had told her what had happened in the night.

"I hope to God no evil has happened to the young man," said the Donna Beatrice, and she was if possible kinder than ever to Teresa, who after a few days began to hope that her dream was nothing but a dream. Late in August—the month of the lion it is called in Italy—they returned to Genoa. The city seemed to bask in a garden of roses and oleander, and to be embosomed in groves of lemons and oranges. But to Teresa the charm of the place was dead, for though she tried to keep her fears at bay, she had the feeling of one who revisits a region haunted by the remembrance of a lifelong parting.

As the time drew near to the day of San Michele she became silent and brooding. On the 25th, however, she got a short note that had been written on the first of the month, hurriedly scrawled on a rough bit of paper, in pencil, and which merely contained the words, "The fishing goes on well, and we are hard at work. My heart, you are always in my thoughts."

Well, it was strangely brief, and left almost all unsaid, but it was a message written weeks after the dream that had filled her with such cruel fears. Teresa took heart of grace, and when L'Allodola was still unheard of in the second week of October, she refused to dwell on the thought of any disaster. But on the 12th of the month she learned that the rest of the fleet had returned. On hearing this the Donna Beatrice went with her to the office of the agents who owned the boats. But they only knew that L'Allodola had not come back, and that she had been last seen within half a day's sail of the coral at which they had worked.

"They did not all come together—some returned 12 days ago, the last only three days back, but that is later than usual," said the head clerk.

"What do you think has happened?" asked Donna Beatrice in a low voice.

The clerk shrugged his shoulders. "We cannot say positively, madam. The boat may have been disabled and put into some port, with which there is no steady communication; or it may have been caught in a sudden squall. There are generally one or two wrecks in the season."

Donna Beatrice made a sudden motion of caution to the man, but Teresa had heard; and after all, it was but giving voice to the terror that had grown her intemperate companion that was with her all day, and hovered over her sleep, and caught at her heart the moment she opened her eyes. But she kept perfectly calm, and when they left the office, instead of getting into the carriage in which Donna Beatrice had brought her with Mariuccia and the Bambino (who was becoming more and more like one of the B—'s lovely boys), she said in a low voice, "Excellency, if you will allow me, I should like to go to San Lorenzo for a little time."

"Of course, Teresina, but are you fit to be alone?" said Donna Beatrice, having her hand on the girl's shoulder and looking into her face.

It seemed as though a pitiless sponge had been passed over it, erasing its soft colouring, its happiness, and all the bloom of first youth.

"Oh, yes, Excellency, quite fit—it may be that I shall have to be mostly alone all my life," said the girl gently. Donna Beatrice would rather have seen her more passionate in her sorrow. But Teresa remained unmoved until she reached the little chapel in which she had prayed beside her lover on Holy Friday. It was quiet and dim, and there was no one near her as she knelt down . . . "O, buon Gesù e Madonna mia addolorata vera madre di misericordia miserere nostri" (O, good Jesus and my lady of anguish, the mother of pity, have compassion on us) was all that she could utter, but her tears flowed fast and took away the stoniness of her grief, and hope once more revived.

"Cospetto, why should one believe people are lost because they are late in getting back," said Pietro to her that evening after telling tales of ships that had been missing for months, and then sailed safely into port.

"I have not given him up," said Teresa, and she went about her duties day after day without a murmur, reserving all her tears for that daily visit to the chapel of the Madonna, where she seemed to leave her worst fears and gather up fresh hope and courage.

Ten days after Donna Beatrice's visit to the office her husband was promoted to be major-general, and appointed aide-de-camp to the Prince of Naples for that season, dating from the first of November. It was necessary that they should leave for the Eternal City almost at once, as there were many preparations involved in this change of social life. That afternoon Donna Beatrice went once more to the agents of the fishing boats, but this time alone. She found that the worst fears had been confirmed. A merchant ship had picked up some timber-broken wreckage bearing part of the name L'Allodola. On returning home she went into the day nursery where Teresa was sewing.

"I have come to tell you, Teresina, that we are going to Rome in a few days," she said, as Teresa put down her work and rose on seeing her mistress enter.

"Yes, Excellency, but it would not be possible that I should go— I must wait for Carlo," said Teresa hesitatingly.

"But, poor child, if he is not to come?" replied Donna Beatrice, with infinite gentleness.

"Excellency, you have heard," said the girl quickly.

And then she listened to the news that had come, and though her eyes dilated and she trembled a little, she did not utter a sound. After a few moments she said very slowly—"The boat is wrecked—yes—but, excellency, I do not believe that the blessed Madonna would deceive me. No, it is true, she did not promise me in words, but she heard me when I asked her to help me in small things, and would she turn away, when I pray day and night that Carlo should come back to me?"

Donna Beatrice had in her college days in Chicago taken more than one prize for logic. Even without such proficiency it would have been easy to show the weakness of Teresa's position. To point out, for example, the disasters that have befallen Christian nations in the very gravest matters while the worshippers in a thousand churches have prayed in vain for deliverance. But, instead of making any attempt at reasoning of this kind, Donna Beatrice hastened away, and made her eyes red with crying. She felt forced, however, to return to the question again next morning.

"How are you to stay alone in Genoa, Teresa? a young girl like you without any relations."

"There is always the Madonna at San Lorenzo, and besides there is old Francesca," answered Teresa. "I thought over it last night when I could not go to sleep," she went on, gravely. And then she told Donna Beatrice that Francesca was an old woman of the best character, who lived in a small room on the same flat that Concetta was in—a tailoress, who got work from some shops, and lived on fivepence a day; "not in grandeur, it is true," added Teresa, "but it is enough. I could take a little room near Francesca, and dress marionettes. I have learned from Concetta, and she says that I have great quickness. Besides, excellency, I have saved more than a hundred lire in your service, and I have plenty of clothes for a long time to come."

"But, child, I must be plain with you; suppose you wait and you wait, and Carlo does not come, what then?" said Donna Beatrice.

"Excellency, you have come from a country where the Madonna is not so well known; she simply could not treat me like that," answered Teresa, softly. From this attitude she could not he moved, and finding this Donna Beatrice decided not to sublet for the present the palazzo she had so munificently furnished in the Via Balbi.

"After thinking the matter over, I am sure it will be best to leave Pietro and Concetta in charge here until we see whether Rome agrees with me," she said to her husband. "You see I have never lived in it before for more than a few weeks at a time."

"Everybody is well in Rome during the winter," said the new major-general with mild surprise at this sudden change of plan.

"But, my dear friend, I am not everybody, and if the malaria attacks me, why I must at once flee back to Genoa, where I have been all the time like a fish in water."

A young and pretty woman who has had millions tightly settled on herself and her descendants, must be allowed a few caprices, and, of course, Donna Beatrice carried her point. She knew that the alleged motive must carry weight, whereas the real one would have appeared to her husband too wildly extravagant, even for an American heiress. Pietro was a great favourite with his master, whom he had served from the time that both were boys, and the major-general would not have consented to leave him behind, except for a weighty reason, such as taking care of a valuable property. So when Pietro and Concetta were installed as caretakers in the palazzo, with Teresa left in their charge until she should recover from the effects of the shock that had fallen on her, no one dreamt that the real reason of the arrangement was to give the girl a home with the best friends she had in Genoa, while she waited with the forlorn hope that the Virgin would work a miracle in her favour.

But on the day before the family left for Rome, Donna Beatrice summoned Teresa into her boudoir. "Sit down here, my child," she said, pointing to a low, easy chair, and the girl, with the innate breeding of her race, sat down opposite her mistress, without demur or awkwardness. She was thin and pale, with great dark circles round her eyes, but there was no despair nor hopelessness in her face.

"Teresa, I want to tell you a secret," said Donna Beatrice in a low voice.

"Excellency, it will go with me to the grave, if need be," answered the girl.

"Well, it is this. The Palazzo is left unlet and Pietro and Concetta in charge, entirely for your sake."

"For my sake, excellency," stammered Teresa, in bewilderment. But in very few words Donna Beatrice made her understand the situation; when she did so she was for a little time overpowered.

"Oh, excellency, what can I do to show you my gratitude," she said through her tears.

"You can promise me to give up looking for Carlo, if he does not come by the end of the year. You see, Teresa," went on Donna Beatrice as the girl sat with a dumb fear on her face, "the Madonna and the Saints, and God, who is greater than all, may be very good, but they do let some very queer things happen in this world; and all we can do is just to go on with our lives, and make the best of them."

"So Teresa gave her promise, that if at the end of December no tidings came of her lover, she would on New Year's Day come to Rome with Pietro and Concetta. But the interview left the impression on her mind that despite the Donna Beatrice's goodness, and unbounded generosity, she was after all a heretic, who did not be believe much in the Madonna's ability to help in the hour of trouble. Yet as the weeks glided on she herself began to realise that however powerful the Virgin may be, there are some prayers she does not answer. When November closed in, and no signs or tidings came, the conviction fastened on her like a heavy hand touching her heart, that Carlo was really engulfed in one of the waste places of the remorseless sea.

Then for the first time she became subject to fits of quiet heart-broken weeping. But they passed, and she controlled herself to go through the daily routine—so much time in the open air, so much at her devotions, and so many hours sewing with Concetta, making little robes for their mistress, that would be needed in the nursery early in the coming spring. As for Pietro, he kept himself employed by going over the 40 odd rooms of the palazzo in rotation, and maintaining them in the same speckless order in which they had been kept when the family were in occupation.

In the middle of December the agent to whom the letting of the palazzo was entrusted, came to show a Russian prince over it, and he took the residence from New Year's Day. On that afternoon Teresa went to the chapel in San Lorenzo, but when she knelt down as usual she could not utter a word. She looked in a strange way at the Madonna—that woman with the benign face, before whom so many human creatures, mortally wounded, prostrate themselves with cries of endearment and entreaty. An old woman with a dingy red and yellow handkerchief, tied over her snow-white hair, threw herself down beside Teresa, weeping most bitterly. The girl looked at her for a moment and the words rose to her lips, "She will not hear you." The next moment she was horrified at herself, and rising hastily, she hurried out of the cathedral.

She went down the Via Lorenzo, and then by the Via Alberto to the harbour. There were so many ships there, big and little, that had come safely from the far ends of the earth. O, mother of compassion, why not the one for which she had prayed day and night? . . . And there were others coming in all the time. She watched them gradually drawing nearer and being ranged in position. Those that were passenger ships had often-times groups of friends awaiting them, and joyful cries of greeting and recognition would be heard. But here came a weather-beaten felucca— the paint all stained and blistered and peeling off, some spars broken, and the sails ragged and torn.

"See that wretched little ship, as melancholy-looking as the devil; it must have been wrecked, and then vomited up by the sea," said a well-dressed bystander to his companion. Teresa overheard the remark, and she watched the felucca with painful interest. She threaded her way round a large vessel the better to observe the belated-looking new-comer, which was towed into an obscure corner behind an angle of one of the quays. It was boarded by a Custom-House officer, and then two men came on deck, ragged and unkempt and bare-footed, and began to scramble across an intervening boat on to the quay. Teresa gave a low cry, and then stood petrified. She wondered vaguely whether her sorrow had turned her head, for at the first glimpse she caught of these two most miserable-looking vagrants, the thought leapt into her heart, "It is Carlo and Tista." When they stepped on the quay she knew that this was no wild delusion, but the solemn truth. She tottered towards them, and if Carlo had not caught her in his arms she would have fallen to the ground.

"Oh, Carlino, Carlino," was all that she could say for a few moments. A little crowd began to gather round them, and so they made their way to a more retired spot, behind an old marine store, close at hand.

"Did you think we were lost?" asked Tista, when Teresa was sufficiently recovered to greet him as an old friend.

"What then could I think, when we found L'Allodola was wrecked?" answered Teresa.

"Wrecked," exclaimed both men in an awed tone. Then before they told a word of their own story, they learned from Teresa all that she knew concerning the lost vessel.

"That cursed Sicilian has met his doom, God is just," said Carlo, almost in a tone of exultation.

"But Carlo—all the other poor men, and they had people praying and waiting for them as I waited for you," said Teresa, in a broken voice. This side of the question shamed Carlo into repentance of what he had said. After all he had but fallen into the trap that few avoid when they glibly talk of Divine intervention in human affairs.

"And you two were not wrecked at all," said Teresa, gazing at one and then at the other, each equally destitute. Then she found how prophetic her dream had been. On the night she had dreamt it Tista was put in irons by the Padrone, who throughout the ill-fated season had behaved more like a demon than a human being.

"It was a miracle that I did not kill him," said Carlo. "I knew that I would strangle him and throw him overboard if we stayed any longer. That was why after Tista was released we both got out of L'Allodola one night when the dawn began to come into the east, and swam to a fishing smack that was within a few hundred yards of us. They landed us in Tangier, and there we were put in prison for a theft we never committed. But we were runaways, and could not speak a word of French. At last they found that we were innocent, and they set us at liberty. We worked our way back on that boat, which for more than a week of the voyage was every moment in danger of being swallowed by the waves. So here we are, my life; beggars, but alive and hungry."

"There is an osteria not far away," said Teresa, slipping her little purse into Carlo's hand. He looked at it with a half-melancholy smile, saying, "All your mother's evil proverbs have come true, little one."

"O, blessed Madonna, not one of them," said Teresa joyfully. They rose from the planks of timber on which they had been sitting, and went to a small inn near at hand.

"Come first to the cathedral, and then with me to the palazzo, where you will find all that you need," said Teresa after the men had drunk and eaten. On the way to the cathedral she went into a branch office and sent the telegram which Donna Beatrice has since shown to so many of her country people. "O, excellency, the Madonna heard me. Carlo and Tista came back from a hundred graves this morning."

www.ingramcontent.com/pod-product-compliance
Lightning Source LLC
Chambersburg PA
CBHW071512110726
47908CB00003B/814